cleanskin

Gay Lynch has published short fiction, run playgroups, and taught creative writing. She lives by the sea with her husband, and is completing a PhD on South Australian Irish immigrants in the 1850s. *Cleanskin* is her first novel.

cleanskin
GAY LYNCH

Wakefield
Press

Wakefield Press
1 The Parade West
Kent Town
South Australia 5067
www.wakefieldpress.com.au

First published 2006

Cover designed by Liz Nicholson, designBITE, Adelaide
Text designed and typeset by Ryan Paine, Wakefield Press
Printed in Australia by Griffin Press, Adelaide

National Library of Australia
Cataloguing-in-publication entry

Lynch, Gay.
Cleanskin.

ISBN 1 86254 703 3.

I. Title.

A823.3

 Government of South Australia

Arts SA

 fox creek

 Publication of this book was assisted by the
Commonwealth Government through the
Australia Council, its arts funding and advisory body.

It is in point of fact, a difficult matter for men to realise the extreme importance of social discrimination which seems outwardly insignificant but which produces in women moral and intellectual effects so profound that they appear to spring from her original nature.

SIMONE DE BEAUVOIR
The Second Sex

Squeaky Beach

Salt water coursed through Madelaine's veins. She drew in the sea like a drowner. On black days it took her and shook her and she flailed in deep water: salt on her face, hair in her mouth, sobbing into the wind when she should have been at home with her children. On other days when the water was still and solid as a painting, and yachts lay like bright handkerchiefs between the buoys, she set herself against the canvas, like a signature.

After they arrived at the house by Boston Bay, Jerome had led her to the water gently, as if she were a child. On hot nights the sea was soft, and whickered against her fingers as his hands curved down her backbone. He had stroked the curve of her belly, watching the little fish that would be Georgia, undulating beneath the taut sheen of her bathers. He had kissed her face and hissed warm breath into her ear – breath as soft and fruity as the sauvignon-blanc they'd just demolished. Madelaine had felt languid, not unstable. Not at all. Things were different then.

Now, she brooded over the perfect swathe of cornflower-blue sea beyond her window. Boston Island floated like a cheerful dumpling in the bay. But the city of Port Lincoln hemmed her in. Madelaine scanned the rooftops on the lower reaches of the street, and at the window's edge caught glimpses of the silos and the baggery. Clouds of grain dust swelled and drifted over the chutes. If she were walking, she would hear the grinding of the machinery, the barking of dogs, and the shouting of workers. She might see weather-beaten peninsula farmers whose crops were sucked from silos into the boats at the wharf. One way or another, Port Lincoln's future was bound up with the sea; there was fishing and there was export grain. Madelaine sometimes felt like the city: alert to the mood of the sea and weather, dependent on them to deliver service.

'Madelaine.'

She jerked her head around.

Jerome slammed the fridge door. 'Are we out of milk?'

'Use the long-life,' she called.

She'd tidied up and swept the floors. It would have to be done again, when playgroup left, or Jerome would mutter, It would never be tolerated if adults pissed on the floor, stood on the furniture and threw food. But Madelaine didn't like to discipline other people's children. When they came, with all their wheels and bags and noise, she felt inert, as if the house were being colonised.

She sighed and stirred her cold coffee before dragging herself into the kitchen. There seemed to be disappointed half-drunk cups all over the house. And she was fed up with washing machines, phone calls and unwanted visitors.

'So, coffee day?' Jerome folded the newspaper, smoothed the folds, and tossed his coffee in the sink. He didn't do long-life.

'I hope Nell doesn't bring one of her bleeding souls today.' Madelaine bit her lip. She loathed herself when she was mean. Nell was a good, good person. She put in volunteer hours for the women's shelter, the nursing mothers, sea rescue. She collected money for Amnesty International, and world famine relief. Nell had 'think global, act local' emblazoned on her heart. Why did Madelaine want to slap her?

'What would you do then, about life's inequities?'

Madelaine was wounded by the lilt of sarcasm in his voice. Had a shadow of regret crossed his eyes?

Perspiration glistened on her upper lip. Be damned if she would lay herself open for Jerome. He was smart enough to find his own way in. 'They think Nell really likes them. But soon enough she dumps them. Or collapses in a heap herself.'

'I thought you girls cared about each other. Unlike we men.' He pecked at her cheek. 'I'll be late tonight, so please, eat without me. Meeting at six, then I have to prepare for tomorrow's hearing.' He eased his briefcase under his arm and picked an apple from the bowl on the sideboard. 'Remember the Trellaggan case? Twelve-year-old girl, eating fish and chips on the foreshore and whammo, dragged over the retaining wall and sodomised. Almost impossible to interview, of course. Stares at her feet and says nothing coherent. Probably wouldn't have presented if the aunties hadn't brought her in. How the hell am I supposed to represent her? Poor girl.'

Madelaine felt ill. 'It won't make a scrap of difference.' She wiped down the sink with angry hands. 'He'll get a bond and if her family can't protect her, he'll be sniffing along the jetty after her within a week.'

'Too right, and if that's the way he expresses himself, he's carrying a truckload of damage himself.'

Madelaine stood motionless in front of the kitchen window,

biting her lip. 'Come home as early as you can.' She lifted her head again and felt tears welling.

He put down his case to seesaw his tie in front of the hall mirror. 'Have a good day then. Spend it any way you like.'

Madelaine stuck out her chin. 'Dayum. Ah shurely thangk yo mite be right. Ah'm fixin' to sweep mah cage. Will yawl git me some more likker?'

'If I were home with the children I'd sit in the garden and read a book, let them play.' He touched her cheek with his hand.

'But you're not, are you. That's the point.' She turned her face away.

'Stuff you then.' He smiled sweetly and slammed the front door. The BMW roared down the drive. *Such a child to drive a car like that.* He made her so angry she could spit. With a sick kind of longing she dreamt of sliding under water, sea lapping over her head.

Happiness. Madelaine vaguely remembered something resembling it. Once, Jerome had borrowed a mate's boat and they launched it at Billy Lights Point. While Jerome drove, Madelaine swung her video camera in glorious unprofessional arcs from sky to sea, taking in birds and land and mysterious underwater stirrings. The wake of other boats slapped against the hull until Jerome gunned the motor, and they surged between the white-edged furrows, heading for the other side of Boston Island.

Georgia had sat contentedly, sun-blocked, sun-hatted and life-jacketed like a small yellow duck. If they dangled her over the side she laughed and flapped her fingers in the water. They had all laughed, at everything. Then Georgia snoozed in the cabin and Madelaine sat at the prow, wind throwing back her hair, cool spray on her face, salt licking her legs and arms as they ploughed out to sea.

'Why do you love me?' she had fired over her shoulder. Jerome, deafened by the wind, doffed his hat and blew her kisses. They had anchored behind the island and waded through the water with a basket of sandwiches and wine, Georgia gurgling at Madelaine's hip.

The sand had squeaked underfoot as Madelaine placed the baby in the centre of the small beach and used bent driftwood to build a playpen.

'Don't you move, or there'll be big trouble.' She waggled her finger. Georgia dribbled, and tugged at the wooden bars of her prison.

As the tide rushed out, Madelaine and Jerome bent over in the water, legs astride, tossing cockles into buckets. What happened next became Jerome's famous story:

'My demented wife, prancing up the beach with a crab dangling from her finger, blood everywhere. Retired hurt from cockling, didn't you, Mad … Couldn't put your finger on why!'

Revenge was sweet enough when they boiled the crab and the cockles on a driftwood fire. She snapped open the crab with her fingers, and juice ran over her wrists. There hadn't been much flesh, but she shared it with Jerome. He had opened a dry white. Cross-legged on the sand, they had passed the bottle back and forth, and scrabbled in the billy for food, like children might play with a bucketful of snails. Georgia snoozed on, covered with a towel.

Replete with wine and sun and love, Madelaine had laid back in the crook of Jerome's navy fishing jumper, wishing that she could stay forever. But a malignant chunk of sadness broke off inside her as if it had been there all the time, hardening in her underbelly, putting pressure on her organs, crowding out the happiness. She had pushed away from him, clambered up, and hit the beach running. At the water's edge she screeched, 'I wish I was indigenous,' and began pulling off her clothes.

'You want to be anyone but Madelaine,' he had called. 'And you're brown enough.'

She waded out until the water ringed her chest, laid back, and when something brushed against her, squid perhaps, felt the cool fingers of the sea lift her up and rock her. The current tugged and she swam half-heartedly against it, sensed herself drifting along the coast, away from Jerome and the baby. The sun glittered on the beach. When she focused on the shore, she had seen Jerome jump up, a hand at his brow to scan her progress in the glare.

He had beckoned furiously and Madelaine had struck out for the shore, swimming as if her life depended on it. Breath ragged, eyes on the little dot that was Georgia, she had forced her way across the rip until at last she felt sand beneath her feet. She staggered onto the beach to gather up her clothes. Her legs were shaking. Jerome had reached out to her and although the island was deserted, pretended to cover her before he pulled her down beside him.

'You okay?'

She had burrowed her face in the hollow of his shoulder.

In the late afternoon, when the sun slipped behind a cloud and a heavy sky rolled in, Jerome stood up reluctantly. 'We'd better go,' he said. 'The water is chopping up.'

They decanted a sleeping Georgia into the cabin. Thigh high in churning water, Jerome pushed the boat out while

Madelaine swung the wheel for home. Wind blew hard behind them as they cut behind the island and across the bay. Awash with a queer kind of happiness, Madelaine had bowed her head to stare into the swirling depths. Always, the sea moved her.

'Pass the camera,' she called.

'Silly girl, you'll drop it in. Let me steer then.'

Back then, she had loved their almost wordless days, when being and doing were enough, and Jerome had not carved up their relationship with specious talk.

Madelaine's

At ten o'clock, when she heard the banging of car doors in the street, Madelaine half rose to look through her lounge-room window and reached for her video camera between the cushions on the sofa. Hovering above the balcony rail, she panned the sunlit sea until she identified the voices on the street – Jo and Danica – and lowered her camera. She had rung Danica, who by some process of elimination was her closest friend, to bring some milk. Madelaine liked Jo well enough. Her husband, Doug, was a prick, but she was lovely. Jo could put anyone at ease, and sold designer-label clothes at Jansys.

Jansys was not a place for children. Grubby fingers could ooze a trail of God knows what across cream silk and pale taffeta. It was a place to shop alone. Madelaine usually shepherded children behind the toy box while Danica tried on size-eight eveningwear and posed awkwardly before the mirrors.

'Should I bring it home? Show Vlado?'

'Why the hell not?' Madelaine juggled an armload of toddlers as deftly as a bin lady handling bottles.

Jo was always kind. 'Just gorgeous on. You could wear that anywhere.'

Danica trailed back to the fitting room.

'What about you, Mad?' said Jo.

'Count me out. I haven't a clue about fashion. Pauline's the one to speak to about a consumer-led recovery.'

Madelaine liked to have a few well-cut clothes and wear them all to death – for years if necessary. Today she was wearing a pair of tailored navy pants, and a white shirt.

White, Madelaine and children, don't mix, her mother might have said. But anything could be made white again; it was only a matter of bleach, and time. In any case, she was over her mother. Her father, now that was a different matter.

She leant against the balcony and angled the camera: Jo was standing on the footpath next to Danica, who was balancing a large nappy bag and a litre of milk as she struggled to lift the children from the car. Madelaine moved downstairs with one eye pushed against the rubber viewfinder, bypassing the garden, gliding over the watchful sea, circling the scrum of children wobbling on the gutter. Sonja cried softly and tugged at Danica's arm. Madelaine opened the front door.

'Pause. Thanks for bringing the milk. I'll carry it. You grapple with the prisoner.' Madelaine flopped the camera onto her chest. 'How are things?'

'Not so good. I'm tired,' Danica sighed.

Madelaine pursed her lips in sympathy, and used the back of her hand to stroke Danica's cheek.

Inside, she passed mugs of coffee over the breakfast bar. 'Straight in the vein, or is this okay?'

'Today, you shouldn't joke,' replied Danica, looking grim. She stood near her children, waiting until they settled like timid birds at the Duplo table.

Jo shimmied onto the over-stuffed sofa at the window.

'This is the life, Mad. I could be in Amalfi glancing up from my book to reach for another glass of red, deliberating over how I'll cook the fungi for dinner.'

'But we're not, are we,' said Madelaine. 'Besides, I expect girls get raped on the beach there too.'

'Oh, is Jerome representing that girl in the news?'

'He's representing someone today. That's all I know.'

'That poor, poor girl. Was she from up the coast?' Danica swivelled to face Madelaine.

'I don't know.'

'What are they going to do for her now that will make a difference?' said Jo.

Madelaine had been fiddling with her camera. She lowered it and marched forward to snatch a toy from Paige. 'That's naughty. Jason was playing with that.' Paige grinned up at her mother. 'Horrid little beast. She's quick,' said Madelaine, pretending severity.

Jo chuckled.

'One word from me, and they do exactly as they please.' Madelaine winked at the others.

'I know the law can hardly protect people before something happens.' Danica gnawed at her fingers.

Surprised, Madelaine glanced up at Danica. *Who would have thought her such a dark thing? Worrying away over social justice.*

'At least it should discourage repeat offences,' argued Jo, looking at Danica with sympathy.

'I don't believe it does,' interjected Madelaine. 'Victims may not even win in court. I'm all for primitive solutions.'

'I bet Jerome's colleagues would love to hear that,' smiled Jo. 'Let's change the subject. We could talk politics – before Pauline arrives. What did you think about Hayden outsmarting Fraser, opening the way for Hawke to have a go at PM? All for the sake of the party. Doug is full of it.'

'That's the Labor party,' replied Madelaine. 'Would you give up your political career without a fight because some suits – boiler suits, dinner suits, what's the difference – had decided to sacrifice you? I never was very good at team sports.'

Jo laughed. 'Think of the alternative. All that scare-mongering about our money being safer under the bed than in the bank, three billion dollars left the country, blah, blah, blah . . .'

'Never mind Pauline, shouldn't we wait for *Nell* before we discuss politics? Then we can take notes,' said Madelaine, who feigned interest when Jerome read extracts from the paper over breakfast. She began filming again, paused to lift a small hand from the lens of her camera, and stooped to kiss the upturned face.

'Madelaine, I thought you and Jerome were staunch Labor party members,' laughed Jo.

'Jerome is one of the faithful.' Madelaine looked deadpan as she ducked her face out from behind the camera.

Jo smiled. 'How many are there? Faithful.'

'About a dozen. Slight exaggeration. God, it's so bleakly conservative here.' Madelaine drummed her fingers on the side of the camera. 'But I've never been in an electorate where my vote made any difference.'

'Nor I,' said Jo.

'Helloo, we're in,' Nell warbled from the front door. She levered her large body and a twin pusher around the door, unloaded an Oxfam carry bag, and puffed as she shepherded two small boys up the stairs.

'Quick, change the subject,' Madelaine said.

'I hope you're all coming down to Jansys this week,' Jo piped in. 'The new season's Crawford and Cutten have arrived.'

'Already! It's not even autumn.' Danica looked doubtful and continued chewing at her fingernail.

'Yes. The most beautifully tailored jackets and pants, and jewel-coloured shirts,' said Jo.

Sometimes, at the shop, Madelaine would pick up a dress and make a point of looking interested. Occasionally she bought something because fashion was Jo's livelihood.

Nell wore large Asian shirts in primary colors, to disguise her bulk. She rocked at the top of the stairs like an over-laden ship. Pauline, her two noisy pre-schoolers in tow, slid in behind. She touched her hair and waved at Madelaine's camera. Nell bent over with difficulty, clucking and patting the heads of the children clinging to her leg, then smiled at the grown-ups. Nell looked soft, mumsy, but she was tougher than a hammerhead shark.

They were all there: Madelaine, Danica, Jo, Pauline and Nell.

'How are we all? Ready to divulge the excitements of the weekend?' Pauline held her breath, glancing from person to person around the room. 'Any goss?'

Madelaine rolled her eyebrows. *Someone who could be so rude to people's faces should never need to gossip.*

Pauline rolled words out in front of them, savouring her pregnant vowels, her breathy tone. 'Ai love plehgroup. I meet all sorts of people who would noormally never come into my awbit.' Madelaine admired her nerve, but if she slid into her I-love-your-little-house routine, she would have to kill her.

Danica's cheeks flushed red as she took up the sting of Pauline's comment.

So sensitive. Poor Danny. Intelligence is no protection. Madelaine ducked from behind the camera to blow her a kiss. Nell was delving into her craft basket, pulling out strands of Danish flower cotton, comparing colours through her thick bifocals. Madelaine continued filming, zooming in on Danica's face, allowing it to fill the screen while she watched for the inevitable waves of terror. Pauline always made Danica loathe herself. Madelaine wondered why she bothered.

While Pauline laughed and told stories and made dry asides, Danica chewed her ravaged fingers. Pauline was always impatient and dismissive, her long painted nails dancing around like butterflies, resting on her skirt, circling a button, caressing her throat. When Danica complained of feeling tired or worried, Pauline lobbed the ball straight back at her feet.

'Why don't you get some help around the house? You can obviously afford it.' Or, 'Perhaps aerobics is too much for you. Take a break? Or some Prozac.' She dismissed Danica's half-hearted arguments.

During Pauline's monologue, Danica had stopped fiddling with her fingers, and was staring as if hypnotised by Pauline's face. Madelaine zoomed in. Wide-eyed, ingenuous, Pauline's eyes sought out the camera. Madelaine waited for something, anything, that might save her friend. Then she put aside the camera, leant forward, and soft as the flutter of a bird's wing, stroked Danica's hand. She pressed her lips against her ear, and whispered, 'Never be afraid of silence.'

Pauline laughed.

Danica swallowed hard, tried to look away, but couldn't.

I should make a film, with gothic subtitles to denote Danica's thoughts: Why does she hate me? I wish I hadn't come. What will happen now? The camera would glide from the eyes to the trembling mouth to the twitching fingers. Then it would cut to Danica waking in the night, battling against something bearing down on her chest. Danny would lurch up in bed and reach for pen and paper to write a letter. The camera would linger on her tear-soaked, scrappy page:

Dear Pauline, I was tired. I was nervous ... about something else. I'm sorry ...

'Why should you care what she thinks?' Madelaine once said to Danica. 'She's just a dipstick.'

It had been after the playgroup at Jo's, when Sonja had fallen from the top of the slippery dip and landed on her head.

'You can't take your eyes off them for a minute,' smirked Pauline, pressing a packet of frozen peas to the bruise. Sonja found screaming therapeutic.

Rather than abandon Danica in her misery, Madelaine had led her and all four children to the toyshop.

'How unfair,' Danica had complained, subsiding among the jigsaw puzzles. 'I was loading up the car when it happened.'

'Rewind. Whose children have had the most spectacular fractures? Be honest.'

'I know – Pauline's. But ... Don't touch, Miranda.'

Danica leapt into the air, slam-dunking a flying china doll back onto the top shelf. Madelaine bluffed the toy manager with a look: say one word, and I'll never spend money here again. Danica shepherded her daughters towards the door.

Madelaine tried to tell her not to worry, that they were all just acting in a play in which the sets were small, and everyone wanted to leave but they were trapped, for they needed each other to pass the time.

'I'm not trapped,' Danica had said. 'This is what I've

always wanted. Later I'll work part-time, but for now, I want to be a good mother.'

Madelaine grinned. 'The world is closing in.' Then, carrying Paige and hauling Georgia behind her, much to Danica's alarm, she had plunged out into the traffic, crossing the road in three quick strides. Almost airborne, Georgia squealed. Cars braked behind them. Glancing over her shoulder, Madelaine had seen Danica heading towards the pedestrian crossing. *Dear girl. Always so anxious.*

That had been a month ago. Meanwhile one playgroup had merged into another, and here they were again. Madelaine sighed. They were all trapped. Like goldfish, in front of the big open windows of her family room. The same five women gobbling oxygen, hoping playgroup would sustain them through another week.

Madelaine stopped musing and used the zoom to focus on Nell's thin lips, her pudgy face. Nell was setting Pauline straight, in a discussion about work and marriage. Nell was earnest in a lethal way — like good drugs. *Should I fast-forward or shoot the pair of them?*

'Motherhood is a role, like fatherhood,' said Nell.

Pauline registered the hit and smiled graciously 'I loathed working. So stressful. I like being a mum.' Her fingers fluttered at her throat.

'Maybe so,' said Nell, 'Forgive me thinking of the ironies. Your parents stood on a production line to pay for your education. They worked their backsides off to put a boat in the driveway and a pool out the back, and they produced someone like you, who never wants to work again. No offence.'

'Well, that's a mistake you feminists make. When both

people in a marriage are working a job-and-a-half, life is craaazy. Then there are families where no one has a job at all. No one is getting up in the mornings. It suits me to support my family – at the moment. Hugh is totally unreliable, I know, he can't help it, and I don't want to be exhausted.' Pauline examined her nails minutely. 'I might go back to nursing, one day.'

'True blue?' Nell was embroidering tiny pink rosebuds onto a wash towel.

Madelaine winked at Danica and whispered, 'If you were on Prozac, you'd miss all Nell's nuances.'

'Let's be friendly, Nellie. No offence taken, but,' Pauline responded. 'I'm intelligent. If I hadn't been a woman, I might have studied medicine.'

'Of course you could have,' said Nell, 'But now you have love, and love bought you privilege. And whatever else it is, love is location, location.'

'That's awfully cynical, Nell,' threw in Jo. Nell ignored her.

'How many opera singers and mud wrestlers do you think Hugh met on his ward rounds?' Nell continued. 'Doctors invariably marry nurses.'

Pauline threw her hands in the air. 'What were you hoping for? A selection panel?'

Madelaine subsided on a chair by the window, and watched a fishing boat glide across the bay. *I wish I was on it. Making my way to the open sea.* Nell and Pauline. Nell and Madelaine. Pauline and Danica. *What is the point of all this sniffiness?* The playgroup girls were nice, in their different ways, and funny. In a new city, with no friends or family, she would never have coped without them. But it was sometimes tedious, the brushing past each other in enclosed spaces, the familiar choreography, the scripted sentences. Like synchronised swimming.

Every time Pauline acted patronising, Nell went for the jugular; the playgroup was her baby – social work and child care rolled into one. Nell would make a good social worker – nothing fazed her. In fact, apart from her voluntary work, she still worked occasionally for money, filling in for staff at the health centre. It was just awkward with Czaba, Nell's husband, working there as well. Child care was a problem and Madelaine wasn't putting her hand up for that, any more than she had to.

Madelaine knew that Nell had met Pauline and Hugh while paddling on the beach one hot summer's night after dinner. Czaba was a physiotherapist, so he had a nodding acquaintance with Hugh. Nell bulldozed them home for coffee and checked out Hugh for his particular attitude to women's health. Madelaine could imagine Pauline tapping her long red nails on the laminex arm-plates of Nell's 1940s smoker's armchair, taking in the picture of a dumpy pregnant girl and the clutter of her living arrangements. She would have wondered why Hugh allowed himself to be taken in. Madelaine was surprised Pauline had stuck with playgroup. Child care seemed the obvious answer. *Is there something else I've missed?*

The fishing boat appeared to have stopped on the eastern side of the island. Perhaps they were catching pilchards for bait. Madelaine thought about Danica's family, the Divjaks. Under cover of darkness they had travelled in fishing vessels through the islands of the Dalmatian coast, away from their country and the communists. Danica's father's family had disembarked, walked across the Istrian Peninsula and along the coast to Italy. Jeleni, Danica's mother, had come via camps in Austria, to work as a domestic in Australia on a two-year contract. Danica had whispered to Madelaine that because of this, she could never complain to her mother that the lines at the supermarket were too long, or that she was always carrying heavy bags, when here she was, living in the land of plenty. Jeleni thought material things staved off misfortune, were a measure of self-esteem. And Australia was safe.

The year they met, Danica had taken Madelaine to the family mansion on the hill, where a life-sized family fresco graced the Divjaks' hallway. Much later and with Danica's permission, Madelaine had directed her camera to glide from one proud face to another, and then to sweep into the living room, chock full of rococo flourishes, and Italianate marble.

Grandfather Dragon had straightened up, pointing to his roll-top desk. 'Antique – custom-made by master craftsmen – out on Whalers Road.' He inspected the rims of his finger-nails, slicked back his hair, and dipped his weathered, golden forehead to the task at hand: making money – the purchase of fishing licences was carefully calculated. Madelaine had watched his stubby pencil skimming over the pages of his ledgers.

So, there you had it, Danica and Pauline, the daughters of struggle, both living in the land of plenty.

What a motley group. Nell has gathered most of us on the beach. No doubt read a book about playgroups and organised one within the week. At first Madelaine, glad to get out of the house, had thought they were all interesting, in their way, but after a while the sameness of the sessions wore her down, the trailing like emus behind the children, the petting and picking up. Nell thrived. Madelaine wished that she could be as admirable every day, packing and unpacking great bags of food, toys, handiwork, ideas and activities.

'Are you going to the hospital ball, Madelaine?' called Pauline from across the room.

'Not if I can get out of it,' she answered, returning from the window.

'What about Jerome?'

'Jerome? I remember him. Isn't he stuck in a flight pattern that loops to the office and back?'

'So he says,' Pauline murmured. 'You could try and bust him. Take a swab.'

'Don't go there, sister. I know what you're getting at. Smarter women than me have hit the deck. What of Hughie, then?'

'Doctors are notorious. The more complicated their lives, the better they like it. Besides, they want to help people – suckers for a good line. As a precaution I check on him; ring the hospital and the clinic.'

'Are you serious?' Madelaine raised her eyebrows.

'Half. It's immensely reassuring when he's where he said he'd be!'

'Hrmm.' Madelaine leant forward, a dark cloud of hair drifting over one eye. She lowered her voice. 'Sex is a bag of monkeys anyway, don't you think? Noise, mess, squalor. I sometimes ask myself if it's worth it. Would you be bothered, sleeping with someone else?'

'Of course I could. The first few weeks of a love affair are tantalising.' Pauline arched her neck, and ran her fingers through her hair. 'Think back, you poor old thing, to when you were entranced by your own perfume, by the music ... the wine playing havoc with your judgement ...'

Madelaine laughed. 'Did you read books like that when you were a teenager?'

Pauline knelt, and bounced a small bottom onto a clean nappy. The toddler made a fist at her.

'Oh you ... I thought a swollen member was a politician, not something to pivot off when ballroom dancing. And of course, I wouldn't do it, play up I mean, unless I was hellishly unhappy. I've invested too much time and effort to throw everything away for excitement.'

Intent on mischief, Madelaine slid forward along the carpet, and lowered the camera into Pauline's face. 'If we played the car-key game after a playgroup dinner, whose keys would you lunge for?'

Pauline raised her eyes, playful, mouth bristling with nappy pins. 'Jerome's?'

'I'd take Vlado's,' Madelaine crowed, forcing Danica's attention.

'Take him where?' said Danica, spooning yoghurt into Sonja.

Madelaine shifted the camera from Pauline to Danica's face. 'If you could command any of our husbands, princess, who would it be?'

Danica bit her lip. 'Hugh, I suppose; save on my medical bills.'

'Are you girls being smutty?' Jo was fiddling about with batteries in the belly of a truck.

'Certainly not.' Madelaine backtracked. 'Are you going to the hospital ball, Jo?'

'I wish. I think it would be gorgeous, but could you see us affording it?'

'Rather elite, don't you think, Nellie?' Madelaine swung

the camera back with a flourish and knocked down a Duplo tower. 'Darling, sorry, Maddy will help.' She laid the camera beside her and began rebuilding. *Will Nell respond? She is such a prickly pear. Takes everything so seriously.* If not, Pauline could be relied upon. She was on the hospital fund-raising committee and bound to spit. *How far will she go?* The week before she had told them what a shame it was that World Vision children didn't come from nicer countries, so their sponsors could visit them. Nell had almost choked on her whole-wheat muffin.

'I can't see a problem with the ball – anyone can go.' *That was predictable at least.*

'A lot of people I know couldn't afford to.' Nell picked up her embroidery, peering at her design, affecting boredom.

'If they really wanted to, they could. Just give up gambling or alcohol for a couple of months. Priorities,' argued Pauline.

Nell glared at her. 'I know families who could never afford to go, and eat as well. I've written to the paper because I think it stinks.'

'You're such a prude, Nell. Why shouldn't people who can afford it have some fun? Think of the money we'll raise. It'll be a damned good start on a new operating theatre. Everyone will benefit,' said Pauline, threading breakfast cereal on a shoelace necklace for her son.

'Too true, but these are essential services, the government should be providing them. Thank God your lot were voted out. Inflation has dropped, the economy is improving, and we now have a government with some interest in social justice. Give the string back to Rupert, Pauline. You're not supposed to do it for him.'

Pauline coloured and passed over her busywork. 'They'll never control the unions; wait and see. Wages will sky rocket.'

Ear-piercing screams aborted the conversation. Pauline rushed to prise her youngest son's hand from his face, revealing several teeth marks dripping blood. 'My God.'

Nell tracked her guilt-ridden son, who had retreated to the toilet, clutching his truck.

Danica looked shocked.

'Children of pacifists can disappoint their parents too,' said Madelaine, flashing a wry smile at Jo, and sliding away to make more coffee. Jo frowned and fiddled with her watch. A sober red-faced Nell returned. She'd been crying. Madelaine watched her force a wary reconciliation between the biter and the bitee.

Slouching on the counter while the water came to the boil, Madelaine watched their faces. It was a sour note to end the morning on. Nell would beat herself up, then rationalise. In the instant, Pauline had played wolf-mother, but later she would laugh it off. *They look sleep-deprived, the lot of them. They should all go home for a nap. Take their kids too.*

No such luck. Pauline made a dash to the delicatessen for sausage rolls and pasties, and they'd extended morning tea into lunch, relaying the children past the sauce bottle, through the high chair, and via the flannel. At one o'clock, Madelaine grimaced, fiddled with her camera and looked at her watch. *Leave, please leave.* Pauline's boys were squabbling over a bike and Sonja was snuffling at her mother's knee. Nell and Pauline were agreeing in an animated way about the city's lack of child care. Paige had fallen asleep in a pool of warmth behind the sofa. It seemed they were in it for the long haul. Madelaine was over 'plehgroup'.

The Film Studio

Thank God, they've gone. By two o'clock Madelaine had raked the toys into the centre of the room, sorted them into containers and vacuumed all the crumbs off the carpet. It took more than an hour. Three streets away, Nell would be contending with a dozen visitors whose kids would rush like a deluge through her house. And she would listen to them and make coffee. God knows how *she* managed.

Madelaine was exhausted and had put Georgia and Paige to bed. No doubt she should work out like Danica. Some time after she had arrived in Port Lincoln, she had enrolled at the gym and gone to a class. After half an hour she couldn't keep up with the instructor and she worried that her heart and lungs would explode. Aerobics was fierce. Pregnancy gave her some excuse to abstain and she had never bothered to return.

At three, she dithered about transferring footage from camera to videotape, smoked three cigarettes one after the other, then stripped off her clothes and pulled on her bathers. The day had heated up and she badly wanted to go for a swim. She crept up on the mirror in the bedroom and prodded at her flesh. Not much had changed over the years. No doubt she lacked tone, but life lacked tone.

Since puberty she'd felt a surge of power when people noticed her in crowds, or stared at her with expectation. There had been power before puberty too, but that hadn't been nice, not nice at all. She'd learnt to veil her anxiety and still herself, to hide the rabbity terror she felt when her father's eyes locked with hers. When she met Jerome, it seemed he only wanted to please her, and she had found this inexplicable. Reaching deep inside herself, she had searched for a virgin wish to offer, a pure thought untainted by the manipulations of her father. Now Jerome was impatient. He wanted something *now* alright.

Madelaine had never imagined marriage, let alone children. Bailing out of school in the dying weeks of her final year and winning a job at a film studio had been the first terrifying thing she'd done – the first step away from her father, and the classics degree he had mapped out for her. He had taken it badly, become severe with parishioners waiting at the manse door, and asked them to respect his privacy, God was testing him.

The week before she took up the job, the rows had been excoriating. As a show of faith, she had taken her volume of Catallus to read by the sea at the end of their street. But he was not appeased, and she could feel his eyes boring between the slats of the venetian blinds, tracking her along the foot-path to the sea. The weather had been hot and humid. She made a nest between two large boulders and hunched over the book. Latin words had ricocheted in front of her eyes until her head thumped with tension. Even the sea was wilful, with its choppy waves. Bales of seaweed formed on the beach. She had put the book down and swam out past the holiday crowds, as far as she could go and still crawl back. That night she pushed her chest of drawers across her door, and shook in the bay window while her father raged, and her mother begged him to come to bed and leave the girl alone. Everything Madelaine did that week underlined his disappointment in her. But, finally he withdrew to pray in his study; she had won.

'There's no future in this job, Madelaine,' her father had jabbed at her as he dropped her at the studio on the first day. He bent to graze her cheek. 'You're just a glorified office girl.'

For a fortnight she had limped from the car like a beaten animal. What had her employers seen in her when they interviewed her?

'That's an ever lovin' daddy you got, Maddaliiine,' joked Bart from sound. 'Dropping you off, picking you up.'

Tears welled in Madelaine's eyes. 'It's over the top, I know.'

'Spook, you need to get out, leave home.'

He was right.

'When I go to Thailand next month, take up my rent. Eight weeks to get a taste of feelin' groovy, sister.'

Packing quietly, late at night, she planned her way towards it. There would be no going back.

Madelaine had liked the work at the film studio: answering the phone, juggling bills that stretched the overdraft and thirsted after grants, greeting the cheerful untidy crew, ferrying them coffee and Jim Beam and coveting their jobs. One day when she had slid dreamily onto the old theatre seats at the back of the studio and eased her shoes off, Jerome had arrived. She had seen him standing in the doorway, a tall man with dark shoulder-length hair, an ordinary jacket over a grandfather shirt, a briefcase in his hand.

'Go home,' yelled the crew, waving their arms at her, deciding that she knew him. She blushed. How kind they were, how clever, and how lucky to be making art. She would have liked to make a film herself. Nothing pretentious, just interior scenes of ordinary people bowed down by their inconsequential secrets. She had leapt up quickly, not wishing to disturb the work, to usher the strange man who became Jerome, into the office. He asked the way to a factory behind the studio, where he had arranged to interview a client.

Men had made her nervous then. Jerome had leant against the office doorframe, his eyes intent on her face as he took in her directions. Before he left, Jerome had recognised Bart across the room, said he knew him from school, and wanted to catch up with him when he wasn't working, when would she suggest? She took his card, planned to tape it to the cover of the office diary, pass it on when Bart was free. She had turned it over in her hand and watched him go. Jerome Rawlins of Burrell and Partners, Barristers, Solicitors and Notaries, turning down the alley behind the building. When he swung his head to look at her she drew back into the office and closed the door.

He turned up again the following week at Friday 'happy hour'. Madelaine registered him shouldering his way through the fug, to where she was draped over a broken set piece, sharing a joint with Bart. They kicked on, the three of them, at several wine bars and coffee lounges, until the early morning hours of Saturday, when they drifted into the city market for European coffee and pastry. Friday nights became a regular thing. She began to look for him at six, when he arrived with his coat slung over his shoulder, his fingers caressing the beginnings of a five o'clock shadow, the evening paper spilling out of his briefcase. He was nothing like her father.

It seemed a long time ago. So much had happened. Of

course, there had been a honeymoon period, but now she was hurtling over the speed limit and feeling self-destructive.

Now she wanted to make disturbing films: narratives punctuated by heaving seas, blinding winds and drowning men; lost children rolling their belongings in garbage cans along the shoreline; frail bodies spewing from the emergency shutes of planes. She visualised epilepsy-inducing opening scenes where popping light bulbs swung like rosary beads, old clergymen and their stoic wives beat against glass walls and hurled their lumpy bodies at ropes just out of reach. The music would be melancholy, off-key, probably sax, cello, haunting flute. Madelaine could see herself, hand-held video camera bobbing in front of her like an extra character. *Am I in trouble? Plenty of people dreamt their art. Am I hallucinating?*

Jerome had bought the video camera a week before Georgia was born. The baby gig had been something he was set on — the camera just another sweetener.

'I don't think I'm ready for a baby,' she'd procrastinated the year before, newly arrived in Port Lincoln, peering at job columns in the newspaper.

'The timing's perfect. Take a break for a few years. Think about film courses down the track,' he said.

There being no happy alternative — she couldn't see herself working in hotels or haberdashery, let alone anything agricultural — she acquiesced.

'To tell the truth, Mad, country people can be conservative. I could lose business if you take their kids' jobs. I don't agree with it but I can understand it.'

After the baby-making, she lay on her back, legs in the air to hold in the sperm, maximising the perfect timing, watching light dance on the ceiling.

Jerome was proud, he said, of the way she spat both children out and emerged serene, through blood and chaos. She had ridden cascades of pain like waves, licked the salt from her hands like a wounded animal, her own survival paramount.

Disdaining the mirror and definitely the video – she was no auteur after all – she felt the babies hadn't come from her at all, were just some elaborate hoax, played out by Jerome and the hospital staff. Later, when soft hands gripped her finger and absurdly wise and trustful eyes stared back at hers, she had capitulated. For what it was worth, she would love them.

She shrank against the bedhead, sipped black tea, tried not to think too much about it. Some mothers just weren't good cows, the doctor said.

'Let's try the bottle,' a nurse said kindly.

Madelaine nodded and sighed as she handed the wailing bundle over.

'Try and get some sleep.'

How could she sleep, knowing that Jerome was disappointed?

A mewling Georgia had tugged at Madelaine's nipples. Early attempts at feeding had been sabotaged by an image of her father sneering in a corner of the hospital room. A great churning – half languid, half gripping – had begun in her womb. Then worse, the awful thought that she would have to face lactation Nazis. Nell was Kommandant, and 'breast is best' her dictum. On the way home from the supermarkets, Nell's enormous blue-veined breasts, engorged with anticipatory milk, dripped through her lumpy clothing. Czaba, Nell confided, liked to suck as well. Too much information.

After hospital, they had mostly been good babies. She enjoyed seeing them tucked in the bassinet and pram, like precious jewellery in a satin-lined box, and she had tiptoed in to brood. They were awesomely whole and perfect.

On the screaming days, when nothing settled them, she had rocked the cradle too hard. Her teeth clenched, and her brain registered alarm as they landed against the slatted sides. She left the room for their protection, heading down the narrow passage and closing all the doors between them.

Town Beach

Vlado had gone to the boat. Danica stood in an old track-suit and slippers at her kitchen window. *Where's the dog?* She scanned the cement planter boxes, the borders of newly planted palms. *Too quiet.* He'd been there to eat his breakfast. *Damn Hugo.* Slamming down the saucepan she was rinsing at the sink, she stormed into the yard. *Damn, damn, damn, you bloody, useless, expensive fence.* Sure enough, another hole in the brush, and she was sounding like her mother. The back door banged behind her as she ran to the road to call him. He couldn't be long gone.

She found him nosing under the neighbour's camellia. He glanced over his shoulder, watching her warily for a second, then tucked in his tail as she neared, and shot across the street. Danica held her head as a car braked and swerved, and the dog bounded away.

'Hugo!' Now she would have to wake Sonja, and Miranda would be rebellious about leaving the television. The bloody dog could get run over one day. *But please not yet. Vlado is away on the boat so much.*

Fighting temptation to leave Sonja at home, she lifted the drowsy body from her cot and carried her to the car. Madelaine shopped while her children slept. They never woke in less than two hours, she said. But there were house fires on the television news all the time. Little kids burnt to death in a back bedroom. Jeleni would never forgive her.

The car crept along the street leading to the esplanade. She wound down her window and called, 'Hugo, you filthy, beastly dog.' And he would be filthy, reeking of blood-and-bone, or something equally putrid. Why had they bought two kilos of white fluff? And why hadn't Vlado had him de-sexed?

'Huuugoo,' sounded shrill. Danica ducked her head over the steering wheel. A list of his indiscretions hammered through her brain. Miranda unbuckled her seat belt and began to grizzle about *Teletubbies*.

Danica was prepared to bargain. 'I'll buy you a nice bagel.'

'But I want to go to the torlet.'

Parking the car by the wooden steps to the beach, she scanned the shoreline. The beach was pale and empty, as viscous as egg white. She would have to get out. Shielding her eyes against the early morning glare, she jogged halfway to the water to search, when suddenly she caught a glimpse of him playing with a mud-coloured terrier by the jetty piles. She sprinted back to lock the car.

'Sit still. I promise to only be a minute.' She took off her slippers and pattered down the steps to run back across the beach.

Just within earshot, she called and caught his eye. Then, half turning, she called again more softly, heading gradually up the beach towards the car. She gambolled, threw sand and laughed back at him. It often worked. *He's just a stupid dog. Brain the size of a pea.* All that effort to get out and he'd throw it all aside for a game. Sure enough, he came bouncing after her.

31

'Good dog, good boy,' she threw, over-animated. Then as he neared, she lunged, grabbed a handful of his coat and muttered, 'You little bastard. I'll chop you and your fishy smell into my brudet one day.' The dog panted happily as she reached out to pat him and he catapulted into the back seat to lick the children. *He can be sweet.* She just hoped to God he was boosting not busting their immune systems; Miranda already had a cold.

Back home the telephone rang as she grappled with the back door keys, Sonja's sodden bottom on her hips. The dog's lead had tightened round Miranda's legs and she began to cry. Danica bent to free the child before rushing to pick up the receiver. The phone was dead. Standing at the change table, lips compressed over nappy pins, she swore when it rang again.

'It's me,' said the voice.

'Hello. Madelaine is it? How are you today?' Danica tried to sound upbeat.

'Are you alright?' Madelaine always knew.

'Oh yes. Things are at sixes and sevens. Is that what you say?'

'What's wrong?'

'Just the usual: nappies and grizzling; the dog broke out and I've missed my aerobics class; I've just brought him from the beach, in my slippers.'

'Poor you.'

'Miranda's sneezing, I think she's got a cold, and if I don't get a good night's sleep tonight, it will be the end of me.'

'Let me shoot the dog. We'll take the kids out to Whalers, and push them off the cliff. You and I should get along nicely then.'

'Oh, Madelaine. You shouldn't joke.'

'I'm not joking. You should do something about that dog. Every time I'm at your gate, he tries to shoot between my feet. Last week I had to push my foot into his mouth. Get rid of him.'

'I love him, mostly. And it's not his fault — he can't help his hormones.'

'He's not even a proper dog. More like an animated tampon.'

'I paid a lot of money for him, and I wouldn't feel safe at night without him,' Danica wailed.

'What would he do if someone came? Lick them to death?'

'God knows. Madelaine, I have to go. Miranda's got a chair ... she's climbing on top of the fridge. Did you ring for a chat or something else?'

'Just to see how you were. Let's go to the beach tomorrow.'

'Sure. I'll have to get someone in to look at the fence today.'

'Ten o'clock then, before it gets too hot?'

'Yes, fine. Will we meet where we usually do?'

'Absolutely.'

'Madelaine, I have to run. Miranda ...'

Billy Lights Point

God, look at the time. Madelaine had slept in. She had heard the toss of toys from the cot, and baby chatter from the bedrooms before the fluoro numbers on the clock-face had begun to mean anything. Muzzy with sleep, she had hauled Capri pants over bathers and fossicked for a white tee. *Hell, did Jerome say goodbye, graze my cheek, look in on the children even?* She remembered nothing. She pushed on, ignoring ammonia smells as she pushed plump flesh through the holes in baby garments.

Within twenty minutes she flipped out, tossing an arm-load of towels, fruit boxes and apples into a bag on the back seat of the car. Men travelled light, even with their children. Just threw them in the car – no sun block, drinks, nappies, baby Panadol; if the kids were lucky, a wallet to pay for any emergencies.

When Madelaine arrived, half an hour late, Danica was huddled with her children on the sand, biting the inside of her cheek.

'Darling I'm here. Get over it,' Madelaine said.

Danny rose and picked up a printed beach towel. Holding each end of the towel behind her outstretched arms, she turned to face the water. The towel flapped once and hung still.

'You look like a mother cormorant drying your wings.'

'I can't stay long.'

'Sorry.'

Madelaine lit up a cigarette and lay back on one elbow to video her children, prancing in the perfect sand, dancing in the ticklish water. What a good wife and mother she was, taking the children on an outing to the beach. Now she could smile a gleaming, successful, toothsome smile. Georgia cantered across the sand, her three-year-old face upturned. 'Mum, Paige's got smelly pants.'

'Gorgeous.' Madelaine gripped her camera with one hand, pretended to rear up at Paige, and stubbed her unfinished cigarette in the sand. What was one butt when the city council had shelved plans for a sewage-treatment overhaul? Her neighbours had told her horror stories of effluent over-flowing into the street and onto the beach. Madelaine rifled through her bag for a wet cloth.

'Alright, I'm coming, chook. Back you go. Keep swim-ming.' She raised her eyebrows at Danica.

Madelaine felt brittle enough to snap as she marched towards the water, her grotty child in focus. Shell grit crunched underfoot. Tiny crabs the colour of fingernails plucked at her toes. Sure enough there was a squishy, misshapen parcel in the seat of Paige's bathers and a less than winsome odour. Madelaine plucked the baby up and kissed her hard against the neck. Paige scrabbled at her hip, and Madelaine scowled before shading her eyes with one hand, to stare across the water.

Holiday-makers were backing their boat awkwardly down the ramp. *Probably never done it before by the look of them. I bet no one will poo and spoil their day.* So happy and noisy, all expensively dressed like magazine cut-outs, waving champagne bottles over their heads. It was such a beautiful day with the sun beating down on the water and gulls bobbing on the toffeed surface. *Which way will they go?* Out past Boston Island or back towards Thistle or Goat? They'd come back tired and dry-skinned, the women cross with the men.

She rinsed her fingers in the water before levering her white swimsuit out of nooks and crevices. She tugged her towelling hat lower over her face. Paige cantered away, naked and rinsed.

'Seagull'll bite your bum,' Madelaine called. Half alarmed, Paige skittered under a towel. Madelaine strode up the beach in search of a bin, dangling a tightly wound and knotted plastic bag.

When she returned, Danica smiled sympathetically, her uneasy body slumping inside a two-hundred-dollar swimsuit from Jansys. Then she rose and stepped away to shake out her towel before she wrapped it around her waist. *Why doesn't she ever look at home in her body?*

'I need to go, Madelaine. Vlado came home last night. Not that I'll see much of him. The boat'll probably need its engine rebuilt or . . .' She hung her head.

'That's the way of it. Jerome is always bloody tired. Know the secret of a happy marriage?'

Danica didn't always get Madelaine's jokes. She hung her head on one side, peering up at her.

'It's a secret,' Madelaine hissed.

Danica snorted. She looked letdown. 'Are things worse?'

Madelaine rolled her eyes, and mimicked Jerome: '"Law is serious, Madelaine. Its interpretation changes people's lives."'

'What are you going to do?'

'God knows. He can hide out at the office but where can I go? To the deli to pig out on choc, like you?'

'Don't.'

'You're such a fragile piece. I don't know why I took up with you in the first place.' Slinging an arm around Danica's shoulders, Madelaine dropped her head to rest her nose against her friend's. Danica was hurt, and pressed her lips together as she gathered up a whining Sonja.

Later, back home, Madelaine retraced her flight path. She had rushed out too fast and the house was a tip. *My God, what was I thinking of? This is my workplace. I'll have no credibility.* She ran like a rat looking for the control panel, in circles from the kitchen to the bathroom, to the laundry, down the passage, and back again. She scurried here and there, flapping and mumbling, clearing and tidying surfaces, shrieking at Paige and Georgia until she dispatched them, clutching bottles to their cots.

What a blessing to afford technology. Machines hummed, digesting dirty dishes and gammy nappies. She could run the whole segment backwards like a noir film, or fast-forward it like an old one. She could take a stagier role, and crash spreadeagled on the kitchen floor, knock herself out under an avalanche of dirty dishes, her hysterical exhalations lifting the fringe of her hair. It wasn't always bliss, being fully conscious.

Madelaine poured herself a glass of wine and eased onto a stool at the breakfast bar. It was past lunchtime. She should eat. *What will be the least fag to prepare?* Tipping her glass back, she swilled wine around in her mouth like wash, then smelt her armpits. *God, I stink. And I'm covered in sand.* The beach had seemed a good idea the day before. Everything was more difficult with kids in tow, and it wasn't Danny's fault that things had fallen flat. Madelaine had been late and they had both been tired. Now the wine was going to her head, and she swayed experimentally. She decided on an afternoon bath. *How decadent.*

She rolled on her belly in the tub. Crossing her ankles, she slipped sideways against the hollow-sounding sides of the bath, and curled up with her head in the crook of her elbow. Her hand dangled uselessly until she felt the beginnings of a cramp in her wrist. Tiny circles of grease winked at her from the surface of the water: her own sloughed skin perhaps, or simply perspiration. When she blew on them, the circles bumped against each other, and reflections of the overhead lights lurched about between them. A perfect coil of dark hair floated towards her face and she breathed from the back of her throat. The skin of the water ruffled, indented, bounced, as her breath passed over.

Jerome poked his head around the door. She rolled onto her back, soapy debris slurping at her edges, and stared at him. *Why is he here?*

'Are you ill?' *That wasn't very polite.* She tried again. 'What's wrong?'

'Late lunch. I love your map of Tasmania.' He lifted his eyes from her body. 'Kids asleep?'

She rose, and turning her face away, shook water from her sides, like a horse, and stepped out. He withheld an outspread towel, then stepped forward to fold it around her. He pulled her hard up against his body until she stumbled on the edge of the bath, splashing water on his suit.

'Let's not have a hissy-fit – just a cuddle,' he said, quirking an eyebrow and dabbing at his jacket.

She sighed. Nuzzling at the side of her neck, he tugged her backwards out of the bathroom.

'Remember. A hard-on is not a sign of personal growth.'

Would he have the grace to look apologetic, to shrug as she released her hair from her tortoise-shell clasp and hunkered down? It was of no consequence. He was like a big dog snuffling and panting as he nosed her towel aside.

Not so often now, more before the children, she had grown excited when she felt his fingers teasing fabric aside, moving it softly between her skin and his. He had been a warm and solid presence. She'd locked herself against his hand, and angled her head to reach for his lips.

'How was it this time?' he'd grin afterwards.

'You don't want to hear about it, I know,' she usually said.

'I do, I do. Tell me how it was: deeply menstrual, raw, like a cat dragging its bum over rough surface, crashing like falling water? Humming? Sobbing? I'm always interested!' Perhaps he was.

'Liar.' If she licked at his face or chest, he pushed her off. 'I don't recoil afterwards, like you,' she said.

'It's true, release does give me that what-the-fuck-am-I-doing-here sense of being.'

'Like a rutting stag.'

'Ah well.'

It seemed to her their conversations ran along predictable tracks, derailed on the same bends. She bit her tongue.

'What's wrong now?' he said.

'Nothing,' she replied.

Today Jerome would have the world at bay, no more than a distant glimpse over the flesh of her shoulder. He believed in love but wanted more. In the face of his greed, she felt resigned. Afterwards he stood naked at the window, a man surveying his yard as he idly scratched his penis. Then he turned his head to check the bedside clock. 'It's two. I'm supposed to see someone – ten minutes ago.' He stepped sideways to gather up his shoes and socks.

'And when will you be home?'

'No idea.'

Madelaine stared through him.

'Haven't a clue and I'm late now.'

Is he implying it's my fault?

She heard the car reverse down the driveway, saw him raise his hand without looking up at the house, then swing the car towards the city centre.

The sun moved behind a cloud, the sea had settled heavily in front of the bedroom window, and shadows flew across the lawn. Madelaine lay sticky and affronted, an earring lost in the sheets somewhere, the bedclothes broiled and mashed. *Men are lucky.* There was no coaxing or sweet unfurling. It was a handicap, he said. Why should she believe that? He came to her in faux self-loathing, desperate to be unburdened. How clever to wheedle. Who could be angry then? Intimacy crowded her inner spaces. Breathing was hard some days. Her world was shrinking. Her mother would say she was lucky. But what would she know about that?

Hot and irritable, Madelaine dripped into the bathroom. The tiles were cool under her feet as she peered into the mirror. She didn't much like her face after this kind of sex: mouth in a grim line, teeth clenched. Not so many years ago, the face in the mirror had been flushed and soft, the lips full and hot, and the hair wild around her head. He used to like to see her twisting about beneath him.

'You're enjoying this, aren't you?' he said once, as if it gave him power.

Inland

Last year in April there had been ear infections, erupting baby teeth, sleepless nights and bucket loads of millipedes massing on the porch. They had decided to go away: a few days alone, for respite. Conversations uninterrupted by the phone, and having nothing to do but get lunch would lift their spirits, Jerome said. Madelaine hadn't wanted to go, had rushed down to the water at the last moment and thrown herself in for one last wallow. Bitter cold, the sea had wrapped its arms around her, attacking her skin first and then her bones. She had pounded up and down, fighting the crosshatched waves and the stinging wind that made her eyes stream faster. She swam until her skin tingled and her feet cramped and she was resigned to hauling herself back up the beach and home, to pack for a holiday she didn't want. Jo would have the children, Jerome said. He had already asked her.

He had taken her inland, away from her beloved sea, to a bed-and-breakfast mansion. They dumped their luggage; his suit bag sprawled over her overnight case.

'Now, please?' he urged from the four-poster bed.

'I'm quite tired.'

'I'm thinking of you. I don't want to bother you later.'

He tugged at the hem of her jacket, all sly fingers. 'Don't you want to?'

She licked his neck, and received a rush of grateful kisses. No doubt he could bang up against her while babies howled, doorbells rang, and children cried out that the dog couldn't breathe and the Cocoa Pops were lost. While she sneezed, bled, cramped, sobbed, recovered from childbirth. He was very focused. As he dropped his head to latch on to her nipple, she thought about his mother – wondered if she was the dark spectre of Jerome's erotic life. *Weaned late or early?* So unfair, to blame another woman. *I refuse to be his mother.*

Cleaned up, they walked straight out into the khaki bush, stopping only for sandshoes and a glass of water. An arm slung round her shoulders, he looked tired, boyish. Now that he'd had his way, she hoped he wouldn't fight with her.

Housedogs followed at a distance. They had acted more like cats, circling behind them in the scrub, then appearing suddenly beneath their feet, tripping them up and disappearing again. Trailing bushes with hard dark berries lined the creek bed. Tendrils strayed across the path, snagging his linen jacket, catching on the hem of her pants.

Concentrating on the dappled path, she picked her way round pocks and mounds, stumbling and inadvertently clutching at his arm. This pleased him. Tiny bush birds scurried in the undergrowth, hopped ahead of them along the path. Madelaine could see them on the periphery of her vision, whirring, dropping, and skirmishing like insects.

They crossed at a ford. Small worn stones remained firmly anchored. Large ones wobbled about, splashing water on their shoes. She reached out to hold Jerome steady, laughed, willed their civility to hold. Apart from the trickle of water and the occasional raucous cry of crows, they took the deep silence of the bush on their shoulders. It was almost palpable. A mesh of gum leaves held the sky at bay. Suddenly, they heard the slightest sound, the whispering of parting grasses, followed by a guttural growl. Jerome jumped back, and seized a fallen branch. Madelaine stiffened, drew in her breath and half turned to take in the shadowy silhouette of a large buck kangaroo, his cocked ears moving like radar. Four females nosed the air behind him, their shoulders hunched in concentration, their paws crossed like ladies at tea, before whisking up their tails to bound gracefully away.

'God, that scared me.' Madelaine reached out her hand to catch Jerome's coat.

Pleased, he slid an arm around her waist to steer her back along the homeward path. 'Glad we came?'

At the last bend, when the turrets of the bed and breakfast loomed over them, and the grey flanks of its west wing grew visible through the privet hedge, he released her and unzipped his pants. Leaning back on his heels and holding his penis, he shot straight up the trunk of a gum, and smiled. She took in the silky skin, the large vein, the cocky boy part of him, happily absorbed. *Am I feeling maternal after all? Is this how his mum felt, that it was awfully cute, a boy pissing?*

Later, light rain fell as they drank tea on the verandah. Mist drifted through the gums and the beginnings of their conversation leapt from the children, to stories from playgroup, and on to aggravating neighbours as if a torrent had been unleashed. But it petered out and they were at a loss. Tangled in the bath, her toes on his chest, his bracketing her hips, steam in their hair, they trickled in orange oil, and soaked for an hour, before taking dinner in the library, among the guns and war medals. Stumps crackled and spat in the fireplace, lighting the wine in their glasses. Through course after course she willed the talk to please him, for them to avoid the usual flashpoints until they swayed tipsily off to the giant bed, and the cabbage-rose wallpaper. During the night, land breeze whistled at the dormer windows and Madelaine longed for the sound and smell of the sea. *Was I born longing?* She felt paralysed, as if time had slowed, and she could die here, alone with Jerome.

The next morning she woke to find him chugging over her, mouth at her ear.

'Sorry. Do you mind?'

That April, marriage had seemed like a garment that she had once slid into easily. It had looked nice, but chafed on odd occasions. Now it no longer seemed to fit, and she wondered if she'd grown. Later, while they lazed in bed, she stroked his back.

'Isn't this how it should be?' he murmured at her shoulder.

'Yes,' she lied, thinking of soft cheeks and the faint ammonia morning smell overriding the scent of the sea. A part of her hardened against him: a kernel of despair.

Port Lincoln Leisure Centre

Danica swung her red Audi into the gym car park, completely alone at seven am, not a clamouring child with matted hair and crusty eyes in sight. Vesna, Danica's mother-in-law, had scooped up the greying cereal bowls dripping at the breakfast bar, raised the bedroom window sashes on sour morning smells, and waved Danica away: 'Shoo.'

There were not enough words to describe the release that came from working out. She clumped in rubber-soled shoes across the slippery tiles beside the pool, and smiled at early-morning swimmers. The great membranous wings of the centre's roofline stretched above her. The smell of chlorine was strong. She moved along the mezzanine walkway past half a dozen people rowing and running on heavy machines. In the next room, local footballers were working with Jadron, their weights coach, an old friend of Danica's from high school.

'Danny!' he bellowed through the door and over pumping music. The footballers turned their heads like birds on a rail and ogled her on cue, while Danica tugged at her hooded sweatshirt and waved. Jadron was small, compact, beautifully muscled, and had won a junior body-building competition when they were sixteen. Much to her mother's horror, Danica had helped him wax his legs and chest.

'Jad,' she mouthed, using the reflection of her body in the glass partition to straighten her posture before turning into the aerobics room.

She dropped her bag in the far corner, rolled off her sweatshirt and pushed out a few calf stretches. The air conditioning was chilly on her skin but she would soon warm up. The room was almost bare with floor-to-ceiling mirrors at the front and *Sports Illustrated* girls on the wall.

While Danica waited for the instructor to pad in, bearing her mat and ghetto blaster, she moaned about the new timetable with a small dark girl who often came to the same classes. The girl was quiet, rarely said a word unless Danny spoke first, but she always worked up close to the front mirror, facing her reflection. All through the routine, the girl's eyes never left her body, as if she were having a love affair with herself. By contrast, Danica threw surreptitious glances at the mirror, as if throwing stones on the Gaza strip, as if she wanted to run away in fright. Neither exercise nor diet shifted the bowl of her belly. She sucked in, tightened her muscles, and looked away dissatisfied. *Is it having babies?*

The warm-up music rolled over her in a lovely wave and she strode out to meet it, swaying and bending, flexing and relaxing her muscles, her misery quieting, her body obedient. Her boots tapped against the sprung floor. As she lifted her diaphragm, her heart and lungs shifted gears, her breasts settled beneath her leotard, and her upper body stilled, keeping the balance when the pace picked up. She felt mechanical and graceful, strong and weightless, by turns.

As she attacked the beat, the music held her, and she was only half aware of passing footballers with towels strung around their necks, staring in. Perspiration glinted at her temples and neck, grew in a damp patch at the base of her spine and between her breasts. She concentrated on breathing.

Vlado would hoot: 'You concentrated on breathing. Right!'

The instructor was talkin' the talk: 'Grunt', 'Yes', 'Wooah', 'Push it up.' Vlado would fall on the floor laughing if he were here; he would be making stupid jokes about sex.

Too bad. Aerobics made her feel powerful. If only she had more control on other days. Little hands were always clutching and pulling, breaking and soiling. There were so many long lonely days and nights when she was desperate to stride out of the house, down the road, and away. But she couldn't. Well, she wouldn't. She shouldn't.

She sighed during the cool-down stretches, and smiled at the thought of Vesna, who helped with so much generous pleasure. When her own mother came, Danica was up at six, hanging nappies, vacuuming and tidying in preparation. She retracted into herself, away from the waves of her mother's disapproval, and went to sit by the window in defeat, draw furiously on a cigarette. Jeleni was like a baying wolf scenting failure through sleet and rain and dust. But she didn't know everything. Danica had found a way to manage.

When Danica returned an hour later from the gym, Vesna beamed: 'You're feeling good?' Her broad face was arranged in good-natured folds. 'Your darlings, they are happy.' The children sprawled in front of the television. *Far too close, but . . .*

'Thank you, Vesna. If only Vlado was around at more useful times.' *Why did I say that to Vesna?*

'Ahh, we women stick together. That is what family is for.' Vesna laughed. 'You want coffee?'

'No, oh yes, alright,' Danica corrected herself. 'We'll have one together. I'll make it. You sit down.' She measured

Turkish coffee into a long-handled saucepan. *I drink too much coffee.* When the girls were younger it had punctuated her day. Black and sweet and gritty – she had reached for it like a lifeline.

Vesna lifted the lid on the saucepan gently vibrating on the hot plate. 'I have cooked brudet and egg pie for your dinner. What a day you have; nothing to do but play with your babies. Do you go many times to the playgroup? It is not too much for you?'

'It is good Vesna, to go out and meet people.'

'What sort of people though?' Vesna's mouth turned down. 'In our families this is a wonderful time to have hard work, to watch the little ones grow.'

'I miss the shop, Vesna. I know it wasn't much, but . . .'

'Work! You have work. You have everything a wife could want. Those other girls, they have to work to buy things. Not you. My Vlado is a good provider.'

'Yes I know, but I might need to work . . . soon.' She sighed. 'I know, I'm lucky. When I think of your lives . . . but things are different now. Some men help at home.'

'Owww! Who would want that, Danica? They are just a nuisance . . . underfoot. Remind yourself of this, when the boats are in, and he is at home. Men are interfering with everything you do, wanting attention. Imagine him clucking and cleaning around the house all day. Would you like that?' Vesna tugged at her black crepe belt, which strained under her enormous bulk. Danica couldn't bear to look like that – or like Nell. She would rather diet all her life.

'I hope you will enjoy your dinner. You are so thin. How will you conceive a son when you are just skin and bones?' Vesna chuckled, elbowing her gently in the side.

'You're all in such a hurry. Sonja is only eighteen months. Still a baby, and you want me fat again,' she laughed.

They bent, touched cheeks, hugged. Danica could feel Vesna's breasts against her, thick and heavy like pudding.

'Hvala, Vesna. I really appreciate your help. Dovidenja.'

'Dovidenja.'

Later, Danica noticed that Vesna had shifted things around, remade the babies' beds and placed a leaking pot plant on the sink. *I suppose it doesn't matter.* Danica slipped into the shower feeling flat and tired. *I haven't seen anyone for days.* It seemed her treks to the bakery, and the playgrounds, were out of sequence with the others'. She would try the supermarket. *At least it will break up the day.*

Nell often said, 'Come for a coffee.' But dropping in felt rude. Other people did, she knew, but what if Nell was sick or sleeping, or the house more chaotic than usual?

'Yes, I might,' Danica always lied.

There were often sad people at Nell's. *What if someone thinks I'm one of them?* Nell encouraged confidences and was terribly personal, asking alarming questions, drawing people out. Pauline joked that taking a black eye to Nell's for afternoon tea gave more pleasure than a plate of Amaretti biscuits, and that she had once had Nell enthralled with a tale of strawberry enemas, and of Hugh binding her to the bedposts with bandages. Nell probed happy people for a history: a gay brother or a dominating mother.

Not only that, in the supermarket, Nell pounced like a terrier on the contents of people's trolleys, nosing out flowered loo paper, ozone gobbling spray cans and plastic carry bags. Nell looked after water systems, sustainable practice, world peace, the endangered and the oppressed. Danica was afraid of inciting her holy wrath. There were so many things to consider. Multicultural sins were Nell's only concession: strong coffee, in moderation, well-salted olives, thick cheeses.

Sonja's chubby knees swung from the baby-seat of the trolley, and Miranda wobbled crabbily behind. Shopping with children was no snack. If the trolley cruised too close to laden shelves, Sonja sent cans crashing to the floor, snatched things up and chewed until the packaging was soggy. Danica had tried to make it fun, lingered between the rows of toys, bought treats and paperback picture books, but when the trolley was almost full, Miranda had let out a banshee wail. Lately Danica had been on first-name terms with the floor manager who carried the toilet key.

When Czaba materialised in the queue at the checkout — thankfully alone — Danica pushed the chocolate donuts behind the breakfast cereal. *Would he dob me in?*

'Hello, Czaba. How are you? Morning off?' She inclined her head, tugged at her black stretch pants. *Are they too tight?* As if he would notice. Like Vlado would say, Nell was so fat she couldn't get out of her own way. Danica felt nasty and cheap for even thinking such things. Nell had diabetes. Her weight wasn't her fault.

'Yes, Nell's unwell.'

Danica bit her lip. 'What's wrong with her?'

'Urinary tract infection. Her blood sugar went haywire. How have you been?'

'Well enough. This is not my favourite place.' Sonja erupted from the trolley. Danica leapt forward, caught her by the legs and buckled her chubby knees back through the leg holes of the baby-seat. Sonja threw her arms around her mother's head, messing up her hair. Thumb in her mouth, Miranda slid her other hand inside her nickers. Her eyes glazed over. *God, Miranda.*

'I'll let you go.' Czaba bounced a finger on Sonja's chin, and winked at Miranda as he wheeled away.

Hell, Czaba's boys sat in the trolley without moving or speaking. *Were they breathing?* Sometimes the most undeserving people had dull, stolid children who quite unjustly turned out to be intelligent as well. Biting was their only vice. Miranda reached for a chocolate bar, which Danica intercepted millimetres from her mouth, and placed higher on the shelf. Indignant, Miranda threw herself to the floor. *So unfair of the supermarket to place it at the checkout. Don't any of their staff have children?* Perhaps she needed chocolate too. After all that aerobics, one couldn't hurt. She reached up and took one, slipped it beneath the milk in the trolley and in the same swift movement, bent to smack Miranda's legs and haul her to her feet. Danica glared at the checkout girl. *Hurry up, you stupid little bitch with your seven ear studs, and your stupid have a nice day. Have one yourself.*

What is wrong with me?

Rustler's Gully

Jo's three-year-old daughter Willa stood on a chair at the front screen door, all spoggy hair and eyes, uncertain. *Why did she open the door? Of course, she's frightened.* So, Madelaine waited, confronted and confounded by Doug slamming his fist against a kitchen bench. *Jesus! What a fracas.* Nonplussed, fingers curled around the screen-door handle, she wished she could rewind, withdraw, leave, but after several unpleasant seconds, she pushed the door open with great care and stepped forward to scoop up the child. Jo moved sideways, clutching at the wall.

'I'll be back when you've calmed down.' Doug heaved past Madelaine at the door, nodded, 'Madelaine. Sorry.' His car screeched out of the driveway.

Jo crossed to the door and held out her arms for Willa. 'Did you hear?' she whispered to Madelaine.

'Jo, I did, I'm sorry. Not much. Willa opened the door.'

Jo pressed her lips against her daughter's head. A baby cried in another room.

'I'm just returning the plate you left at playgroup. Are you alright?'

'I'm not supposed to cry in front of the children. It undermines his relationship with them. His mother rang to tell me.'

'Outrageous.'

'How about, if I talk to my friends about him, he'll call the police?' There was a crackle in Jo's voice.

'Do you think he's seriously unhinged?' They both giggled. Madelaine liked the inappropriate way people laughed during angst-laden moments.

'I'm so exhausted. He never helps. I know I don't work full-time, but I do take every night shift with the children.' Jo smoothed down her clothing and sighed. 'Shall I make a pot of tea?'

'Just a quick one. Will he come back?'

'Later. He'll go to the yacht club first.'

Madelaine slipped along the passage to the baby's room, pushed the dummy between his lips and tucked him in.

'I think he's going to settle,' she whispered to the girls who had followed her in like a trio of soulful angels.

In the kitchen, Jo sliced and buttered yeast bun, then licked her fingers. 'Thank you, I think the noise disturbed him. He's very tired.'

Madelaine boiled the kettle.

Jo wiped her eyes with the back of her forearm. 'We've been at Doug's staff picnic,' she said. 'I organised the food, the drinks, the kids, and packed the car. Before we left I asked him if he could carry out the picnic basket.'

Madelaine nibbled a piece of bun and raised an eyebrow.

'"Later," he says, "I'm watching the golf." The picnic was awful. Willa vomited and Doug ignored us.'

'Jesus, Jo. What can you do?'

Jo began to cry again. 'I don't know. I used to think I could be the shock absorber, trying harder, helping everyone, but I'm so tired.'

She pushed her chair back from the table and reached behind her for a tissue. 'Let's talk about something else,' she sniffed.

They spoke despondently of late holiday-makers clotting up the car parks in the shopping streets, throwing rubbish into people's yards. Madelaine poured the tea and passed juice to the children. Jo calmed down but, in the end, Madelaine didn't like to leave without returning to the dire subject of Doug. It would look heartless.

'Did he do anything while you were at the picnic?'

'Complained that I brought too much gear, that I wasn't talking to the right people, and that the baby coughed too much. I'm worried he has asthma, like Willa.'

'But did Doug have fun?'

'Yes of course he did!'

They both laughed.

'Dear God, Jo. If there's anything I can do. Not that I have any answers, none at all. In fact I'm the last person to ask about anything . . .'

Jo turned the cooling teapot in slow circles. She brushed hair from her face and closed her eyes.

Madelaine tipped the remains of her tea into the sink and gathered up the children. 'You're so far from your family here, and I know there are some people who like their families!'

'I do, actually.' Jo smiled

'Must be time they came for a visit.'

'It's worse when they come. I feel humiliated.'

'You could move on.' Madelaine wondered if she could.

Jo held the door for her and shook her head.

'I'll be alright.'

Boston Bay

There was always wind at the Divjaks'. Even on a summer's day, dry grass and cereal dust from the wharf skirmished on the patio before settling in the corners. On blistering north-wind days the hanging pots swung out wildly before they crashed, throwing clouds of earth and foliage. In the winter the wind was savagely cold, howling around the seals on the great sliding doors, spraying salty invective across the glass.

Madelaine liked to watch Danica with Vlado's family. At first they seemed so hard working, happy, and uncomplicated that she was jealous. But if she thought about it properly she knew that wasn't true. All families had problems, especially if they came from a country where war had pitted neighbours against each other, east against west, Allah against a Catholic God.

Madelaine was an outsider, but when the boats were in, the men tempted her with dark European chocolate, tiny cups of strong coffee and bracing šljivovica, their big fishermen's bodies leaning across the counter. Their eyes followed her as she moved around the room. Even the old boy would leap up when she arrived, offer her his hand, and hold it for that half-second too long.

'Madelaine,' he would say, his eyes shining with welcome. 'Good morning. Good afternoon. Good evening.' *Always so polite.*

Otherwise though, Madelaine was not privy to the kind of talk where voices rose and shadows flew across the faces of members of the family – when men turned on their heel and women withdrew to the kitchen. Even for a privileged guest there were only glimpses. With the best intentions, to protect each other, families plastered over secrets. *I should know . . .*

Danica was laughing, looked content, but who would really know? Her children too, playing quietly with the Divjak cousins on the Italian-tiled floor, under the umbrella of their extended family. *They're damned good children.* Danica complained that they were demanding, but perhaps at home they were agitated by *her* anxiety.

Today the sky was still, the sea bright and clean and beautiful. Madelaine feasted on it. Not long now and she would be out there, rising and falling between the breaking waves, throwing spray and rolling on her back like a dolphin. Only the faintest breeze stirred the senses.

Vesna carried a gleaming silver tray laden with seafood: export-fat lobster, huge bright prawns from Damir's trawler, and smoked fish on rye with lashings of sour cream. Ice clinked in the big jars of spritzer. Madelaine watched Danica wrapping a cevapcici, and was amazed at how deftly her fingers manipulated the pita-bread. Madelaine knew that food was both her comfort and her torture.

'Come over here, Danica. Bring your very beautiful friend. I will tell you what happened to cousin Tomaislav. Poor fellow.' Patting the seat next to him, Grandpa Dragon roared with laughter. Danica winked at Madelaine and they slid along the bench beside him. Reddening in anticipation, Tomaislav was grinning like a fool as he rearranged his mammoth limbs on a spindly chair. *He's a nice enough chap, but he drinks too much.*

But then, who am I to talk? Madelaine felt like lamb on a spit, he stared at her so boldly, and she glared.

Grandpa Dragon threw out his hands in an exaggerated flourish. 'Last week at the head of the Bight, we were running a lovely school of tuna when who falls in the water? Do we see Tomi poling for his life? No, Tomi, Tomi . . .' He tossed back his head; his laughter boomed across the table. 'Tomi decides he will go for a little swim.'

'I heard,' Danica smiled. 'I hope you saved him quickly, Grandpa. Good deckies are hard to find.'

Grandpa burped and reached for another cevapcici. 'It was very lucky he owed me money or I would have had to let him go.' He guffawed.

Danica caught Tomaislav's eye. 'Your mate, Otto. He was in strife last week?'

Madelaine knew that Danica wasn't fond of Otto, discouraged him visiting Vlado at the house. She winked at her.

'Hah! Silly bloody ab divers, always off their face with marijuana,' interjected Grandpa.

'That's not true,' Tomaislav flared. 'He didn't mean to stay down too long. It's time the city got a decompression chamber. Bloody lucky he wasn't jelly.'

'Picking up ten-dollar bills off the bottom,' snickered Grandpa.

'There have been a lot of accidents lately. It takes too long to fly divers across to Adelaide,' Danica agreed.

Madelaine enjoyed watching Danica bantering easily with her family. No doubt there were underlying tensions but she looked more confident than usual, and more relaxed. She was flirting with old Grandpa. *Would Jerome love* me *more if I played games? Damned if I will. Not even to keep him, or protect the children.*

Danica laid her hand on Grandpa's arm as he raised a match to pick his teeth. He was sputtering like a sea lion, with grease and onion in his beard. He prodded the table with the match.

'Wouldn't need a chamber if they weren't so greedy, and left a bit for the next bloke, eh Danny.'

The old devil.

'Accidents still happen when every precaution is taken,' said Danica.

'And where would *we* be if *we* weren't careful?' he barked.

'With Tomaislav in the water?' Danica smiled evenly.

Bravo! Why does she back off so much at playgroup?

'You're a good girl, Danica, but you don't understand men's work. Lucky we don't need you to help us. You would blow away, off the deck. Have more pitta. Fatten up for poor Vlado. He has no one to keep him warm on shore.' Grandpa raised his voice, 'Eh Vlado?'

Vlado had been listening to a Scottish deckhand in front of the big sliding doors. He swung to face his wife, touching his fingers to his lips in the same motion. Danica blushed at the kiss and moved away to stack plates, gather serviettes, and carry them to the kitchen. *She looks so happy.* Madelaine rose to help her. *What a shame she has to go back to her own big house and be the mother.* Sometimes she seemed too young.

Vesna was in the kitchen humming to herself as she washed dishes, a bright apron tied around her waist. Hard Australian work had made her tough and brought prosperity. After the old terrors of hunger, fear and war, did people still remember how they left their village, their country? Did they wake and scream at night? Vesna and Jeleni wore their contentment like sleek well-fed seals; expensive jewellery glistened between the fleshy folds of neck and shoulder, enormous breasts swelled above the perspiration line, cabriole legs splayed below.

'We are glad that you could eat with us today Madelaine, and of course the little children.' Madelaine scraped dirty plates and stacked them on the sink.

'Thank you for inviting me. I was glad to get out of the house.' *Play the game, Madelaine. They are nice people.*

'And where is your husband?'

'He flew out this morning, to a meeting, but he'll be back tomorrow.' Madelaine gathered up a cloth to wipe the table. 'Danica seems so happy here. She is a different girl, and eating.' Madelaine looked slyly at Vesna.

'Oh, eating. When she was baby she drove her mother mad. Jeleni fussed so much. Then when she was teenager it was worse. That stubborn mouth stayed shut. If her mother ignored, Danica ate even less.'

'God, I didn't know it went back that far.'

'She is better now. Vlado has made her happy, and her children.'

'What did her father think?'

'Jeleni said he would growl, "Eat meat, Danica!" and reach for his belt. Jeleni was always shrieking, "You are silly girl. You will kill yourself. Not to eat is irresponsible. You used to be a good girl." They paid too much attention. I think it is normal for girls to fuss with food.'

'You may be right. She is lucky to have you onside, Vesna.' Madelaine could see Danica laughing at Tomi as she spooned food into Sonja's mouth. 'I never knew my husband's parents. They died before I met him. He was the baby.'

Vesna touched her hand. 'You have your own little family.'

'Yes indeed.'

Once, Danica had told Madelaine that Dragon kept a girlfriend in an apartment near the new marina blocks. And, God forbid, a baby. *Does Vesna know? Is life simple for anyone?*

Never having wanted children, maternal love had taken Madelaine by surprise. The girls had changed her life. Babies are vulnerable. They had forced her to take responsibility, or at least to make a show of it, and she had managed to stay afloat. Madelaine wondered if Danica would be swept along by her family – and their friends – producing babies until a seedy inertia gripped? They could discuss it at playgroup in the morning. Nell would know the answer. For a change, Madelaine would sling a topic on the table.

'Two point two,' Nell would say. 'Two-point-two children per family.' End of story.

Nell's

By morning Madelaine felt ambivalent about going to play-group. Despite an early night, she hadn't slept well. Jerome had rung late to say goodnight and they had squabbled. She had asked all the questions she could think of about his health, his day, his travel, but there had been long silences. She had paced the balcony, smoking uneasily, wondering why she hadn't felt well lately. *I'm not pregnant.* The morning had brought incontrovertible proof of that. Thankfully not another happy accident.

But it would be easier to go out than think of amusing activities for the girls at home. They loved playgroup – were far more sociable than their mother. If a bus pulled up, they'd get on, Madelaine often joked.

When she arrived at Nell's, Danica was preparing the morning tea. Dirty coffee cups were up-ended on the sink. Crockery was always hastily rinsed at Nell's, and put in the dish drainer ready for the next influx of guests. Madelaine grimaced over the deep stains inside the cups, and imagined the conversation when Czaba came home for his lunch. Nell would say, Any chance you could shift some afternoon appointments today? I have to lie down. I'm so exhausted.

Madelaine felt sorry for him, coming home to a dusty house with a sink full of dishes and a wife gone to bed.

Through the window she could see Nell's dog lunging at Danica's hands as she walked to the clothesline to unpeg clean tea towels. He wanted to play but Danny plodded along, her shoulders slumped. *She's definitely peevish.*

Damned if she would wait while Danica fluffed around. She would grab her own coffee. A plastic cup would do. Madelaine selected Minnie Mouse melamine from the cupboard and poured the water in, then reached into the refrigerator. *Hell's tooth!* Which milk should she choose: unlabelled something in a flowery jug, packet milk past the expiry date, or soy? She sniffed the flowery jug: cow's milk? It seemed alright.

Nell's bottles of insulin were lined up behind the jug. One or two mils could kill, she said. And there they were, standing innocently behind the milk. Would Georgia be smart enough to leave them alone? Paige couldn't open the refrigerator door, let alone negotiate a childproof lid. Once, Georgia had drunk a bottle of banana-flavoured antibiotic – loved the taste. Erupted through her nappy, but cleared up her cold. Madelaine pushed the insulin bottles to the back of the shelf. On a whim she plucked one out and slipped it into her pocket. *Will Nell notice?*

Jo, Pauline and some of the children were singing along to audiotapes. Nell and Danica were having a confab at the back door and staring now and then at Madelaine. *God, what have I done now?* She slid behind the coffee table to lift a biscuit, bit into it and slipped it back. *Bloody diabetic.* Then sat cross-legged on the floor behind the couch. *I'll video the children.* Her girls were connecting plastic construction pieces in a long chain. Willa passed the pieces. Madelaine tilted the camera to make a better composition, zoomed in too fast and lost their heads. She zoomed out.

'Is it your birthday next week, Willa?'

'Can't know.'

'You can't know!' said Madelaine.

Snippets of adult conversation distracted her.

'Are you okay, Danny?'

Madelaine saw Nell push her glasses onto the bridge of her nose with one hand and eyeball Danica, who was looking edgy. Nell had Jo's baby tucked under one arm. *God, she's feeding him.* There lay the secret of her babysitting prowess. Breast is best. *Does Jo mind?* Nell lowered her voice and scanned the room to pinpoint Madelaine's location. *Paranoia can be fun. Hah!* This morning Madelaine had thought her world was shrinking. Now everything seemed larger and louder than usual, amplified. Nell looked huge. Pauline's high-pitched laughter penetrated the white noise in Madelaine's ears. She dropped onto her tummy and shook her head hard. Willa thought it was a game and climbed across her back. Madelaine bounced her off.

Nell was always on her case. A week ago, when Jerome and Madelaine had visited for Sunday lunch, Czaba had spent most of the afternoon playing on the floor with the children. Jerome had followed him without enthusiasm. While slicing fruit for dessert, Nell had interrogated Madelaine about why she didn't go to university. To avoid dependence on her father, Madelaine had said, but mostly she hadn't liked the study. She'd passed high school well enough and was considered reasonably intelligent, bright even, but the slog of it hadn't suited her, the way it crowded out almost every other part of her life. The advertisement for the job at the film studio couldn't have been more perfect timing. Of course it had disappointed her father but why should that be a problem to

Nell? Madelaine had fobbed her off. *By God, she's such a ferret.*

Later, over coffee, Nell had latched on to Jerome, and Madelaine had slipped away to kick a ball around the yard with Czaba and the children. Through the kitchen window she could see Jerome's unhappy profile. He was itching to get away as soon as possible. They had argued on the way home.

Now, with a chuckling Willa balanced on her shoulders, Madelaine zoomed in on Nell's face. *She's pretty in her way.* Madelaine had seen photographs of her in her teens: broad open face, square nose, bright smile, penetrating blue eyes, one slightly off at one o'clock. Every dog has their day, Jerome would say. Willa slid off and appeared nose-first in the view-finder. Madelaine pushed her away gently and cleaned the lens with a tissue, half attending to the conversation in the corner.

'I don't think things are going terribly well with Jerome and Maddie,' Nell was hissing at Danica. *Could you speak up! Goddamn the woman. Who had heard her?*

Madelaine wanted to shout across the room, I can hear you. I'm not on television. She glanced around. Jo and Pauline were still singing their hearts out – something about catching a bear. *Safer than a man, at least. Jo should have stuck with bears.* Madelaine turned her attention back to Nell, who had lifted the baby off her breast and thrown it over her shoulder like a small sack of millet. More than likely Nell was business-like in bed; direct, occasionally enthusiastic. Jerome always said that Czaba was passive and Nell a ball breaker who needed a good fuck. But once he cottoned on that Nell was more than happy to discuss her sexual preferences, and Czaba's full range of abilities, *he* was shocked.

Madelaine hid behind the viewfinder and flapped her ears.

'Last week I invited them for lunch,' Nell said to Danica. *That was audible enough.* She looked so deeply concerned. Madelaine snorted. She could hear Danica mumbling something about 'Maddie' coping pretty well, and that everyone had problems. *Thanks darlin'.*

'I suspect there are long-standing beefs and they both need our support, but, Jerome especially.' Nell turned her back to bang on the window at one of Pauline's boys, who was swinging on the clothesline. *Jerome especially! Bloody, bloody! What has Jerome been unloading on her?* If he only knew it, Nell would love to issue him with counselling vouchers, trap him in her bean chair and give him a textbook going-over. It would bloody serve him right.

Madelaine pressed the stop button and leapt up to glare at Nell, but Danny looked absurdly guilty, and dropped her head to brush cake crumbs from her shirt. *How dare they talk about my marriage in that forensic way.* And, it was so unlike Nell to defend a man. *She must really hate me.* Madelaine readjusted the zoom, edging closer. Nell caught on quickly and changed the topic.

'You look tired, Danica. Vlado been leaping off the boat and beating you with dead fish?'

Madelaine mentally labelled her films, 'Mindless Conversation, 1 and 2'.

'Don't be silly, Nell.'

Go, Danny.

'Say he did. Beat you.' Nell pushed on undeterred.

'I would go home to my mother. But I would hate that. I'd feel like a failure.'

'That's a good one.' Nell smirked. '*You* would feel a failure.'

'Well, you don't know my mother.'

'Wouldn't you fight back?'

'There was a brown snake in our yard last week. I nearly wet myself. I'm not great in a crisis.'

'Oh, come on. I bet if one of your girls had come out, you would have turned into a she-devil and chopped it into little bits with the garden rake.'

Madelaine moved closer. She rocked back on her heels to film the ceiling.

Pauline sauntered across the room and elbowed her in the ribs. 'Fascinating cornice, Mad?'

Madelaine lowered the camera and focussed on Danica.

'Who are we needling today, Nellie?' Pauline added.

'We're talking about domestic violence. If it happened to me I would take a firm stand and book Czaba in for psychotherapy.'

Danica shrugged and mouthed 'we' at Madelaine, who suppressed a smirk behind the camera.

'Firm stand.' Pauline laughed, putting an arm around Nell. 'That sounds awfully flaky for a feminist. I'd only need a day to commandeer the plastic and some plane tickets, have a quick interview with Jerome about how to bleed the poor darling dry, and off I'd go.'

They all laughed.

Nell wriggled free of Pauline's embrace and passed the baby over while she rebuttoned her shirt. 'Hugh wouldn't kick a cat. What about you Maddie?' She placed her hand on Madelaine's arm and stroked it thoughtfully.

'Me? You're interested in me? If Jerome hit me?' Madelaine didn't like the way Nell stage-managed conversations. 'First I would change the locks on the house – while he was at work I imagine. And I would laugh at him. Make him see how impotent he was.'

'Why would you do that, for God's sake?'

'It's about power, I guess. I don't know ... I want to win.'

'How would that be winning?'

'That's how I see it ... that's all ...' Madelaine felt dark on Nell and hoped that she would lose interest and pick on someone else.

Nell leant forward. 'What would you do Jo, if Doug took a swing at you?' Her eyes were bright with interest.

Jo placed light fingers on her lips and gave a small nervous cough. 'Sometimes, when Doug's been very naughty – you know, hung-over all morning or disappeared to the football – I think I might deck *him*. Or when I've been up all night with Willa wheezing and vomiting, the baby crying, I still have to work in the morning, and he says something ridiculous like, "You're always too tired to spend time with me." Oh, I feel a boiling great rage.'

'Poor Jo. You are wonderfully patient.' Pauline kissed the baby and handed him back to Jo. 'Willa may grow out of her asthma.'

'It's Doug I need the use-by date for.'

'Splendid Nell,' Madelaine said. 'Now we're all depressed. Thanks for that.'

'We can help each other.' Nell linked arms with Madelaine.

Madelaine shrugged her off. She watched Danica scoffing Nell's sugar-free fruit cake, while looking over her shoulder to see if anyone had noticed. Playgroup always began so well, with everyone laughing and talking as they arrived, starved for adult company. But it didn't always end well. Now Nell's boys were bossing Georgia at a low pine table.

'No, Georgia.' The older boy held his mouth perilously close to Georgia's face.

Madelaine swooped across the room. The older boy reached for another sheet of coloured paper.

'You haven't filled your last page,' she said. Perhaps he would engage with her, and leave Georgia alone.

'You don't have to,' he countered, snatching up two more sheets.

Madelaine pursed her lips and tried another tack, wondering if the boy would turn out like his mother.

'You can't write on the shiny side.'

'Yes, I can.' He glared up at her.

'Well isn't that amazing,' she conceded.

'Oh ...' the boy sighed, pointing at his brother. 'He's not allowed to have glue.'

Having flung green glitter across the page, the baby brother had begun to suck on the glue canister. His brother pushed him hard in the chest and snatched the glue. The boy tottered and Madelaine reached out to steady him. Surprised, he looked up at her and pulled away. Almost immediately he fell backwards into a battle-zone of paper, glitter, scissors and glue. Madelaine decided to pack it in and go home. All too soon, as it happened.

Madelaine's children had only been in bed ten minutes when the phone rang – Danica's keys were lost. They had searched everywhere at Nell's: the bins, the toilet, the family room, the yard. Jo had bundled Danica and her children into her car and dropped them home to pick up the spare keys. Danica had broken in through a back window.

Madelaine, phone squashed between shoulder and ear, searched her playgroup basket and there among all the detritus – crumbs and caved-in drink boxes – was a set of keys. *Damnation.* She had been hanging out to swim, had changed into her bathers. The sea glittered and beckoned from the lounge-room window. Her head throbbed. She could hardly remember what day it was. Since she'd worked at home – yes, every mother is a working mother – one day merged into another.

Who could have dropped the keys into her basket? *Willa, Georgia? Pauline's brats?* Oh, that wasn't fair. Once, Georgia had dropped Jerome's keys in the compost. It had taken days before they had stumbled across them. Now she would have to drive the keys to Danica's, and she couldn't just drop and run – Danica would more than likely have laid out coffee cups and semolina biscuits. Madelaine dropped her head between her knees.

Perhaps she wasn't going to make it after all.

Danica's

Danica was waiting at the front door, detached and pale. She'd put her children to bed. Madelaine noted an empty Ponderax container on the sink. *Vlado must be used to it.* The crazy down-hill slide, the binging for days at a time, until she beat her body back into submission at the gym. The continual anxiety. Madelaine agreed to a coffee and settled at the kitchen bench. She hoped the handover of the keys wouldn't take too long. She was still wearing her bathers under her shorts, ready to fly. The kids would sleep for hours and she could still have a good swim.

Danica moved to the cupboard and shook savoury snacks from the packet onto a silver plate.

'God, that Nell! She makes me feel totally destructive.' Madelaine tapped ash fiercely from the tip of her cigarette, took one last drag, then extinguished the last few centimetres in the ashtray. *Dammit! I'm smoking far too much.*

'I used to wonder why she got us all together. It's because nothing happens to her. She feeds on our lives.'

'She must find me dull,' ventured Danica.

'Danny, you are a wag. You know I love you but do not fib to your friends.'

'No one's beaten me. I'm not fighting with my husband.

The children are over their ear infections.' Danica laughed, looked at Madelaine, as if uncertain. 'My biggest problem is that when Jeleni puts on the *1812 Overture*, her favourite, the dog goes bonkers. Runs around in circles barking his head off when he hears the canons.'

Madelaine stared back at her and shook her head. 'You're priceless.' She leapt to her feet, shoulders hunched over while she lit another cigarette. Elbow cupped in hand, she began pacing up and down by the window.

'Did I ever tell you that my father beat me when I was a girl? Actually, there was more to it than that, and it happened until I was quite a decent age.'

'Did he really? My father often threatened, but he never did.'

'Yes. He liked the ceremony. He would close the door, pull down the blind in a slow deliberate way and slide the strap out of his trousers. He always ran it through his fingers before he began.'

Danica began to shovel savoury shapes into her mouth.

Madelaine spoke as if she was a high-jumper poised for the run-up. She licked her lips and tipped her head on one side. 'He was a fundamental Christian. Spare the rod and all. It was worse afterwards. He would come back to my room crying, begging forgiveness. "Pray for me," he'd call from the doorway as he left. Did anyone ever touch you, when you were young?'

'Dear God, no,' said Danica, scrabbling shapes off the plate. 'But you aren't close to him now, are you? I've never heard you talk about him. Have I?'

'I hardly see him. Just at Christmas. He still bullies my mother, making her do things she's afraid of, like addressing women's fellowship or leading prayer meetings about touchy things. She rings sometimes.'

'I would hate that. Is she like you?'

'No ... Let's talk about something else.'

'Yes. Nell likes to talk about the strangest things. My mother thinks it bad mannered.'

'I'd like to trot out an irresistible confidence for Nell, one that would throw her completely ... or I could make a pass at her.' Madelaine grimaced. 'As a matter of fact, I don't think I could. She's a very unattractive woman.' *No that's not true or fair. But it will tweak Danica's justice bone.* 'Czaba? Maybe? Then she'd start rationalising threesomes, and want to join in.' Madelaine giggled.

'Madelaine.' Danica blushed. 'Nell is kind. I'm sure she means well, really. She worries about us all.'

Madelaine placed two fingers in her mouth and pretended to gag. 'Oh, I hear you. And I heard you both today. Last Sunday lunch was even worse. Nell kitted the children out in plastic aprons so they could smear an entire can of shaving cream all over themselves, and each other – very sensual. Naturally, it was to bolster Jerome's opinion that I'm a cold and unimaginative mother.'

'Surely Jerome wouldn't like to live in such a mess. It must drive Czaba crazy.'

'Ah well, just like everyone else, Jerome wants to have his cake and eat it too. I'd like to see him pull off a whole day with the kids, like Czaba does.' Madelaine frowned at Danica. 'You look pale. What have you been doing? Starving yourself?'

Danica picked up the plate of biscuits, mouth rueful. 'I wish. I was so stressed at Nell's, I pigged out.'

'I saw that. But that was before you lost your keys.'

Danica looked hurt, carried the remaining snack biscuits to the sink and dropped them into the garbage chute.

Madelaine swung back on her chair as if to distance herself further. 'You need to develop a new interest. You're either eating or not eating; it's always on your mind. Can't you think about anything else?'

'Don't concern yourself, Mad. I like to be fit and healthy but it's hard sometimes. Why don't you concentrate on your own problems or, what about Jo's?'

'Prickly, prickly!' Madelaine rested her cigarette on the edge of the table and reached over to stroke a piece of hair from Danica's forehead. Danica ducked away. Madelaine examined the plasticine line under her fingernails – and Jerome thinks I'm not creative – and picked up her cigarette again. 'Amazing isn't it. Jo is a nice girl. She has pleasantly and persistently asked Doug to treat her fairly, and he ignores her. If she asks once, it's an unreasonable expectation. If she asks again, she's nagging. Things she shouldn't have to ask in the first place. Like an adult male *should* clean up after himself.'

'If you make a bad first choice, you lose control. You spend your whole life fighting. Or you leave.'

Madelaine waved her cigarette at Danica. 'Darling girl ... How insightful ... I am gobsmacked by some of the things you come out with. I admit Jerome was partially domesticated when I met him, but nothing else about him is straightforward.'

'If Vesna didn't help me I'd go mad.'

'What a pair we are. God, I'm bored witless. I don't know why I thought you would cheer me up. I may as well take myself off. I'll go home and tease the children, withhold food from *them* or something.'

'Madelaine.'

'Madelaiiine! Excuse me; I'm going swimming. Ring me later, in case I drown and the kids can't dial the emergency number.'

'What time?'

'I'm joking.' Madelaine kissed her lightly on the cheek. 'Love me.'

'Thanks for the keys.'

Madelaine remained irritated by the events of the morning until she strode into the water and submerged herself. A north wind pushed scuds of water across the bay. At the far end of the island a plume of spray skimmed like a sailboarder leaning against the surface of the water. The spray collapsed and built up again. If there really were a sailboarder out by the island, he would be swept away, past the island, past incoming fishing boats and into the open sea. The bay was not benign.

Madelaine bobbed like a dinghy between the waves until she found herself far enough out to feel the sea moving in a great mass beneath her. She laid her head back – it was about trust – the sea forming a black cowl around her face. The sound of the sea swelled in her ears.

Pauline's

Dinner parties: oh yes, people still had them, and they were an ordeal – especially at Pauline's. She always went for broke: pastel cloths, gleaming silver, the Kutani Crane dinner service, and unnaturally coloured florist flowers. *Is there anything more ghastly than blue carnations?*

Jerome was tense, tired and toey. Danica had rung to tell Madelaine that Vlado had left for sea, and that she'd stood crying in the driveway, in her dressing gown and slippers. She'd probably only come to dinner to spite her mother, who viewed babysitters as a poisonous influence and possibly dangerous. Madelaine surveyed the room. Doug had arrived at the same time as Danny. He was showing an unwelcome interest in her heavy gold neck chains. Danica put her hand to her breast and swam towards Madelaine, who kissed her cheek.

'Cheer up. We'll live through it.'

'Sparkling or flat, love?' said Pauline offering glasses. Hugh cruised in Pauline's wake, clutching the bottles. Madelaine elbowed Danica and leant into her face to raise an eyebrow, then glanced back at Pauline. *Very elegant.* Flame-coloured shirt, beautifully cut black-crepe trousers, French nails, bracelet-style silver watch, long chains – heavy metal artillery.

Danica reacted badly to Pauline's 'love' – as if she'd been

looked over, found lacking, and dismissed. She skittered on towards Nell, whose hair was strung in a raggedy bunch, her broad face clean of make-up. She was resting far more cleavage on the tabletop than the Nursing Mothers' Association might recommend. If a dairy alternative was required over coffee, she was out there.

The wine sparkled into Madelaine's stomach and moved straight on into her head. *Gorgeous.* But, Pauline's dinners needed cranking up. People were either full of savouries or drunk before the main course. Jerome slid his hand under her jacket and crab-walked his fingers towards her breasts.

'Nell is looking expansive. Why don't you buy a new dress? Something short and red, with cleavage.' He grazed his lips against the corner of her mouth.

'I'm glad you think we can afford the dress, but what about the plastic surgery?' she teased, feeling hot, surprised and uneasy.

'Always safe-navy, safe-white; you should put some colour in your life.'

She plucked his hand away.

'You're enough colour for any woman.'

'I love it when you've had a wine.'

'You don't always want me to have a *whhhine.*'

'Is that our favourite spelling joke? Come on, relax.'

They moved into the dining room. Danica was placed at the table between Jerome and Doug. *She looks, jumpy.* Madelaine kicked her softly under the table and winked.

'All alone Danica? Vlado working?' Doug said, using his fork to stroke the back of her hand, which she snapped into her lap.

'Jesus.' Madelaine eyeballed him.

Doug dropped his voice and moved against Danica. 'If I was your husband I wouldn't go to the bathroom without you.'

'What are you doing, dear?' Jo sounded annoyed.

'I'm merely pointing out to Danica that she shouldn't have to spend so much time alone.'

'Oh please!' Jo refilled her glass and turned away.

Pauline had placed large platters of stuffed mushrooms, anchovy crostini, braised and rolled eggplant slices and other antipasto on the table. As Danica reached across in front of her, Madelaine smelt her tension brewing. Mediterranean food was a direct link with home. It transported her to a safe place. It was comfort food.

As the evening progressed, Doug continued talking rubbish, mostly to Danica. Madelaine watched him spouting off at her half-turned back. *Too insensitive to read body language, or pig ignorant? It was lineball.*

When Madelaine turned to speak to Pauline, she could hear him blaring at Jerome.

'Look at your wife, Rawlins. She's always in a bloody huddle with someone. We'll never get dessert.' *It will never replace humour.*

Jerome spoke coolly. 'Tell me about ... what is it? Devolution? Devolution in the education system ... and why that bloke in staffing, James Kinnaid is so against it? I heard him speak at a dinner meeting.' *Plop!*

Madelaine admired the way men, with no apology, changed the subject. Women were too polite, acknowledging everything, often building on statements leading nowhere but trouble. And she was grateful that Jerome would not expose their marital warts to a little turd like Doug. She tried to concentrate on what Pauline was saying, about waiting lists at the kindergarten, but found herself distracted, with half an ear flapping to the men's conversation.

'Kinnaid's close to retirement but the timing's bad. The government only care about saving money. His job could go and he might be transferred out.' Doug wiped his nose on his napkin.

'You don't think it's a good idea?' Jerome looked genuinely interested – possibly saw Kinnaid as a client.

Doug ran his arm along the back of Danica's chair. She moved forward, leaning her elbows on the table and resting her chin in her hands.

'There will be more short-term contracts. It might mean larger class sizes, or hiring the lowest-salaried people. It hasn't worked in other places.'

Pauline had stopped speaking. Madelaine tried to think of the last thing she had said, but in the end it wasn't necessary. Pauline had also shifted her attention to the men.

'Now Douglas, if you don't like the heat you should get out of the kitchen,' she called across the table.

'Someone's gotta do the cookin', he replied. 'Anyway, why do you care? You won't put your kids in public schools.' Aggression was always Doug's first line of defence. *If they get onto private versus public education, I'm going to the loo.* Fortunately, a timer went off in the kitchen and Pauline left.

Danica appeared to be contending with Doug's thigh, or at least his stale breath on her face, for she was moving sideways again. Underlining her distress, she jerked her chair back, muttering, 'I need to speak to Madelaine. I'll sit in Pauline's chair while she gets dessert.' She struggled out of her chair, studiously avoiding touching Doug.

'Someone's got their teeth in your tail,' Madelaine grinned, pulling out the chair next to her so Danica could sit down.

Danica stalled. She gripped the back of the chair and looked back. 'If you're feeling kind. Are you . . .?'

If only she would buck up, stand up for herself occasionally. Madelaine plucked at her friend's skimpy dress. 'Sit down, silly. Aren't I supposed to be your best friend?'

Danica flushed and eased into the seat. When she saw Pauline returning, she half rose.

'Stay there,' Pauline commanded, juggling dessert. 'We'll all change. Find new partners.' She winked.

'This looks very Danny,' smirked Madelaine, waving her cigarette at a whole tiramisu. 'Big piece, Pauline. We'll fatten her up.'

'No thanks, Pauline. I won't. It looks nice but I've eaten so much already.'

'Do have some Danica. It's your favourite. You can get rid of it later,' Madelaine goaded.

'I don't eat cake,' Danica hissed, her eyes flicking around the table.

'You do. Admit, it's all affectation.' Madelaine knew all about Danica's eating habits. When Danica came to babysit her children, Madelaine laid out chocolate traps. Afterwards she would find the wrappers hidden at the bottom of the bathroom bin. *Why does it matter to me that Danny lies?*

'I think I should go,' Danica said, looking piteous. 'It's late.'

Madelaine licked her lips and whispered. 'Don't go. Wait. I'm only teasing. You were being so mousey I couldn't resist. It would be much more fun to blame Doug for a terrible night, and he deserves it.' Madelaine lifted a piece of Danica's hair and shifted the cake two places along. 'Don't you hate formal dinner parties. Being trapped in someone's seating plan for hours, life-threatening boredom and having to clean your plate every course. It's kiddie stuff and I'm damn sure it's fattening. You must hate it.'

Danica's eyes darted back and forth as she struggled to maintain control. 'I really should go, Madelaine. I'm feeling quite unwell and, I need an early night.'

She looked like the lady in the crumbly-cheese ad: hairline cracks splintering her face and body; little parts of her dropping on the floor. Madelaine squeezed her hand under the table. *God, what a pair we are.*

Danica's

Fingernails digging hard into the leather steering-wheel cover, Danica reversed carefully down Pauline's driveway. *Did I confide in Madelaine about eating? What a mistake to go out alone. And bloody Doug. Why did I become involved with these people?* Pauline was at best impatient. Nell was kind in a universal way, but hadn't even noticed her distress. Hugh always looked like he was on another planet, politely attentive, marking time until he could get back to the real world, at the hospital or in his garden. Czaba was pathologically quiet, and Jerome had his own problems. Jo had her hands full with Doug. *Doug is an arsehole.* Tears welled.

She made a point of driving slowly. Although she hadn't had a lot to drink, the last thing she needed was to be pulled over by one of the cops that Vlado knew. *How pathetic would I look, crying in the car, my husband away?* It was quiet anyway. Not much traffic. Most of the action before midnight would be in the pubs on the esplanade. She unclenched her teeth, wiped her eyes with the back of her hand, and turned smoothly onto the main highway away from the shops. By the time she reached the safety of her own driveway she could feel emotion rising again.

Pressing the remote control in the glove box, she raised

the garage door, roared in and straightened her clothes before climbing out of the car. 'Thanks Megan,' she mumbled to the babysitter, slumped half asleep on the couch. As the girl's tail-lights receded down the street, Danica threw herself onto the carpet. *Vlado's always away when it counts.* Half the year she was a single parent. What was she supposed to do, stay at home, wear black, visit her mother? She panted hysterically, her lips and fingers tingling. Madelaine always directed the play, asked all the questions. Danica was always responding, never initiating, always grappling for an answer.

She struggled to her feet and marauded through the house. She could hear the soft breathing sounds of the girls in their cots. Miranda was snuffling in her sleep. Danica swung open the refrigerator door and cursed her self-discipline at the supermarket. It was wickedness she craved: chocolate, ice cream, cheesecake, alcohol. Madelaine ran a full bar, but Danica rarely entertained at home. And Vlado had drunk all the beer before he left. Eventually she unearthed a half bottle of maraschino in the pantry.

It burnt the back of her throat as she threw it down in large gulps and fell into a paroxysm of coughing; it was warm and steadying. Back at the refrigerator she considered her best options: risotto, sulking under plastic? It would do, and she shovelled large handfuls into her mouth, swallowing, hardly tasting.

Chew your food carefully. Concentrate on what you consume, in a pleasant setting. That's what they said in maga-zines, whoever *they* were. Nervy scrags who lived on chocolate and Sobranies. What would *they* think of her on hands and knees at the fridge, eating like an animal, with creamy sauce spilling down her dress? It was not guilt that troubled her as she attacked yoghurt, cheese wedges, bread, and jars of things normally far too boring to bother with. Her need to gorge was overwhelming. Afterwards, exhausted, she sat cross-legged on the kitchen floor, rocking back and forth like a baby, dribbling experimentally until a familiar sweetness filled her mouth.

'Never mind darling. Madelaine shouldn't have said it,' she prattled to the haggard and ruined face in the bathroom mirror. 'Even if anyone was listening, they wouldn't know what she meant.' Vomit speckled her matted hair. Retching had ruptured a blood vessel in her right eye. She sprawled across her bed, feet dangling over the edge. A soughing breeze moved a strand of hair across her face. She wouldn't eat for days now.

Billy Lights Point

'How's your relationship with Danica going?' The roads were deserted but streetlights glowed stolidly through the gloom as Jerome rushed across intersections.

'Fine, thanks.'

'Stuck a few pins in her tonight.' He wondered wearily, why he always pursued things.

'Have your fun. I hardly spoke to her till dessert. I admit I did tease her then. Doug had her under his spotlight and she was blinking like a bunny. I was ashamed of her.'

'Oh, she let you down.'

'Don't be a prick, Jerome. You couldn't care less about Danica. Getting at me is the main game. Let's try and be pleasant shall we?'

'Poor Danny. Poor me, for that matter. All we ever did was love you.'

'I do love you but you can never leave anything alone. You're always poking and probing, clawing for marrow.'

'That's rich that is. Danica comes to you for respite, and you offer her confidences to the entire table over dessert. That's what I call ripping into the bone.'

'She must have driven her mother mad, pouting and preening over food.' *If he wants callous, I can do callous.*

'You must really like her. Maybe it's her mother's fault. Ever thought of that?'

Madelaine stretched her neck against the seat and closed her eyes. 'Okay, Freud.'

Jerome tried again. 'Forget Danica. Can we salvage *our* relationship?'

'I hate the way you carve up conversations. Why can't you just say, "You gave me the shits tonight Madelaine," instead of laying our whole marriage on the table like a slab of meat? You sound like the *Women's Weekly*.'

'I'm still asking.'

'I think we have a marriage, if that's what you want to know.'

'We haven't made love for weeks.'

'Now I'm excited; that is such a turn-on.'

'Our relationship is a joke to you. Why don't you want to make it better?'

Madelaine bit her lip. 'You know, you're free to do whatever you wish. I don't make a lot of demands of you. Don't always make me the index for everything you do. Do something for yourself.'

Jerome was driving carelessly, staring bleakly ahead with his arms hunched over the steering wheel, his nose close to the windscreen.

'I don't know why you have this obsession with analysis,' she continued. 'And you're drunk.'

He briefly rested his head, rubbed his eyes and wondered if they should have had children after all. 'You don't care how I feel, do you? Or anyone. If you were any sort of friend you would have gone after Danica. I'm surprised you didn't video the whole episode.' He drove on.

'My relationship with Danica is none of your business. The worst thing I could do is reinforce her attention seeking. She needs to grow up. Get over her family.'

Jerome turned a corner too quickly, deliberately sliding back a gear and over-revving the engine. His eyes flickered and his voice hardened. He would force her interest.

'And I suppose your relationship with your parents is normal?'

She turned her head away. 'Danica would have been better off doing what I did, get some kilometres between her and them. I'm happy with two gulfs and a peninsula.'

'I would have thought you, of all people, would be sympathetic.'

'Well I'm not. As far as I know her childhood was perfectly normal.'

'You wouldn't know what normal is.'

'Exactly. And I wish you wouldn't bring it up all the time. You human rights campaigners love to screw a victim. Do you fancy the rape girl too?'

'You're sick, Madelaine.'

As they drew into the carport, she leapt out and slammed the door, her heels clacking as she stormed up the path. He watched her, felt disconsolate, as if he didn't know her, wishing that she would pause at the door and turn her head just long enough to notice that he was upset. After she twisted her key in the lock and pushed through the front door, he watched the downstairs light flick on and imagined her lighting up a cigarette, pouring herself a nightcap, bruising the children with intense kisses. When the bedroom light illuminated the balcony, he thought of the soft fall of her clothing in the walk-in wardrobe. He slammed down the handbrake and screeched out of the driveway. The car fish-tailed and almost collected the letterbox before dropping into the gutter. *Thank God we don't have a fence.* He righted the car and swung off down the street.

He meandered past the caravan park and towards the wasteland that would soon be new development. *Hard to imagine anyone would want to live out here.* He wound down his window and reached out. A sea breeze blew cool across his arm. He had been hot at Pauline's, irritable. Probably why he drank so much port with the cake. That, and Madelaine, who had ignored him most of the night. He crossed a small bridge and followed the road to Billy Lights Point where he swung the car through the car park and down onto the boat ramp.

The water was inky and emitted a full-bodied sea smell. If the car rolled gently, just a few feet down the ramp, he could close his eyes and slide into the wet darkness. But if it sank slowly he would be caught in an undignified struggle between craving for air and commitment. He drummed his head against the steering wheel.

The lambs-wool cover smelt faintly of perspiration and lanolin, which reminded him of the wool fat Madelaine had rubbed into her nipples to prepare for breastfeeding, and to his horror he began to cry. It would be easy to separate. Two out of three marriages ended that way; nearly every day at work he saw the bitter dismantling occuring between his clients. Splitting up was purposeful and constructive in many ways: a signpost out of the wilderness, an end to some of the worry.

He had hit her twice. Not in a blind rage on the first occasion, but quite deliberately, as if to tip the relationship on its side and look at it, to see if it was operable between different parameters. If they couldn't have a normal loving relationship, he'd hoped to spark a pure response from her. When there was nothing, he had despised himself and she had looked triumphant. He had thought about her father. No doubt his actions lay at the core of it all. Jerome had always wondered if he should put pressure on her to report her father. Not that it would help him now.

After several nights of working late, retaliation had come swiftly. Madelaine had accepted an invitation for drinks, and had bailed him up the moment he stepped through the front door, hoping he would agree to shower and come along immediately.

'No can do. Not this week. You'll have to go without me. This is an important case and I need to spend as much time as I can on these notes,' he said.

She had whisked the notes from under his arm and cantered through the front door. He had been taken by surprise and fallen against the passage wall. She had stood at the roadside like an emissary, pigeon in hand, her eyes never leaving his face until he followed her. Then she threw the notes high in the air. The wind caught some and blew them into the gutter. He scrabbled after them, leaping on them with his feet, snatching at others with his hands, then crawling on his hands and knees. He had cried then too, as he plucked the rest from behind the strelitzia.

He smacked her again, hard across the face. 'Why do you hate me?'

'You're not what I expected,' she had answered, and stalked upstairs in her dressing gown. *Will she go without me?* He was past caring.

Sorting out the papers at his desk in the study, brushing off the shoe treads and smoothing out the folds, he imagined her eyes blazing, her body tight and self-contained, hunched like a watchful cat in the corner of the bedroom. She'd stayed in. Later, when he crawled exhausted under the sheets, he tried to cradle her against him but she was still and cold.

'It's got to stop, Madelaine,' he had murmured in her ear. She had feigned sleep. 'We can't go on like this. We'll destroy each other.'

In the early years of marriage, separation had never crossed his mind. Now he thought of little else. Like any other couple they had argued, mostly about semantics, imagined slights and selfishness, the way she spoke to him and he to her, but he had wanted nothing more than to make it right for Madelaine, for both of them. Now, little passed in conversation, no point of difference, without an overwhelming sense of defeat and bitterness.

At Billy Lights Point there was no moon. Jerome's eyes strained against the darkness, sensing the movement of cloud and water. He climbed out of the car and kicked through the sand, listening to the splash of dolphins breaking the surface of the water in front of him. He tramped along the shore and found he couldn't stop, couldn't think of a single reason to turn back and go home. On and on he walked.

Just before dawn he grew chilled. His trouser legs flapped wet against his legs and he was tired of walking. He had run for a while, but his chest felt tight, his legs like jelly. Terminal patients often died in the early hours of the morning, their bodies being at the lowest ebb; Hugh had told him that. On the horizon the sun was throwing tepid light. He could see the rim of it pushing up behind the sandhills. In front of him the sweep of sand and water and sky was coming into focus in shades of grey and beige, mottled like the eggs of the terns in the dunes. It wouldn't be cool for long. Another warm day was forecast.

What's the point in staying? There's nothing more to gain. He wheeled around and headed back along the beach to where his car remained nosed over the edge of the boat ramp. At home he slept in spurts on the couch until the children woke. There would be a lot to do in the afternoon. Caffeine would get him through.

Madelaine's

Danica's hand grovelled to pull the quilt up around her shoulders. In the morning the room was dark, but grey light suffused between blind and sill. She stretched out, feeling stiff and fragile, and the television in the family room emitted a snowy burr.

Most mornings she had to claw past foreboding to a more cheerful consciousness where she could focus on a reason to get out of bed. Slowly, slowly, she hauled herself across the bedclothes to view her face in the dressing-table mirror. Her blue dress was stained and creased and hiked up around her backside. Her face was pink but her mouth felt sour and dirty. She winced at the memory of her spiralling mood the night before. *At least I always lose a kilo after vomiting. Would they have talked about me running out like that? Had anyone heard Madelaine?* Hugh had walked her to the door, acting normal, but then that was his job. She would ring Vesna, go to the gym, take control again.

The gym was always busy on Sunday mornings, especially in the summer. Sometimes Vlado came along for company, brought the girls, and watched them running water through their fingers and splashing about in the toddler's pool while Danica worked out. Older dripping, leggy children ran past them on their way to the water slides and diving boards. After Danica's workout she would often find him arms folded, rocking backwards and forwards on his heels talking to other parents, or lining up for hot chips and chocolate milk at the café. Not this day. Thank God for Vesna, who was kind enough to come at short notice.

The class grumbled about working off Saturday-night excess, but Danica felt weak and frail. Despite a glass of water, nausea hovered oppressively. Hugh had told her once, that when she lost her body fat she was running on endorphins, natural drugs that killed pain. He warned her not to abuse them nor take residual fitness for granted; she could hit the wall.

So far it had never happened. By the time she danced and kicked her way through the high-impact section of the routine she was flying, her mood improved, her body tough and responsive. When the class was over she decided she was strong enough to go to Madelaine's, make an attempt to shame her into an apology. She hurried out.

At the house, Danica strode across the lawn feeling long-legged and fit. Her shoes clumped across the patio tiles. She was confident.

Madelaine appeared at the door in a pair of jeans and a navy sweat. 'I haven't even showered yet and you've been up knocking yourself around. What a masochist you are.' She peered into her friend's face. 'Are you still upset?'

'Of course I'm upset, and I want to talk to you about it, Mad.' Her voice quavered. *I'm pathetic.* What had happened to her bravado? She glanced over her shoulder as it retracted behind her, stranding her sweaty and dishevelled on the verandah.

'Oh for goodness' sake. Why do you always do this?

Everyone's got it in for me this morning.' Madelaine drew an arm around Danica's shoulders and hauled her impatiently through the door. 'Jerome and I had the dickens of a row last night. He spent half the night sulking in his car, God knows where, but that's what he said, and now I have you reproachful on my doorstep. I wish you wouldn't take everything to heart. There is such a thing as normal banter between friends, isn't there?'

'Normal banter.'

'Okay, I overstepped the mark. Alcohol does it to me every time. I actually don't think anyone heard me, about you sticking your fingers down your throat. And be fair, I didn't use those actual words. Please, let's just forget it. I promise I'll try to be good from now on.'

Danica tipped her head on one side, listened hard for domestic sounds and bit her lip. *Where is everybody? The girls should be up by now.* She should have known better than to expect a real apology. 'Where's Jerome?'

'Languishing in the bath. Come in and have a coffee. It might make him behave.'

'No, thanks. I want to go home and shower. I just needed to clear the air.'

'Well, you've presented yourself and I've cleared it for you, so there you go. Beetle home and fix yourself some morning tea. I'm sure you've earned it. I'll come round this afternoon and see how you are.'

Danica felt her voice wobbling dangerously as she said goodbye, and turned to go. She felt dismissed, like a silly child. It would mean nothing to Madelaine.

Danica's

Much to Danica's surprise, Madelaine had arrived in the afternoon, to make amends. Danica had been culling family photos and now lay on the couch.

'Revisionist: head off. I'm here to give you a break,' Madelaine bossed, placing her video-camera bag on the kitchen bench. 'Jerome's bolshy and wouldn't come out for lunch, so I offered to leave him. That should get him thinking.'

'What about the children?'

'I had to be quick or I could have been stuck with them too,' she laughed.

'Madelaine. You don't mean that. What will he do?'

'Probably martyr himself all day, let them make an unholy mess. Then he'll be furious with me because he hasn't read his transcripts for the appeal. Never mind all that, blossom. Run and do your face and go for a drive or something. Visit one of our other friends if you can stand their children.'

'Are you sure?'

'Yes, go quickly before I change my mind. Come back at five.'

'The kids are in the sandpit. They're filthy.'

'Go. I'll cope, and so will they.'

From the laundry window, Madelaine watched Danica

dash into the garden to kiss the children goodbye. There was no fuss: not a blink, let alone a cry. Perhaps she hadn't told them who was looking after them – not that they disliked Madelaine. And they were quite used to being left with Vesna. Madelaine removed her fringed scarf, and shook it out as she watched Danica reverse her car down the long driveway. The girl had style, with her white wraparound sunglasses, blonde hair piled on top of her head and tiny halter-top. *Why on earth doesn't she realise it?*

Through the kitchen window, Madelaine could see the kids trundling buckets of water between the tap and a plastic tub. Miranda lurched along the path with one shoulder lifted to counterbalance the water slopping from the bucket. Prattling to herself, Sonja squatted in the sandpit and stirred the water in the tub with a plastic golf stick. Had Danica said they could use the tap? Bloody hell, Jerome would have a fit. Madelaine leant over the sink to rap on the window and swirl her scarf in parody of a wave. Miranda glanced up with a shy half smile as she lumped her bucket towards her sister.

They're busy. Excellent. Madelaine moved into the dining room and placed two dining chairs side by side in front of heavy silver-brocade window drapes. Mounted on chrome, tubular shelving was Vlado's sound system, the speakers as big as garbage cans. *Vlado, so much power.* His system took up most of the side wall. She checked the power, volume and CD switches, then whistled up the dog, who came skulking from the master bedroom and reeking of something nasty. *Pray God, not a nappy.* She tapped the side of her nose with a delicate finger and picked up a silver photo frame to fan the air in front of the dog.

'Something died, Hugo. You?'

Unwrapping the video camera carefully, she checked the film and battery, attached the remote, and propped it against a book on the room's chrome-and-smoked-glass table, facing the chairs. Like a magician, she flung her scarf over the seat of one of the dining chairs and set the CD player for the first track. *Perfect.* She practised lounging in the other chair, legs crossed, lipstick fresh, hair swept up with two bulldog clips from the kitchen drawer, banana microphone in hand. Then she scooped up the dog, placed him on her scarf and pushed dark glasses onto his face.

'Stay.'

Hugo was worried, cocked his head and lifted one front paw. *And well he might be.*

She hit RECORD on the remote bulb and wondered if she could have been a multi-media personality. *No, far too strung out.*

'Good afternoon, viewers. Please welcome my special guest this afternoon, Canis Dopis.' She leant over and shook his dangling paw, then grimaced and withdrew her hand to wipe it on her pants. 'Now threatened, Canis and his ilk should be grateful for any exposure that will improve their standing in the community. In wild and spectacular fashion, Canis has been staking out new territory, defecating secretly on white shag-pile carpets, vomiting quietly on the porches of Port Lincoln's stately homes, and baying at the seaside moon. Last week, urinating on the street, and clearly out of touch with reality, he was picked up and detained by local police. Loved ones maintain that breaking out is a recent aberration and a rite of passage. Care to make any comment at this point, Canis?' Madelaine moved the end of the banana in front of his face. He sniffed obligingly and panted.

'Canis is certainly looking relaxed now, although this could be one of the kickbacks when advertising Bolle sunglasses.' Hugo stood up and Madelaine bellowed, 'Sit mutt!' Agreeably he did.

'As this may be your final public appearance Canis, perhaps you would like me to play a last request. The *1812 Overture*? Certainly. No need to yap.' Madelaine stood and hit PLAY to activate Tchaikovsky on the CD player.

Hugo sat up and barked as the canons erupted. The sunglasses slid off the end of his nose. *How thoughtful of Danica to tell me this endearing little story about the music and the barking.*

'Wasn't that splendid viewers? Isn't Canis a character? Good boy.' She rubbed the back of the remote against his head, and then pressed RECORD one last time. 'Well viewers, no more knocking people over on his rush through the gate. We wish him well as he embarks on life's next adventure.'

She wondered if she should write 'Hugo' on the spine of the video, or 'Playgroup 27'. No doubt 'Hugo' would be foolhardy. If Danica scavenged for chocolate biscuits while babysitting at Madelaine's, she might stumble over the tape with the others on the second shelf of the book case, and become maudlin or curious. She wasn't keen on Madelaine's homemade videos. They didn't do her justice, exposed her uncertainties, catching gauche moments as she fiddled with her clothing, peered at herself in sideboard mirrors, sneaked food, or failed to pay attention to other people's conversations.

'What doin' Maddie? Hooogo?' Sonja ambled into the room, water spilling from the bucket she lugged.

'Really, not much darling. Can I get you something? A drink? A fresh nappy would set you right?' Madelaine sprang up, retrieved Vlado's Bolles, then carried the dog outside.

She dismantled the film studio and the rest of the afternoon proved uneventful. At three o'clock Madelaine rang home, but hung up in a dither when Jerome answered. At four o'clock Danica's girls came inside asking for drinks, and Madelaine felt guilty that they were sunburnt. The shade must have moved while she was skimming Danny's fashion magazines. She rubbed them with moisturising lotion, and read them half a dozen stories on the couch until their mother zoomed up the driveway at half-past five.

Danica felt tired but happy. She had borrowed a pair of bathers from Tomi's girlfriend, and gone out skiing with them and some of their friends. It was the best fun she'd had for ages and she had worked up quite an appetite. She spat olive pips into a silver dish, and dipped pita bread in and out of tzatziki. Sonja had nodded several times, slumped and subsided, head on her plate. There was food in her hair and her dirty chubby fist clutched at Blanky. *God, they're whacked.* Madelaine must have run them in the heat all day. Their faces were pink from the sun.

Miranda rolled her eyes at Danica and slouched in her chair. It would be easy to reel them in like little fish and toss them straight into their beds, but how unsound – their grimy bodies and slimy mouths on clean linen. They would wake sweaty and cranky in the middle of the night.

She ran a bath and cradled them, first one then the other in the crook of her arm, as she splashed cool water on their necks and faces to keep them awake until she finished. Lights dimmed and doors closed, she drank black coffee.

She missed Vlado. If he were at home she would be curled up in her old candlewick dressing gown, hair washed and teeth brushed, watching the Sunday movie while he sat at his roll-top desk adding up accounts, paying bills, writing cheques for wages. If she pretended to be asleep he would scoop her up and carry her to bed. She'd nuzzle against the damp dark hairs on his chest and at the hollow of his throat, while he used one hand to lift the bedclothes.

'Such a baby, Danny,' he'd say.

Danica thought about ringing Madelaine, to see if she'd made up with Jerome. *But what if he answers? That could be awkward.* She drummed her fingers on the bench. *Perhaps tomorrow would be better.*

Madelaine's

When Madelaine couldn't sleep, she bucked and rolled like an angry sea. Head tucked forward, frustrated and itchy-eyed, she plucked at hair, scraped at rough skin, burrowed fingers into her navel, her armpits, her moist creases. She crashed about in damp sheets, smelling her fingers and flicking crusts of dry skin.

Jerome could always sleep, it seemed. He was probably asleep at that moment – somewhere. He had left the children watching television with the old lady neighbour who persistently mooed over the galvanised fence at the rear: 'Maaaadelaine. Maaadelaine . . .' It had taken Madelaine effort verging on rudeness to evict her, and now here it was nine o'clock and he still wasn't back. She stood on the balcony, smoking, feeling glum as she watched car headlights curve around the crescent.

She had often watched Jerome sleeping at night, head thrown back, a fist under his chin, a long arm resting on his hip. He liked to sleep with his breath in her face, a hand on her thigh, encroaching on her side of the bed, heating and dampening it. When she pushed him off he would flop on his back, arms behind his head, snorting inefficiently like a landlocked amphibian.

One night, not long after Christmas, she had written I love

you, in biro on his thigh. The writing wavered down to an extra long tail on the Y, when he'd suddenly moved. Then he lay back again, snuffling and snoring. She rolled him over, her face at his shoulder, tasting the depth of his night-time breath as he flopped his head from side to side.

'What the fuck are you doing?'

'Nothing, go back to sleep.'

'I am asleep. You're crazy.'

Unfair. She jabbed his side with her finger until he squirmed and, clutching himself like a lumbering bear, walked on auto to the bathroom.

The toilet seat clunked against the cistern, urine splashed into the bowl – and out of it probably. He guzzled from the tap and creaked back into bed. Her cine magazine slid from the bedside table and landed spine-side up in the dirty socks and damp pyjama bottoms. She had feared that he would wake and say stupid things that wouldn't matter in the morning, but then decided to clamber over and quietly mount him anyway. Just a few strokes and he would be there for her, responsive, obedient, eager even? He often thought her crazy, clinging one moment, abhorring him the next.

Her belly ached. Why was the sexual feeling always raw on the days before she bled? Because her pelvis churned with tearing tissue? She stared through the window. A gibbous moon threw bright light over the dark shapes of the trees, but she couldn't see the sea.

She hoped he wouldn't really wake. Just enough to make it good. The sudden and precise moment always took her by surprise, when a surge of warmth kicked in, and she became preoccupied too, angling her pelvis, wanting nothing more than to join up all the dots in a circuit of pleasure that tripped around her labia and travelled deep into her body. Sucking at his mouth she whispered, 'Again,' and then inhaled hard against the soft skin below his shoulder, shutting off her airway to intensify the pleasure. His thumb grazed her clitoris as she arched her back, and dropped her hips. She bucked against him, rested, and moved in again, until eventually she tired, and slid her hand beneath to stroke his balls. 'Your turn,' she said. 'Together,' he often said.

In those moments she thought she partly understood men. But they were different, had untidy body parts, and like lobsters were always probing the air, feeling their way, hungry as hell. They stayed half-aroused all the time; she was convinced. Even in their sleep, men simmered.

She had rolled away and pulled up her knees, wondering if the ache of afterwards was worse.

'You right?' he had asked, eyes closed. He slung an arm across her back and stroked between her shoulder blades.

'Shh. Go to sleep. I love you. Thanks.' She had pushed his hand away, lay rigid, listened until the soothing rhythm of his breathing resumed and she knew he wouldn't wake to talk.

The night had been unseasonably cool and smelt dank. She had suppressed a sudden urge to sneeze, and crept from the dampness. From the foot of the bed she had watched him stir, roll over groggily, reaching for the warm place where she should be. Stepping forward, she crashed against the bedroom door, banged her knee, and tried not to cry out. Nevertheless, he sat up, eyes blinking.

'What are you doing?'

'Nothing. Go back to sleep.' She had wanted only to be alone. Finally he settled, and she lay watching the sea through the window, knees tucked up, a hand on her belly.

Why am I standing on the balcony brooding over old sex? She wasn't seriously worried about Jerome. They had fought before. Though, he had never stayed out this late. She stepped inside and poured herself another drink. *It was naughty not to leave a note – bad form.*

That afternoon at Danica's hadn't been such a great idea. *Perhaps I'm not going to make it.* She rested the bottle of wine against her cheek and stilled herself. She wanted to cry out, 'I am still here!'

'Arid thoughts ... arid thoughts ... drink up,' she mumbled to herself, lowering the bottle over her glass. The television blared in the background. From the balcony she could see Georgia throwing cushions across the family room. Bottom in the air, thumb in her mouth, Paige had snatched one up and placed her head on it.

At seven o'clock, as penance, Madelaine had committed to tackling a basket of ironing while the children finished their cartoon videos. Even as a child, she hadn't liked cartoons. They made her feel out of control, completely on edge as two-dimensional characters crashed through the walls of buildings, over the edges of crumbling cliffs, catapulted out of trees and windows. To her alarm they fell back as flat as unhinged doors, to the sounds of clanking saucepans and birds twittering round their heads. They ran and ran, mindless aggressors breathing down their necks. They were bullied, bashed, tortured, burnt and stretched. Cartoons were emotionally draining. And people laughed.

Some women loved ironing in the middle of the living room. Madelaine couldn't even fake happy, while little fingers pulled at electric cords and globs of play-dough orbited the room. Ironing was best done in a locked room, with no more accoutrements than a bottle of Pimms and an ashtray if one could smoke no hands. But, this was penance.

At ten o'clock she gave up waiting for Jerome and lifted the sleeping children from the carpet in front of the television to their beds. The house was hot and unforgiving. She poked her finger into the fuggy air. She crawled between sticky sheets and waited for the low that was supposed to move in from the west. *I'll feel much better then.* A cool breeze would whip past the curtains and nip at her legs until she tugged the sheets around her. Meanwhile, she thrashed her pillow and heaved her legs about the bed in frustration.

The thin moon had dipped behind heavy cloud. Hollyhocks swayed and the tops of the sugar gums stirred. The sky was mottled like marble, with dark-ink spills rushing towards the heavy outline of the island. Beetles cannonballed onto the verandah and cluttered the window ledge. Shovel loads of them kamakazied towards the light, slid in piles under the doors and whirred on their backs like rap-dancers. Dogs yapped faintly at the end of the street. A wet flannel dried hard on the bedside table where a portable fan lifted the edges of a newspaper.

Near midnight, as if she smelt the pending change in the air, one of the girls had woken. Madelaine could hear her prattling as she padded along the passage and into the bedroom.

'I carn sleep when you carn sleep.'

'I will kiss you.' Madelaine pressed her lips against the sweaty child and marched her fingers across her scalp.

'I want to get in wiv you.'

'It's too hot, darling.'

'Where's Daddy?'

'Gone ... out.'

Georgia was wide eyed, uncomprehending.

'Shoo.' Madelaine tapped the buttons of her pyjama top, as if reprogramming her. The child shuffled off.

She could hear Georgia dragging puzzles from the shelves, pushing pieces stubbornly across the wooden floor. No doubt she was lying on her tummy in her nickers or nothing at all, pyjamas abandoned in the passage.

'Go to sleep!' yelled Madelaine. Eleven-forty-four is not a time to play.

'I carn sleep when you carn sleep.'

It was like *Groundhog Day*, and apart from the beetles, there was still no movement in the air. She got out of bed and tiptoed down the passage to the toilet, peeking in at Paige sprawled across her bed, one leg drawn up, a damp towel across her thigh, thumb in her mouth. Georgia lay under the whirring fan, her head flopping over the puzzle.

As Madelaine came into the bathroom, the kitchen clock fell from the wall and crashed onto the kitchen bench. Heart hammering, she had rushed barefoot into the room expecting almost anything. She viewed the wounded clock and its shattered glass with relief, and then hostility. *Why, at the height of a hot, late-summer night would a clock do that? How many years had it been there, doing its work on the wall?*

After she swept up the glass and wrapped it in newspaper, she retreated to the bathroom to splash her face with water. She swung wide-legged over the toilet seat, head in her hands, elbows on her knees, and watched roaches scurry away from the rude fluoro light. She felt a sudden and unassuageable grief.

Back in the bedroom, spreadeagled on the rack of her bed, Madelaine drank more water and downed a handful of pills. At twelve-twenty she felt waterlogged and heavy. Air the temperature of blood pressed against her on the bed. At twelve-forty the blind flapped against the window once, and the smallest movement of air stirred her burgundy sleep shorts against her pubis. *Where was Jerome?* She remembered seeing the little cards in the clock flop over like a football score: ... one-fifty ... two-forty ... three-fifty-seven, then nothing more.

Danica's

Sea and frangipani smells wafted under Danica's clattering bedroom blinds. She had slept well for a change, instead of lurching awake every time the phone rang. She was getting crank calls most nights, usually only one or two but enough to cause distress. *Why is it happening?* No one ever answered. Soon she would have to go to the police and find out how to trace them.

This morning, damp little bodies crawled across her face. She kissed the soft tummies, the pink mouths, breathed in the sleepy-baby smell. Perhaps she might have a good day, stay on top of things, go to Jansys and see Jo. It would not be long before her mother's birthday-dinner cruise. *I should buy something new to wear.* If the weather stayed fine she could get away with a cream shirt; cut like a jacket, perhaps, but light enough if the temperature dropped, to wear under her red coat with the gold piping on the cuffs. Jo would surely have a cream shirt, something different, of unusual cut or with an eye-catching feature. Soon Vlado would be home again.

Hair sleep-tousled and slippers flapping, Miranda returned from the yard before breakfast and tugged at her mother's sleeve.

'Mummy. Hugo is very sick. Ring Doctor Hugh.'

'Is he here, darling? I think he might have run away last night. It was very quiet.'

'He's under the ballerina bush.' Miranda loved the double pink-tutu heads on the fuchsias. 'Come and see.'

'I'm coming.' Danica paused along the way to fuss with daisies by the clothesline, breaking back branches, tidying, trailing the broken pieces in her hand. Half attending to Miranda's excited chatter, she saw Hugo curled under the fuchsia. He looked very clean for a dog that had been out on the ran-tan. Usually his coat was matted with sand and seaweed, or he smelt of blood and bone.

'Hugo. You are a naughty boy.' She touched him softly and then recoiled. He was unusually still. 'Miranda, I think he is very sick. We must ring the vet.' *My God! Could he be dead?* She turned the child by the shoulders and dragged her away by the hand.

Later, the vet scratched his head. 'I'm sorry, I can't help you Danny. He's been dead all night, I'd say. It's likely to be poison of some kind. There have been baits thrown in your neighbourhood, but you say there's no sign of him vomiting or thrashing about?' Danica's conscience battled away at some small relief that she no longer had to deal with him. But bait. Poor Hugo. He was naughty but he didn't deserve to die. Trying not to look into the opaque sheen of his eyes, she reached out her hand and patted him. Miranda buried her head in the dog's fur and howled. *Who would do this? And bait! What if the children had found it?*

She remembered now that he hadn't been curled up on the couch last night, and she hadn't patted him before she pushed him through the back door to his kennel. He hadn't looked back at her reproachfully before he pricked up his ears and ran barking to the fence. He hadn't been inside at all. *When did I last seen him?* Had someone driven past and tossed a handful of lethal mince over the brush fence?

There was no way she could stay alone in the house without a dog. She would have to train another filthy animal, which would lick the children's faces, beg at the table, and steal her underwear to drool over under the bed. Next time, whatever Vlado said, she would buy a bitch, and have it de-sexed. *Is a bitch less likely to take bait? I'll ring Madelaine. She might know.* It would be a good excuse for phoning, and then she could find out if Jerome had come home.

Madelaine heard Danica belting on her front door and lifted her head from the pillow. She groaned and rolled over. *One-thirty, God.* She hauled on Jerome's robe, curled her lip when she saw the overflowing ashtray on the bedside table, and struggled down the stairs.

Danica dropped a newspaper on the hallstand. 'I've been ringing all morning. Are you sick?'

'No. I'm alright.' Her voice was gravelly and she barked a deep congested cough. 'I'd better check the kids ... Oh there now, ain't technology grand? Thank you Georgia, for putting the *Play School* tape on for Paige.' She swung open the kitchen door. 'And there's breakfast.'

Danica stared at the sloppy bowls and up-ended cereal packets. 'Where was Jerome when all this was going on? I don't want to *know* what you were doing.'

'Clearly, not here, hence the newspaper's still on the lawn. You'd think if someone left you they'd have the decency to let you know. There should be rules.'

'Left you ... Madelaine, do you think he has? Has he said so?'

'In a manner.'

'What if he hasn't left you and he's had an accident?' Danica fiddled with the strap of her handbag.

'Dear girl, no, he's alive. He rang this morning, from the office. To tell me he wasn't joking ... about something. I vaguely remember that.' Madelaine shrugged.

Danica wiped away sugar to rest her handbag on the breakfast bar and sat down. 'You must be worried.'

'I'll admit he surprised me. Yesterday afternoon I got home from your house and the girls were with the neighbour. After they went to bed I sat in the dark for hours, big-eyed like a possum, couldn't sleep. Wasn't it hot? Smoked my head off. Hit the Valium in the end, but my body held out. I didn't think it would ever work.' She struck the back of the chair. 'Man, if he had Nell fluffing around and the house a pigsty, or perfect Pauline pressing him to go out every night, he could complain. We had a small domestic after the dinner at Pauline's; I think I mentioned that. He was brimming with angst, and I won't tell you why, but he never gives anything a chance to heal. He's quite deliberately dismantling our marriage.'

'Why would he do that?'

'Because he can. That's his job.'

'No, that doesn't make any sense. But, do you love him?'

'You're such a simple little sausage. What would you know about love, or hate for that matter? Of course I'm disappointed. I tried to please him, but he wanted blood: real tears on the pillow, yearnings and tiny confidences – every night for Christ's sake.'

Danica looked hurt. She stood up suddenly, her lips prim. *She's so bloody sensitive.*

Madelaine dropped her head. 'I'm worried about the children.'

'Worried about the children.' Danica mulled over the words as if they were indigestible.

'Jerome's a lawyer. What if he takes the children?'

'Oh ... but he can't, surely. I know you're upset, but courts always favour the mother. Relax. Go and have a shower,' she said, 'I'll clear up here and put some coffee on.'

Madelaine yawned and pushed her fingers through her hair. 'God I'm tired. And you sound like my mother. Simmer down. Think nice thoughts! Blah, blah ...' Madelaine picked up her cigarettes and lighter from the bench and left the room.

When she returned, the kitchen benches were freshly wiped, the floor swept and coffee brewed in the plunger.

'Feeling better?'

Madelaine plucked at the collar of her white shirt. 'Absolutely. Lucky you came over – lucky for the kids. Did you say you rang me this morning?'

Danica nodded and turned her face towards the window.

'Why? Is something wrong?'

'Well ...'

Such a drama queen. More than likely she's polishing up some little titbit, wondering how best to introduce it.

'I had a problem with Hugo.'

Oh fuck, the dog. 'So what's he done now?' Madelaine immediately stirred several teaspoons of sugar into her coffee.

'He's dead.'

Is she watching my reaction? 'Aren't you pleased then?'

'Pleased! Of course I'm not pleased. Why would you say that?'

She's going to get hysterical.

'I was the one who chased the bloody dog from daylight to dark, and brought him home from all his rorts.'

'Exactly. Now isn't this a relief?' Madelaine grinned shakily and reached for a cigarette.

Danica screwed up her face and bit her lip. *Is she doing that crumbling thing again?* 'How can you talk like that about something being dead? I'm feeling terrible. I'm very upset, and so are the kids.'

'They'll forget him and so will you. Now your friends can visit in peace, you won't have to clean up any more filthy messes, and you won't have to go crashing down to the beach in your dressing gown.'

'Madelaine, I know you have problems at the moment, but God, can't you drum up some sort of normal sympathy?'

'I'll try.' Arms folded, smoke billowing between her elegant lips, she watched Danica' face. *Will she cry?* 'What did he die of?'

'The vet doesn't know. It's a mystery. He said it could be a bait, but there's no sign of it around his mouth, or where he was.'

'A mystery eh? Bloody dog doesn't deserve it. Will there be an autopsy?'

'I don't think they do that for dogs. Thank goodness the kids didn't find whatever it was … if he did eat something.' Danica's eyes filled with tears. 'Hugo wasn't a bad dog, he didn't bite but, he was so much trouble. I think I'll get a female next time.'

Madelaine prodded the air with her cigarette. *The woman doesn't deserve my support.* 'You what? Why don't you just thank your lucky stars that you're rid of him?'

Danica looked aghast, flattened. 'And what are you going to do about your situation?'

'Nothing.'

Danica left to drink coffee with her mother. *How absurd; she doesn't even like her mother.* Her mother would only make her feel worse. Every time Madelaine rang her mother she felt totally destructive. It took hours to recover equilibrium.

Madelaine wished she'd had a chance to film the kitchen floor before Danica had swooped in to save her. Chaos was the key to everything. She had to stay strong.

Town Beach

As one rough day had collapsed into another, Danica arrived to coerce Madelaine into taking the girls to playgroup at Port Lincoln's main beach.

'Keeping them home isn't fair on them,' Danica said. 'I'll help you. It will be good.'

'I look like death. Won't Nell notice?'

'You look fine. And it's windy. No one will notice anything at the beach.'

The beach was almost deserted; summer nearly gone. The bulk of tourists had retreated to their farms and schools; the jetty scene was less gay. Madelaine and Danica arrived first, and followed the children in their rush to pat a topiaried poodle, walking with an elderly couple at the water's edge. When the couple and their dog moved on, Madelaine brought out two bags of mouldy bread for the children to toss, attracting a crowd of squawking seagulls. Paige became nervous and began to cry, and while Madelaine stooped to comfort her, a one-legged gull hopped close by, eyeing them sideways like a cardboard cut out; such a lovely clean bird with bright vermilion beak and soft grey tail feathers. *How does it manage?*

Georgia tossed a handful of crusts at it. 'Poor, poor bird, Mummy,' she said.

Madelaine ducked with her camera as the other birds swooped around, squarking and snapping. Paige leant against her mother's leg, small fingers curling under her skirt.

Nell thought it was important to include outings on the playgroup roster: to parks, playgrounds, beaches. Kids loved being outside and it meant a week when no one had to clean their house, before or after the event. They often brought sandwiches or picked up rolls and buns at the bakery. When the season changed and summer finally ended, the playgroup would abandon the beach for weeks. Although, on some sharp, clear winter days, Nell would do a ring-around, and they would go anyway, the kids waterproofed in rubber boots and puddle suits, wildly joyful to be out of the house.

Pauline, Jo and Nell descended onto the beach together, a spray of kids erupting over the sand ahead of them. Madelaine waved and turned her face deliberately into the wind. Danica had followed Sonja, who was toddling towards a clump of rocks. What a funny group they were, trailing like hobbled camels along the water's edge. Nell ambled along in her Indian shirt, baggy trousers rolled up over her hairy knees, straw hat flapping as she peered over the top of her bifocals at the children. Hands thrust in her pockets, Pauline was striding with Jo across the firmer sand, in white canvas reef shoes and a designer tracksuit the colour of teflon. And diamond earrings at the beach, for goodness' sake. *Hell, she's happy. And money is no object. Why not?* Pauline was listening earnestly to Jo, her dark neat head cocked in the wind. Jo carried her sleeping baby in a sling.

Madelaine could never put money on how Jo was feeling. She was always so warm and pleasant – to everyone. *Just like me ... Jesus wants me for a sunbeam ... to shine for him each day* . . . Madelaine was shining as best she could. It was a big call. Nevertheless, if anyone asked Jo a direct question, she would spill her guts, but with humility. Pauline was the mistress of direct questions. Madelaine could see from the way Jo bravely held her head up and periodically shrugged the shoulders of her pastel rugby top, that Pauline had hit pay dirt. *At least it will take the heat off me.*

The children flew along the sand, crashing through the shallows and scrambling over slippery rocks. *Kids respond to the elements like animals.* Madelaine zoomed in on their excited faces. They were hoarse and disobedient by the sea: leaping and flying, stumbling and falling. Danica fell back and walked beside Madelaine, saying little, camera shy. It had been kind of her to pick Madelaine up for playgroup. *Is she still cranky about the dog?* Snatches of talk rose on the wind.

'You'll have to tell him. You can't put up with that,' from Pauline.

'I don't know what to do,' from Jo.

Nell, half a step behind them, could contain herself no longer. She pushed her sunhat prow first into the conversation, and heaved the bulk of herself around. 'What gives?'

'Same old thing, Nell,' Jo answered. 'Doug.'

Nell nodded.

'I'll take the kids if you need a break,' interrupted Danica, looking eager and tentative at the same time.

Nell was annoyed. 'Or I could take them any time, Jo.'

Madelaine grinned and moved away with her camera, following Georgia, who was dragging a piece of driftwood in and out of the water. Madelaine was surprised that Danica had dared to usurp Nell's role. If a baby was born or a parent ill, Nell swooped down on the family and took away the children, or at the very least she brought a hot meal; nothing fancy, a casserole or spaghetti and a loaf of bread. To be fair, and Madelaine considered herself fair – if a little intolerant – Nell could be a Godsend. Apart from Danica, none of the playgroupers had family within cooee: six hundred kilometres by road or, sink or swim in the gulf.

Madelaine swung the camera away from Georgia, and Danica had to duck out of its path. Jo murmured grateful thanks all round, but Madelaine knew it wasn't what she was after. Madelaine pressed STOP. Once, it would have been good enough to suggest slicing Dougie's nuts off and stuffing them in his ears, or to berate his arrogant way with pronouns – how he referred to *his* money being wasted, doing what *he* liked in *his* house, like avoiding *her* work, because *he* was in a desperate hurry, might soil *his* clean shirt, would do it later. Jo was over that, Madelaine could tell. She was on the move. It was quite impressive.

Having tailed the children down the beach as far as the motel and back, they had meandered back along the water's edge until they were opposite the grassy verge where they had left their picnic baskets. Madelaine had sat the girls in front of her while she unpacked leftover pizza from the night before.

While Nell lugged the sandy box of beach toys, Pauline had carried a kicking, coughing Willa across the grassy verge to Jo's car. All three of them were leaning against the fender, talking almost in whispers. *Should I pay closer attention, or is everything I do too late?* Danica was approaching Madelaine with a shoe one of the kids had lost.

'What are they all in a huddle about now?' she hissed to Danica, who had sat beside her on the lawn. 'Do they know about Jerome?'

'No, I think it's only the Jo and Doug thing. She wants out.'

'Nell!' Madelaine yelled. 'Can you lend me a wet cloth? My children have sand on their hands.'

Nell ignored her.

'Nell, they need to eat their lunch. Germs, you know . . .'

Danica tugged at her arm. 'Mad, don't.' The children giggled. Preoccupied with far more pressing things, Nell grinned and waved.

Kids distracted, Madelaine turned back to Danica. 'Really, Jo and Jerome should get together and whine away some time.'

'He has been offering her legal advice you know. Are you sure he hasn't been home at all?'

'Danica, do you suppose I wouldn't notice my own husband?'

'How's it going?'

Madelaine shrugged.

'Will you ring your parents?'

'Never, ever.' Madelaine chewed the skin around her finger-nails, then stabbed a vicious finger at Danica. 'Why should I, when I've done nothing wrong, be forced out of my de facto workplace to live in substandard housing with *his* kids, *and* start worrying about money?'

'He might let you have the house, and only want to see the kids on weekends.'

'He can kill himself pretending to be a doting father if he cares to, but if I ever smell another woman on my children, he will never see them again.' Madelaine leapt up and slapped sand from her feet. 'So Danny, marriage. Never turn your back on it.'

Danica resolved to tend to hers. If Vlado came home that night she would be especially warm to him. She would prepare a nice selection of mezze: black olives, goat cheese, whitebait crumbed and deep fried, followed by some chicken, perhaps with lemon sauce.

Madelaine's

Madelaine was chopping vegetables. She popped the untidy ends of celery into her mouth and continued slicing. When the serrated knife took the edge off her thumbnail and finger, she winced and sucked at the blood. Pain always brought the child to the surface. Sobbing, she squatted in front of the sink cupboard, resting her arms on her thighs, allowing her head to nod faintly between her knees.

It seemed her father had been right all along; she was an awful person. Even Jerome couldn't stand her now. He was gone. *Gone, gone.* He would probably never come back, and she would be alone forever. Alone would be alright, but what about the discordant voices hammering in her brain?

Just put your nonsense to one side, her mother would say. For hadn't *she* done just that? After Madelaine's delivery there had been an emergency hysterectomy. If it weren't for her there would have been more children. A son, for instance. Her mother might never have had to stand by and watch her husband show unhealthy interest in their daughter. Madelaine knew exactly what her mother thought of her.

It was six-forty-five. All through her childhood they had eaten dinner at precisely seven pm – no discussion. Her mother would be preparing dinner now. Madelaine imagined her stirring white sauce with a wooden spoon, scraping down the sides of the saucepan and adjusting the heat, her other hand turning the pages of an English romance novel. Her face would be flushed from the rising heat, her hair damp at the back of her neck. Madelaine remembered the overpowering fragrance of lavender, the lazy elegance as she stood on one leg, scratching it with the other.

It suddenly struck her that Jerome would have been to see Hugh. *I bet Pauline knows about us.* Both 'Old Saints' boys; they would have waded through a heap of male cant about sensitive men losing their balls in the war, and then pulled their ties together. It was easy to imagine. Hugh had human in and out trays; when someone took a seat he shifted the previous patient out of his consciousness. Jerome would have his full attention.

She ran a film sequence through her head:

(Scene through an open door)

Jerome pushes the information across the desk, uncertain of its reception: '*I've left Madelaine.*'

In an effort to appear relaxed, Jerome has crossed one foot across the opposite knee. He plucks at fascinating ankle hairs and smiles while watching sunlight glimmering on the sea beyond Hugh's window. Hugh interlocks his fingers and listens intently, professionally.

'*So tired of fighting,*' *Jerome sighs.* '*Afterwards she always waits for me to make the words, to reshape our relationship and pass it back to her.*'

'*Are you sure it's not retrievable? Have you thought of counselling?*'

'*She wouldn't come. She's tired of me prodding and poking away, denying our marriage life-giving oxygen. Her words . . .*'

Hah! If she stopped it there and spliced in the one-legged gull, it would amount to the same thing. At least a bird could fly.

In the film, who could play Hugh? He was not conventionally attractive. Remnants of an awkward schoolboy remained in his large neat teeth and his thin, unathletic body. Jerome had told her that Hugh had been bullied at school: the dork, the clever-dick, they called him. No wonder he wanted to help other people.

More than likely Hugh would invite Jerome for dinner, offer him pills, diet and sleep advice, and then they would shake hands. Madelaine wished that women shook hands more often. Warm feelings passed from hand to hand like plugging into electricity.

Hugh's Surgery

Hugh didn't care about cream silk shirts and tapered navy trousers, and nor did Madelaine, but she wore them anyway. They were benchmarks.

'How are you Madelaine? You're looking well.'

She ignored him. Word had certainly travelled.

'I've brought Paige in. She fell down the stairs.'

'Gracious. Do you think she's hurt herself?'

'It's capable of fudging. You're the doctor.'

He felt his way along Paige's arm, watching her face, gauging reaction. She whimpered once.

'When?'

'Last night.'

'Hit her head?'

'Couldn't say.'

They agreed on an x-ray.

Bored, cheeks bulging with jelly sweets from Hugh's jar of treats, Georgia opened the door and disappeared into the corridor. Paige wriggled from Madelaine's lap and followed her sister through the door.

'Wait by the toys for Mummy,' Madelaine ordered, before turning back to Hugh. 'I suppose Jerome's been in playing his violin? He's left me, I've gathered.'

'How are you feeling about that, Madelaine?'

'I haven't missed his wild-card lunges, sexual or verbal. We're both hellishly tired. It's wearing living in a war zone.'

'Would talking about it with a third party help? Me, or someone else?'

'I think you'd better stick with Jerome. He's your patient and I think he's depressed. Turning forty does that.'

'Are you Madelaine? Depressed?'

'Hugh, have you ever stopped and wondered why so many women are on anti-depressants?'

Hugh raised his eyebrows.

'Difficult lives? I don't suppose Jerome told you that he belted me across the face. Did you even take his blood pressure?'

'So you do still care for him.'

'Not enough to go another round with him.'

'What about the kids?'

'At least he can't take them away. They're in my custody. The law will provide.'

'The law will provide Jerome with reasonable access.'

'I don't see why, when he walked out.'

'They are still his children. He loves them. Take good care of them, Madelaine. Kids soak up unhappiness.'

Madelaine leant across the desk and breathed into Hugh's face. 'They won't be any more damaged than we are, and you know it. Jerome and I, we've left each other stranded. Isn't that the saddest thing.'

Danica's

Danica opened her back door to Madelaine's children. 'Come in chickens. Paige, what have you done?' She fingered the plastered arm.

'Tiny fracture,' said Madelaine following them in, an arm around Paige's shoulder. 'Hugh showed an indecent interest in my business with Jerome. To think I used to feel sorry for him living with Pauline. Apart from mine, do you know any marriages where people don't deserve each other?' she said, shaking her head.

Nonplussed, Danica shrugged.

'Jerome has clearly told Hugh everything.'

'Did he say so?'

'No, of course not. Ethics, you know. But it was as plain as the nose on his face. And that's plain.'

'Coffee?'

'Yes please, I'm desperate. Here darlings, take these chippies outside,' she said, reaching into her bag and passing packets to the children. 'Five minutes before we have to go, I will call out. Early warning.'

'You're a villain, Madelaine, undermining my children's healthy diet.'

'That's the price you pay for my friendship. How are you?'

'Very well, thank you.'

'Happy you, then.' *She's awfully prim. Is it still the dog?*

'Poor Paige, she's always backed down those stairs like a little koala.'

'Who knows? When she's crabby I generally give her a wide berth, tell her to take herself off until she's better company. What would an experienced mother suggest, check her ears and worm her?'

'Madelaine, don't be tough. Listen, Nell knows where Jerome is living.'

'That'd be right. I should have asked her straight away.'

Danica blushed and lunged for her coffee. 'Jo's been there.'

Madelaine looked shaken, wobbled the milk jug over her coffee. 'Holy cow, Danny. I can see Nell peering through the shrubbery. I should pay her.'

'I'm sorry, Mad. I didn't know whether to tell you, but I thought Nell might anyway – '

'Yeah, and call it sisterhood,' Madelaine finished for Danica, and nibbled on an almond biscuit, knocking her cigarette on the edge of the ashtray. She crossed and recrossed her legs.

'He wouldn't have had time for an affair, would he?'

She's so naive. 'People from all walks of life do. Every wife thinks she would notice something.'

'Jo's unhappy, but she's so nice. And she's a friend.'

Left hand cupping her right elbow, Madelaine stood up and looking venomous, paced up and down the kitchen. 'It would be typical of him to fall for someone so insipid ... so Christian, like my mother. Someone who'd feed his ego all day and tolerate minor cruelties.'

'Doug is not Jo's fault,' said Danica nervously. 'She didn't pick him out for that. You don't think that, do you?'

'Jesus, Danny. I don't know. I used to feel sorry for her but this changes things. Who says she didn't cash her chips in early with Doug? Not enough confidence to wait for Mr Right?'

'Perhaps it's not true about her and Jerome. How could she face you?'

'She did come around once, to drop off a playgroup roster. I was bone-weary and she and Jerome were having a good wack, excuse me, reminisce, about their ... "alma mater". I took it as a bonus and went to bed.' She blew smoke out in front of her and stabbed at it with her cigarette. 'I went to a private school you know, but I've never heard so much talk about it, until I came here. It's incredibly pretentious and totally meaningless.'

'You don't think they did something then, in your own lounge room? Jo and Jerome?'

'No, hell they wouldn't, would they? I was just rewinding to see if I'd missed anything.'

Bay Motel

By the time Madelaine thought about making 'Flight from Form', the film about her husband's departure, all her goodwill had evaporated. She wondered who was pushing her buttons. Surely not still her father? Lucky him, to have God on his side. She decided to start with an opening scene in a motel:

Jerome throws his briefcase through the doorway, and subsides against the jamb to survey the room. He looks rumpled, his jacket shrugged round his shoulders, as if he's slept on the office floor.

Madelaine will pan between objects set against the besserblock walls, occasionally zooming in:

Yellow plastic lampshades [zoom in], *a burnt-orange tweed-look lounge suite* [pan past] *and rusty stains in the vanity bowl. A dusty unframed print of a luscious Tahitian girl, frangipani tucked behind her ear* [zoom in].

Cheap and tacky, and Madelaine didn't mean the girl.

He runs his fingers through his hair and lugs his airline suit bag onto the bed to drag out jocks and toothbrush.

The set would be minimalist – orange, seedy. Placing condoms on Gideon's legacy might be overkill. *He's just left home, for God's sake.* An empty pizza box, Coke bottles. She would linger on the double bed, tilt up, pan across to the door and out. The next scene would be at the yacht club.

Jerome is at a laminate table making cosy conversation with Jo and Doug as he stares at the chalked menu board. Doug is pink and voluble, spitting half-baked malice at Jo, who's smiling her sweetest good-leather, real-gold, quality-fabric trademark smile.

Perhaps Doug would have the decency to wait until Jo left the table before telling his joke to Jerome, about how you can tell when private-school girls come – their pearls rattle. More likely Jo would get up, perhaps to top up her lipstick, and Doug would pretend some deferential interest in Jerome's conversation.

The dialogue was predictable:

'I see that rape case comes up next Friday. Full of foul revelations?'

'Not pretty, but there's a process.'

'Do you ever get paid in such cases?'

'Legal aid.'

'When I first went out teaching I thought I could change the world. Even wanted to. I know better now. I always thought it was nurture. Now I've seen a lot more nature.'

'We're all blameless in a sense: parents being after all, the products of their parents. Most people have a go, try to make a life despite the difficulties of their childhood.'

Pompous prick. If she had really filmed it, she would have rewound and deleted it.

The barman hails Jerome. There is a phone call for him in the office. On the way back he stands at the bar and orders more drinks.

Are we having a good time yet? Madelaine bit into her fist.

Doug and Jo are spatting. Blah, blah, blah! Doug is locking his bullying eyes with hers. His tie is loose. His lips are moving rapidly, viciously, below the froth of beer under his nose. Jerome makes little effort to disguise his irritation. Jo turns her wedding ring around and around on her finger.

And well she might.

She dabs at tears with a tissue, keeps her feet together under the table and hangs her head in shame. Jerome will know that she is paddling wildly below the surface, scrabbling for a shred of dignity. His round of drinks arrives. Doug snatches his glass up and moves to greet someone at the bar. Jerome pulls out a wad of notes and pays the waitress.

Well done, to be so cashed up so soon after you leave.

Doug exits left. Jerome places a rum and Coke on the coaster in front of Jo.

Nice. So who is supporting whom?

Jo smiles a watery smile. 'How are things with you?'

Who says that? Fuck, it doesn't matter.

'About the same as with you apparently.'

Jo drops her head and jerks it up again. 'Do you mean?'

Brought up so well, not to ask outright.

'I've left Madelaine.'

He'd done it now; untethered assertions often fly away and become part of the natural order. Madelaine sighed and pursed her lips.

She tried to visualise the next scene without crying:

They manoeuvre through the yacht-club door. Jerome catches the door above Jo's head and leans against her as she swings through. They get in Jerome's car. Madelaine follows their journey along the main road, concentrating on the flurries of dust, the dark head shadows outlined against the rear window, the glowing tail-lights sliding into the crescent.

Back at Jo's:

Jo and Jerome are perfectly framed on the living-room couch, the salmon fabric highlighting her blonde bob. He dabs at the tears on her face.

Madelaine decided the conversation should be banal:

'You can't go on like this.'

'I know I have to be tougher but it's difficult without much money and with dependent children.'

'Those are just bread-and-butter issues. Make an appointment with me this week and I'll explain all the legal ramifications.'

Jo ducks her head. Jerome lifts her chin and hesitates, his lips almost touching hers, until she registers intent and in the fraction of a second accepts it and goes to meet it with interest of her own. Their lips meet in a salty companionable nudge and leap away.

The baby cries.

That would dull their passion. It was a shame Jo had to have the best role – certainly Madelaine had felt sorry for her, but as compensation it was excessive.

Madelaine's

Thank God, the children are asleep. Madelaine had woken at four and spent half the day lolling with her feet up on the couch; thinking, thinking, getting nowhere. She hadn't even dressed. The kids had been good, not demanding. They were great kids, even Paige with her broken arm, who had to be carried up and down the stairs. It wasn't their fault, but one more hour with them and she would have slit her throat. Her moods were vile. Her marriage had come apart at the seams, and she couldn't find the thread.

Glancing down, Madelaine lifted the folds of her blue velour dressing gown away from her legs. Black stubble rasped under her fingers. Her nails needed cleaning and her hair was dirty. She glanced at the empty brandy balloon and sighed. Five minutes earlier there had been a warm, incandescent curve of golden liquid just below the rim. *Such a fleeting pleasure.* Did she feel ugly because she *was* ugly or did she *get* ugly because she *felt* ugly? *Can unhappiness make you ugly? Will another brandy keep me calm?* Would it prevent sins from seeping out?

When she was little, her father told her God would punish her. She had thought he said God would punch her, and ever since, like Woody Allen, she was always on the lookout for a descending fist. Like Woody, she was afraid of death, or was it life?

Heaving herself out of the chair, she scooped up her glass and trudged towards the bar. The bottle was almost empty. She'd have to do something about money soon. She'd never actually had money. They had accounts in the shops in town but Jerome doled the rest out in cash.

Here's a couple of hundred, Mad, he'd say. Get something ritzy for the races. For a long time it hadn't felt like *her* money, and when it came from his trousers, hanging over the end of their bed, she had felt like a whore.

Nell had her contribution to the household all worked out for arbitration – forty-six-and-a-half hours of child care, thirteen hours housekeeping, sick leave, award rates for sex, and time-and-a-half for anything kinky. Madelaine had never cared that much. Not enough to lobby for joint accounts and mortgages. She'd never had escape money sticky-taped under wardrobes or secreted in biscuit tins. Not like other women she knew.

Damn, the doorbell. Lurching up, she threw out a deep-seated bronchial cough, crossed her legs and steadied herself. *Why do I reach for so many fags and draw on them so hungrily? And who would call at this hour?* She felt as if she were in a play – a farce, at least – and threw out her hands to an imaginary audience. *Am I drunk?* Padding down the hallway, she gurgled mucous in her throat and coughed again. Near the landing to the stairs, she leapt back in fright. *Hell, he's in.*

'Rang the bell to announce myself.' Jerome bounded up the last two steps. 'No answer. How are you?'

She stared at him. *How am I? How am I?* Licking her lips and feeling distinctly disadvantaged, she pulled her gown tightly round her legs and pushed her hair back with one hand. *What an arsehole.* 'I'm as well as can be expected. And you?'

'Fine, thanks. Starting to get my life in order. Do you need anything?'

'How thoughtful of you but when we finished the cans and packets last week I gave the women's shelter a ring.'

'You didn't.'

'Of course I didn't you bastard. And why are you looking so pleased with yourself? Has Jo been rattling her pearls?'

His chin dropped in surprise and he scanned the floor. *Good. He's uncomfortable.* Waiting for him to speak would be delicious. But she was too angry, and flew at him with fingernails drawn. He fell back under the sudden weight of her assault.

'How dare you look so smug!' she yelled. '*Oh no Madelaine, there is no one else. It's me. I have to move on for all our sakes. The tension is making me ill.* You hypocrite. And all along you've had the hots for Miss Jo Priss, Miss I-think-life-means-well Priss.'

He doubled up as she kneed him in the groin, and ducked about as she punched his ear, his throat, his face. He raised his arm to fend off the rain of blows.

'What are you on about? Who told you this about Jo? I didn't leave you for Jo.'

She let her hands drop to her sides.

'Madelaine, you're right that Jo has left Doug. I have given her some advice, and I needed to talk to someone too.'

'I deeply resent you discussing our personal problems with her. And I hear she's been visiting your flat. I didn't even know you had a fucking flat.'

Jerome shrugged.

'What bloody gall, to think you can just pick up with one of my unhappy friends. Isn't it enough to bust up our marriage without having a go at hers as well?'

'You know their marriage hasn't been worth a pinch of shit for years.'

'All your information about that, was filtered through me. She's never left him before. Tell me you're not sleeping with her.'

'Madelaine, you couldn't have known it, but over the last year or so, I've seen her professionally – off and on. We met somewhere, recently, realised we were both in the same boat, offered each other moral support. It wasn't sinister.'

'That's geek talk.'

Madelaine felt air escape from her lungs against her will. Cold, nauseous blackness oozed through arteries and veins, banked up against shunts, spun round valves.

'It's really over, our relationship, isn't it?'

'I'm sorry, Mad, but remember, I don't feel good either. Haven't felt good for a long time.' He ran his fingers through his hair and dropped his head. 'When you want to, we can talk about our financial responsibilities. You don't have to worry. I'll do the right thing.'

Her face deliberately impassive, she pretended to think it over, then picked up her camera and flipped off the lens cap. 'Why should I accommodate any of this: this failure of ideals, this compromise of dignity, a sloppy financial solution, and Jo as well?'

'Madelaine, I miss the kids. I want them to come and stay a weekend with me.'

She pressed RECORD and stepped back. 'No way. Why should they? This is their home. You want to take everything from me.'

Grimacing, Jerome pushed his hand over the lens of the camera. 'You use that thing as a weapon. Turn it off, love. Be civilised. We're mature, intelligent adults. We can work this out.'

'No damn fancy lawyer-talk will convince me that I have to let Jo near my children.'

She bobbed around him, documenting what she feared was their final scene. What would she call it, 'Coda'? He had run his fingers along the video titles on her bookshelf once, and said they were crazy. 'Dogged Run', 'April Sea', 'Phrasing'. To her they made perfect sense. God knows he had bought the camera to busy her with making records of the children's development, documenting their life together – 'Funniest Home Videos'. *Well, they're that.*

'A father has a right to see his children.'

'A father's right ... What about a father's responsibility? Where have you been all these years? At the office, at the cricket, on someone's boat, that's where you've been.'

'True, I work long hours, but I haven't been such a bad husband. You could have made a little happiness for yourself.'

'We don't do happy here.'

'Intelligent people can occupy themselves, that's all I'm saying.'

'How long? Seven years like a princess? Seven years of bad luck? Out.'

Madelaine stopped thumping him, and Jerome had stared hard at her. As if in sudden pain, she had taken her fingers to her throat and cried out loud. When she retreated behind the camera again, she started crying. He reached out to touch her shoulder and she flung his hand away.

'We'll be alright, Madelaine. This happens to a lot of people.'

She stalked him down the stairs, filming as she went. Her face was locked against the viewfinder as he closed the door softly and flung himself into the night.

When Jerome was gone, Madelaine backed against the door, fists clenched at her side. She'd done her best: kept the house tidy, the children neat, didn't spend a lot of money, wasn't demanding of his time, didn't complain about wet towels on the bathroom floor. She had no one's worst faults, but she had to admit it didn't sound positive. One of her children was crying. Did Jerome know that Paige had broken her arm? If he cared about them so much, he should have demanded to see them. Perhaps she had knocked him off kilter and he would come back.

Smiling sweetly, Jerome acquiesced from a photograph frame on top of the sound system. She lifted him down and used a felt-tipped pen to draw on a moustache and beard and then black tears and a halo. *Relationship cancelled due to lack of interest.* She added peaky ears, a large lower lip and a satanic black cross, embedded in his heart. *Bastard.*

When they first married, Jerome and his ego thought they had her measure. She knew he hadn't expected a saccharine gush, but he hadn't considered for a minute whether he was up to the challenge.

Madelaine threw back her head and howled, then wiped her nose on the sleeve of her gown. *Fancy crying over my father at my age.* She knew what he would say: What God has joined, let no man put asunder. And: In this dark hour, let us pray Madelaine, for you, and for your little children. He would demand that she ask God's forgiveness. He would guide her along the path of contrition. *Cant, cant, can't.* Examine your conscience, he would preach. Do all you can to conciliate with

Jerome. Do not let pride stand in the way of your redemption. Restore your marriage. Jerome is a good man, and we know that you are not always a good girl. He would grasp her shoulders and pull her to him and the awful smell of aniseed jubes and Lifebuoy soap would make her gag.

Jerome had suggested once that he refer her on to a colleague, who would deal with her father in the courts. She would need to talk to him and see what kind of case she had.

'Don't,' she'd cried. 'It doesn't matter now. I'm fine.'

She pushed a lit cigarette into Jerome's battered photograph, turning his nose red, and watched the bright glow eat into his face. If only she had burnt her father like that – the childish eyes that lit up for God and Madelaine; the paunchy body, soft under his surplice; the shock of hair and the large fleshy face. And for all those years ago, when he had trapped her mother. In wedding photos she looks stiff in her finery, her smile forced as if he had manipulated her from behind, his boyish hand up her dress.

Jerome was supposed to be life's reprieve and carry her away from Father. Instead he had perceived her as an asset, her body a draught to drink, her beauty a refuge to slide into. A stronger man could have passed her up. Weakness and his ego made him think he'd make a go of her.

And now he'd quit, retired hurt, and his acquisitive eyes were on her children. She balled her fist and tried to shove it in her mouth. *What can be done?*

Danica's

Later that evening Madelaine telephoned Danica.

Danica rushed to the phone, her heart skipping a beat as she wondered if she would hear another unnerving thunk.

'It's me.'

'Madelaine?'

'Jerome's been a-visiting. He used his key. Crept in like a husband. I heard someone on the stairs. Scared me witless. There I was in my dressing gown, in complete disarray. When I saw his face I was half relieved, half furious.'

Danica imagined her seated at the black-wood phone table in the hallway, legs crossed, a brandy balloon swinging in her hand. The speech was definitely slurred.

A long silence ensued.

'Are you alright?'

'I'm not very alright,' Madelaine answered childishly. 'He dodged around that slippery Jo question, but it wasn't an unqualified denial.'

'You asked him, straight out?'

'I did.'

'Poor you. What happened then?'

'I screamed like a madwoman, and hurled myself at him.'

'What must he think?' *Madelaine is so extreme.* It would be better if she just cried, let Jerome feel sorry for her. Danica looked at the clock. It was almost time for her favourite television show, but friends came first. *God, it's hot.* Her hands were covered in melted chocolate. She put two more squares in her mouth and licked her fingers.

'I have no idea. Once it would have excited him. Later it would have made him angry . . . Now he just wants to leave.'

'Do you think he means it?'

'Appears to.'

Danica stifled a yawn, covering her mouth with her fingers. 'I'm so sorry, Mad. Are you sad? Well, of course you must feel . . . all those years . . .'

'I feel *something* for him alright.'

'What if you asked him to try again? Could you just say sorry?'

'Sorry . . . interesting . . . I think I'll just get quietly rotten.'

'You're drinking now, aren't you?'

'Certainly, what else at this point?'

'Don't drink too much. What about the kids?'

'Danny, it's night-time,' she giggled.

'Madelaine, I don't know what to say. I've had a terrible day myself.'

'Poor baby. Food issues?'

'Don't be cruel. I had a fight with my mother.'

'If we're in the queue, I'm ahead of you for a parentectomy.'

'She said Miranda's cheeky. Said she would never have allowed her children to speak in such a way to their grandparents. With Vlado gone, I don't need my mother dumping on me.'

'Don't worry. More than likely she's jealous.'

'I can't help it. I love her, but she makes me feel a failure. I feel hopeless.'

'Tell her to take over for a few days, and we'll shoot off somewhere together.'

'I couldn't leave the girls.'

'Wouldn't, you mean! Fill yourself up with pills and bourbon and stagger off to bed. Like me.'

'You haven't been taking pills, Madelaine?'

'No, that's right, I haven't. Silly old me. Hugh gave me the lecture about that.'

Danica heard Madelaine humming softly to herself. *She is such a trial. Those poor little girls.* But a husband walking out would be such a shock. All couples fought sometimes. Jerome wasn't playing fair. *I would be angry too.* Danica broke off another double square of chocolate.

'Madelaine, don't take anything else tonight. I'll come around in the morning. We'll talk.'

'Don't worry. I know you can't come ... can you, Danny? I'm the only mother who leaves her children home alone.'

'Madelaine, don't.'

Danica bit her lip and waved Miranda back to bed.

'Stop worrying. It's not a test. Madelaine's acting foxy but you're quite safe,' Madelaine slurred.

'I am worried. But what should I do? Ring me if you get desperate, promise; I'll get Vesna for my kids. She'll understand.'

'Fine. That's dealt with then. We have a plan. As a matter of fact, I feel much better. I might take a long bath, and float my bottle like a ducky. I haven't dressed at all today.'

The receiver banged down in Danica's ear. *Hell.*

Danica put the phone down and sat in front of the television with half a punnet of ice cream. It was spoiled somehow, but she ate it anyway. The phone rang three times. The first time she leapt up and spilt the ice cream. No answer. Twice more. Nothing. Danica took the phone off the hook and put herself to bed.

She fell into fitful sleep, and dreamt that she and Madelaine were driving a red Lotus on a European motorway. It was raining lightly, and their hair flew out behind them as they roared around hairpin bends. Climbing through a mountain pass enveloped in cloud, the car lurched unexpectedly and screeched on two wheels across the centre-line, into the path of an oncoming truck. Danica screamed. Hunched over the steering wheel, hair standing up around her face, Madelaine laughed. Rivulets of water ran down her face. Her skin was white, her mouth a red slash. She clenched her perfect teeth as she hauled the car away from the truck, and crashed through the metal barrier. They plunged into an endless abyss. Danica woke, thought she was still falling, lunged for the light switch, her eyes wide with terror, her heart thumping. Then she slept a heavy, dreamless sleep and woke feeling thick and fuggy-headed, her limbs clenched so rigid they were aching.

Louth Bay

Dressed in trademark navy, Madelaine stepped from her car with as much grace as she could muster, threw her head back into the salt spray like a spring filly, then crunched along the gravel path to Jo's door. The timber-framed asbestos-clad beach house was distasteful to her, or was it only because she caught a glimpse of Jo washing dishes at the kitchen window? Jo glanced up, smiled, and reached around the draining rack to open the battered aluminium flywire door, kicking it free when it caught at the bottom.

What a fabulous opening scene it was. Madelaine would call the movie 'Kitchen-sink melodrama 1'. *If only I'd brought my camera*. But then Jo would never go for a big film denouement. And Madelaine would find acting, directing and operating the camera very stressful. Perhaps she could come back later, in the early hours of the morning; she could swing her camera through the garden, along the walls of the house and onto the beach, utter an on-set commentary. If she didn't succumb to the temptation to scream and hurl herself at the windows of the house, it could work.

'Different style Jo, but I note your touches,' pattered Madelaine, gesturing towards a seeding tub of verbena on the doorstep, and a collection of pink shells overflowing from a basket. 'Winton at the window – it's the wow factor.' She ran her fingers along the row of floral china pieces on the sill. 'This a permanent move then?'

'Semi I suppose. You know I've left Doug, do you?'

'Don't play silly games, Josey.'

Jo sighed.

Perhaps she didn't realised that such things were supposed to be unpleasant.

'Where are the children, Maddy?'

'Nell whisked them away. And yours?'

'Playing on the beach with Sandy, the friend I'm staying with.'

'More useful than Doug then. Don't know why all girls aren't gay.' She laughed loudly and then focused on Jo's eyes. 'But then you don't think so, do you? You're going back for sloppy seconds.'

Jo smiled nervously. 'I can see Madelaine, that you want to speak frankly. Would you like some coffee?'

'Not especially. If you would, hop to it.'

'I think I will. I'll only be a minute.'

Madelaine sauntered round the room, peering and poking. 'Such eclectic taste. Crass to copy I suppose. Do you steal *ideas* from other people too?'

'Yes. From books, magazines and sometimes other people. *You* have good taste.'

'Oh no, I'm very simple. After we moved in, our place looked like a morgue for weeks. All white walls and spartan spaces. Jerome found it noisy and unwelcoming. I dug up a few things to please him, but I'm not like you, with all this clutter of cloths and china. I'm not a homey sort of person.'

'You like clean lines, Scandinavian wood perhaps, or abstract paintings.'

'Modern is something I'm definitely not. What about what you're doing with Jerome, is that modern?' She leant against the living-room wall and lit a cigarette.

'I'd like to speak openly with you, Madelaine. It is true Jerome and I have become close friends. I'm sorry you don't like it. I can understand that, but he was there at a bad time for me. Both our relationships were in trouble.'

'*You* are the trouble in Jerome's and *my* relationship. He's never left me before. I should have guessed someone else was involved.'

'Jerome didn't leave you for me. I know he's told you that . . . he was unhappy.'

'People always say that.' Madelaine yawned. 'Even if it were marginally true, you must know that you are a powerful reason for him to stay away.'

'No, Madelaine. We're friends.'

'Poor, poor, Jerome. And Jo. But what about me? I too, am unhappy. And here I am stuck in the wings while he struts about, discarding roles and eliciting sympathy, making *friends*.'

'You heard what happened with the rape case? He was very down.'

'Surprise me, the kid got off.'

'Guilty, put on a bond.'

'Jerome expected nothing more.'

'He was flat for days.'

'Law's like that. There are compensations . . . like you.'

'I wonder, Madelaine, if talking is going to be productive. You're upset. Let's leave it, shall we.' Jo rose and moved towards the door. Madelaine sauntered after her.

'Listen up. If you want to pretend some esoteric bloodless

relationship with my husband, it doesn't worry me. But it doesn't fool me either. Get involved with my children and you *will* be sorry.'

Jo reddened and twisted her handkerchief between her fingers.

All quite satisfactory really. Dignity was a very subjective thing. Neither of them had even raised their voice. Madelaine leant forward to butt out her cigarette on a doyley. *So impractical.*

Madelaine's

Jerome was always such a grump about the camera. Half the time Madelaine couldn't remember whether she'd filmed scenes or not. She had called Jerome, but figured it was better not to go to the beach yet. That film would have to be made later, but she could write the script. Labelling a new tape 'Divine Intervention', she imagined Jo in a taupe crushed-linen suit, waiting in a restaurant for Jerome. He had been reluctant to meet, so perhaps he had planned a significant announcement after dinner. No doubt it would begin with one of those bleating greetings that helpless men enjoy: Cow of a day, just can't seem to get on top of things anymore. Then I go home to that little red hellhole and I haven't got a clean shirt, the ants are in the honey and I'm out of loo paper. Poor darlings – goddamned needy and not highly evolved.

Jo had always been a tolerant person. Sand in a man's office shirt was a giveaway, but she would be oblivious. When Jo and Doug had arrived in Port Lincoln four or five years ago, he had been boyish and exuberant. At parties he would throw Jo over his shoulder, kneading her flesh and peppering his conversation with sexual connotations. Madelaine bet he was not a bit like Jo's previous boyfriends. He was good old Doug, and everywhere he went there was backslapping, jokes and buffoonery. Jo would have felt like part of it. Not Quiet-sensible Jo anymore, but Isn't-life-hilarious Jo, and Isn't-it-crazy-that-he-loves-me-so-much Jo. But it had all worn thin. If there hadn't been sand in Doug's shirts, there would have been lipstick, and the year there were lime-green nickers wedged behind the rear car seats, Jo had gone spare.

When Jo got tired of it, Doug had spent his verve on other people. Jo became the wet blanket who wanted him to hand over the keys, stop drinking and come home. She hankered after a family man. *Too bad, how sad.* Then along came Jerome, promising nothing much, and Jo had made the leap of a desperate woman. How would that go down at the cricket club, where Doug had a smallish following? In sporting circles only men were supposed to make the moves. Madelaine wouldn't bother making that film—been done a hundred times before. The men got all the best roles.

If only she had a tool on her video camera, to make a silent movie with still shots, and voice balloons. So much more fun than narrating scripts on empty sets with absent characters.

Perhaps she could film Jo at the Jansys end-of-summer sale. She was good at her job, extremely sharp. She knew which matrons took five garments home to think about, wore one or two of them on the weekend, and brought them back spot-cleaned and sweaty.

Madelaine thought she might go to the next Jansys sale, try a lot of things on and leave them in a muddle on the change-room floor. She could mix up the sizes, but Jo was more than likely used to that. If she brought home an armload of silk shirts, black crepe trousers and beaded tops, what would happen when the bill lobbed on Jerome's desk?

Powerhouse Beach – Dusk

Jerome straightened the papers on his desk, lined up pens and pencils with his favourite letter opener. Sitting upright all day made the muscles in his neck spasm. He'd heard of people pulling muscles while in their office chair. He eased the chair out from under his desk, plucked his grey sports jacket from the hook behind the door, grasped his briefcase and flicked the light off. *Late.* At least he didn't have to cook for himself tonight. He wondered how do workingwomen get themselves a meal. Always too late for the shops, too tired to even find a recipe, let alone cook it. Now that Madelaine had rung, he'd be even later. Never mind, had to do the right thing. God knows what she wanted. She sounded awfully strange on the phone, soft and fluttery and unsure of herself. Could he please come round at seven, to talk?

At Madelaine's, he tapped on the front door. *No doubt I shouldn't have barged in on her the other night. Quite likely made her aggressive.*

'Come in,' he heard her warble from the direction of the bathroom. Peering warily through the door and feeling hot and clammy, he loosened his tie and stepped into the hall. Vivaldi's *Four Seasons* rippled from the sound system. They'd always rocked Georgia to sleep with it. Never failed.

'Won't be a moment, Jerome. There's a drink on the shelf. Help yourself.'

'Kids asleep?'

'At quarter-to-eight – of course. How quickly you forget routine.'

The drink was strong. Nice scotch, and he'd probably paid for it, so why not? He sluiced it down and pottered round the kitchen where everything was strangely orderly. *Madelaine must be feeling better.* There was fruit in the bowl, a ragged bunch of flowers lifted from someone's garden, on the sill, and a complete absence of laundry or cupboard clutter.

She crossed the room to graze his cheek with hers.

'I thought we might walk to the beach. I need to talk to you.' Her hair fell in a long rope down her back. A magnolia was tucked in the feathery tail of it and he could smell fresh toothpaste and her favourite French perfume. Gold leather thongs glowed against her brown feet, and a cream silk shirt was tucked into her oldest black skirt.

'I haven't got a lot of time, Madelaine.'

'I suspected that, so I brought a snack.'

Like a peasant, she slung a roughly woven basket over her shoulder. If only she was that uncomplicated. *But peasants aren't simple either.* He admonished himself for thinking that.

'Alright, I won't be ungracious, but let's make it fairly snappy shall we? I have a lot of reading to do tonight.' That was a given, but he didn't need to tell her about driving on for dinner.

Madelaine lifted her camera from a hook on the hallstand. Jerome swung around to face her. 'I'm not an actor. If you bring that thing, count me out.' He immediately felt hot and frayed. His heartbeat quickened and he felt short of breath. She acquiesced, ducking to lift the camera over her head and place it back.

Pre-children they had often walked arm in arm to the Powerhouse Beach and sat on the rocks, with a beer beside them, and fish and chips warm in their laps. They had watched small figures march up and down the wharf, carrying goods to the big boats from Japan, South America and Russia. In the daytime the baggery chutes whirred and chugged, filling the vast holds with peninsula wheat and barley. In the night stillness, the silos, great tomb-like monoliths that housed the grain, reared massive against the skyline.

Before them had lain the great long lonely wharf from where they could hear odd splashes, and the curses that flew from night fishermen hunched over their rods, kitbags at their sides, an array of mussel shells and hooks spread across the wooden struts. Twin lights glowed from the farmhouse on Boston Island. Trawlers puttered through the moonlit water, on their way to net the stirring prawns.

At dusk, they had seen sailors walking past the ancient boarding houses, heading into town in search of fun. There were only pubs. A few local girls might be willing for a promise or a dream. Jerome had told Madelaine about the busy ports in Europe he had visited in his twenties; Genoa and Calais, for instance, where whores mouthed smoky obscenities and sang softly with their skirts rucked up.

After his outburst about the camera, Madelaine had marched off and they had walked along the road at a cracking pace, mostly in silence. She had cut a long winding path to the beach, skirting tussocks and hopping stones. Jerome felt increasingly uneasy and struggled to keep sand out of his best shoes. The confluence of man-made shapes set at curious angles around them unnerved him. The power-house, industrial fences, signs and symbols, reminded him of dark detective tales. He searched out the unstable but familiar shifting of the sea, the soft grey curve of the horizon, half-lit by a soaring yellow moon. *The bloody place is beautiful.* Everything resonated until they stepped away from the road and down to the beach, and Madelaine smiled. Jerome felt immediately wretched again. His life was full of contradictions.

Dusk was falling by the time they arrived; the beach was empty and the water swished sadly. Sandals in hand, Madelaine picked her way to a sheltered space between two boulders, where it was secluded, dry and safe from the tide. Jerome shoved his hands in his pockets, glanced about uncertainly, wondered if he would have to dry-clean his suit pants afterwards, as she patted out a small rug and offered champagne and potato crisps.

'Bon appetit,' she said. 'Salt is essential by the seaside. Say it three times.'

'Why are you so cheerful, Madelaine?'

'Here, drink and I'll tell you.' The champagne bubbled over the side of the glass and effervesced in the palm of his hand. She leant over quickly and surprised him by licking his fingers.

'Nell took Georgia and Paige for the whole day, so I could set my house to rights. The floors are scrubbed and so am I. Last time we were together . . . it wasn't nice.'

She drew his hand along her ankle, calf and thigh, then lightly took away her own. 'All smooth flesh. I've been plucked like a turkey.'

He grinned. 'Good for you.'

She trickled her fingers from brow to hip and ducked her

head in mock contrition. 'Facial, body scrub, massage. I'm pared down completely – quintessential me. Drink up.'

Only vaguely remembering his empty stomach, he'd gulped whisky at the house and now champagne. *Nerves. Will she hit me this time?* If he had to bail out again, how awkward it would be walking back to his car, with her flapping and squealing like a bat behind him. 'I haven't eaten dinner yet, Madelaine. I'm light-headed.'

'I've brought food.' She laid packets of crayfish sandwiches in his lap. Despite his best intentions he attacked them hungrily, reaching again for his glass. They would suffice as entrée. He would have to call in late.

'Can we just for the moment,' she continued, 'forget our problems and pretend we're Jerome and Madelaine of old, nestled in amongst the rocks, no children, no responsibilities.'

'You make us sound like Ken and Barbie on a picnic!'

She pouted. 'Jerome, try at least.' Leaning across his body, she pointed to a massive grey ship anchored near the wharf. 'Look at that flag. Egypt, do you think? Do they buy our wheat?'

'I'm not sure.' He could smell her perfume.

'How was your day?'

'Busy. Did you want to discuss something specific?'

'I'm after a more civil footing. I haven't been sleeping well. I've lost momentum.'

'I haven't been happy for a long time. I feel too exhausted to begin again, if that's what you're asking.'

'Forget it tonight then.' She inclined her head sadly, her voice ebbing, then flowing again. 'We'll hitch a ride to Egypt.'

She turned aside, topped up her champagne, and then moved squarely back in front of him. Personal space had never bothered Madelaine. Jerome could feel her breath moist on his face. A stricken streetlight flickered behind them. Dark clouds had crossed the moon and shadowed her eyes. He could see champagne glistening on her lips.

'What do you want, Madelaine? What is all this about?'

'Nothing too frightening. I'm after something to savour later, to smell on my body when you're gone. I can do uncomplicated.' She seesawed his tie and flicked open the top buttons of his shirt.

He sat motionless, his breath ragged as she dipped her finger in his glass and slid it inside his shirt.

'Madelaine, I doubt there's a point.' *I could just get up and walk.* He'd done the hard part.

'You look so tired. Why do you work so hard? It's a shame Gregory won't get off his arse and do his share.'

'Don't say that, Madelaine,' he snapped. 'It's more complicated than you realise. People don't ask to see him.' While he spoke, he was conscious of her hands at his shirt, at the waistband of his trousers. She was spilling champagne all over him, licking it off his neck and chest. He would reek of booze. Beneath the surface, rational Jerome protested feebly: *Stop now. I feel uncomfortable. It's way too late.*

She exhaled in hot little puffs, rose up on the balls of her hands, and began moving her breasts against him, pushing him back into the sand.

'Madelaine, this is not a good idea,' he said through his teeth, gripping both her arms in an effort to wrest control.

'It is, I promise. Kiss me,' she begged, her mouth opening over his. Moving both his arms to encircle her skirt, now bunched up around her bum, she moved his hand as if he were a blind man, from naked hip to inner thigh, and breathed hard into his face. The faintest movement of air stirred tendrils of hair around her face. She closed her eyes and arched her back to throw off her shirt. Her arms shuddered in the evening breeze as she latched onto him like some furious flailing sea creature. He lay quite still and thought about his options, but in the warm and enveloping moment, they all seemed good. He had always liked it, the moving inside her.

'Jesus, Madelaine,' he groaned.

'That's not romantic.' She bit hard into his lip.

A stubborn part of him leapt away, nagged and resisted, struggled for control. A dog whimpered in the seagrass. The streetlight flickered one last time and died. *What will I gain from a moment's pleasure?* But his loins had commandeered his brain.

He moaned and rocked, his body driving back his doubts. The cloud covered the moon again, and he could see only the outline of her face in the darkness. Then she pushed aside her bag to clear their picnic space, and they careered between the rocks, her nails pressed hard against his flesh. They rolled, twice, stayed connected. Jerome could feel her scrabbling for her bag beside them, before his back came down hard on the rocks beneath them. She put her arms around him and rocked with him, kneading and pinching the flesh of his back. They moved again, and he felt sudden pain.

'Madelaine, for fuck's sake.' Something was digging into him and he struggled to pull away. Madelaine was astride him, panting with exertion, her face banging against his, blocking out the paltry light. Her elbows on his chest constricted his breathing. He gulped away a feeling like indigestion – the lobster? He tried to turn his body but she had seized his face in both hands, and was kissing him hard on the mouth. Then, using her hair, she wiped saliva from his face.

'Madelaine, ease up. You're hurting me.' Sand crunched beneath him. His back and side stung. He could smell ylang ylang and lobster. Under him felt damp. Hair tangled around her face, Madelaine whimpered and gagged as she always did. Had she spilled the wine with all her roughhousing? *What's got into her?*

At the very last ridiculous moment, and feeling faintly nauseous, he knew that he was going to come.

Powerhouse Beach – Dawn

The air was electric and the humidity high when a coil of smoke mushroomed over the city, braced for the wail of the siren. Flowers wilted and vegetables went to seed. Concrete paths emitted heat that penetrated shoe leather. A change brewed behind the western blocks threatened by fire. Boston Island snoozed in the bay, like a lazy wombat.

Big Swamp bird life soared over the grey tussocks and dirty subsiding trees, then vanished with the water. It had been a long hot summer. European trees dropped their leaves. Great dry gums crashed to the ground and splintered. There had been bumper crops last year – all forgotten. Backs were turned on the dying paddocks. With each day of waiting, more farmers ploughed for seeding and watched the topsoil drift and twirl around the contours of hills. Their desperate prayers brokered opening rains, and when it fell, they would turn their glad faces up like flowers, to drink it in.

Hugh missed the early-summer, midday hum when chooks cackled, bees hovered around the passionfruit vine, and the dog lay contented in the sun. Late summer threw him into anxious, edgy moods. He was flustered by the heat, and the body that was pegged off from the public, on the scorching sand in front of him, wasn't helping. It lay unnaturally, face down, knees pulled up, an arm cradling its sandy head. Boring as men's suits were, there was something familiar in the cut of this one, and later Hugh berated himself for expecting a broken drunk. When he arrived, a policeman was standing to one side, his cap in hand, the sun pelting down on his blank red face and perspiration running down his neck. Another officious man, presumably a plain-clothes cop, was hectoring him about procedure. They had all shaken hands.

Hugh grasped a twisted arm, tucked it under and neatly rolled the corpse. As the body flopped back into the sand and settled legs akimbo, Hugh pulled back sickened, his heart lurching.

'My God, Jerome Rawlins,' he said. 'He's a friend of mine.' He fell to his knees beside him, feeling for a pulse, desperate to override the stillness of the white flesh, the gobs of sand adhering to the face, the closed eyes and bluish lips.

'Hell, it is too. I've met him in court. I'm sorry, doc,' said the detective, raising his eyes at the cop. 'I just got here myself or I would have warned you. Would you have expected this?'

'No! Oh, no.' Hugh dropped to his knees, his customarily professional expression drawn back in agonised contortion. His eyes bulged and his mouth hung open, exposing large even teeth. 'There's no blow to the head or any obvious injury.'

'Ambos'll be here in a minute to take him to the morgue. We need a death certificate?'

'Can't write a death certificate until I establish the cause of death. You know that.' Hugh held his head in his hands. 'The whole scenario is so unlikely. Drugs? Alcohol? Drowning . . . doesn't look steamy enough for that. He's been under a lot of strain lately. He could have taken something, but why here?' As he selected and discarded possibilities, all unlikely, he felt as if his head was swivelling.

'You can have a better look out of the hot sun.' The detective mopped his brow vigorously. 'I'm sorry, mate.' He shrugged. He was a big man, and ill at ease; Eyre Peninsula was isolated and mostly quiet, so apart from an occasional drowning, shark attack or road accident, there weren't many bodies.

'Shall I contact the wife?'

'I'll do that, if you like. She's a friend of sorts.'

Hugh trudged back to the car, hot sand glittering beneath his feet. Sunlight shimmered in front of his eyes, like an aura, and he swayed as he snatched off his tie, rolled it up and put it in his pocket. Taking out a handkerchief, he wiped his sweating brow, honked his nose and dabbed at his eyes and face. He was shaking.

Madelaine's

Explaining to Madelaine that her husband was dead was not something anyone would relish. He knew Madelaine well enough to anticipate some extravagant displacement. He just hoped she would redirect her emotions at him, not the children. Hugh ran his fingers through his hair. *Hell it's hot, and what a bastard of a morning.* He hoped his staff had shifted all the appointments he'd walked out on. Sauntering round the side of the house, he peered over the fence. *Ah yes, I thought I'd heard something.*

'Hello there, Georgia, Paige. Where's Mummy?'

They were playing with a hose in the sandpit, not a stitch on them. A sodden grey nappy lay abandoned on the edge of the wooden sleepers bordering the sandpit. Little monkeys. Not even a hat, and it was so hot. How on earth had Paige lifted her pyjamas over her now rather loose plaster?

Surprised by a man's voice, Georgia stared up at him.

'Where's Mummy, Georgia?' Paige's glance skidded over him as she continued happily sloshing water with one hand in her saucepan. *Most unlike Madelaine to allow this.* He picked the little one up, dusted her bottom and wedged her on his hip.

'She's in bed. I can show you,' volunteered Georgia, leading him through the laundry and along the tiled hallway to the stairs.

Modern domestic arrangements never failed to astound Hugh. The children lived downstairs almost in their own compound, and the parents slept and lived upstairs. Pauline had a yen to do the same but he'd always quashed it. In his old-fashioned family they had all jangled along together. Parents' retreats were unheard of then. Training children to shower and sleep and play in their own quarters wasn't affordable. Nasty antisocial modern idea. How did children learn anything? By osmosis?

After stepping gingerly through the surface litter of Duplo and muesli-bar wrappers, he climbed the stairs.

'Madelaine. I'm in. It's Hugh.' He hesitated as he broached the landing. Georgia padded softly forward.

'Georgia, go and tell Mummy that Doctor Hugh needs to see her. It's very important.'

Sand falling from her flanks, Georgia waddled across the carpet to the main bedroom.

She was back within a minute.

'Mummy said, go away, she's sick.'

'Madelaine. It's me, Hugh,' he called again. 'I think she thinks you're playing,' he bent to whisper in Georgia's ear. 'Go and get a tee shirt for you and Paige. It's very hot outside and Mummy will be disappointed if you get sunburnt.' Indeed, he sincerely hoped this was the case. Georgia looked pleased and smiled up at him, but took no action.

Bleary-eyed, hair tousled, her dressing gown wrapped loosely round her tall figure, Madelaine appeared at the bedroom door. 'Hugh. I'm sorry. I'm not with it yet.'

'Had a late night?'

'Not especially,' she said vaguely. 'Come downstairs and I'll get a glass of water. Then you'll have my undivided attention.'

In the kitchen, she tiptoed to the sink, surveyed the clutter of drink packets and spilled food, and filled her glass at the tap.

'I wasn't feeling very well last night. I popped a few of those sleeping tablets you gave me, with several glasses of whisky.'

He tutted. 'Madelaine, I've told you not to take that sort of medication with alcohol. It's dangerous.'

'I slept like the proverbial log, but I sure feel like death this morning. Will things ever be normal again, Hugh?'

'Ah, I've brought news Madelaine. Not very nice news, I'm afraid. I think you should sit down.' He lifted Paige onto a chair at the plastic play table and passed her two pieces of Duplo. She looked unimpressed.

Madelaine curled herself up in a corner of the chesterfield, her knees drawn under her chin.

'Fire.'

'I was called out by the police this morning, to examine a body. It's wretched Mad, but I'm afraid it was Jerome.' Tears welled in his eyes as he struggled to control his voice. *Just what she needs, her doctor falling to bits.*

'Jerome, a body! You're having me on?'

'No. I'm afraid not. He's dead, Madelaine,' he said grimly.

'That's ridiculous. What's he dead of? He's far too young to die.'

'I couldn't agree more. How long since you've seen him? Was he well?'

'You'd have to ask Jo that.' Her head slumped to her knees. 'Oh God. This is too much.'

He felt sorry for her then, and reached out to place his hand on her arm.

She leapt up and staggered away, teetering against the walls on her way to the bathroom. He could hear her violent retching. By the time she returned, her face was ashen, her hair and face damp.

'I'm sorry, Madelaine; this has been a terrible shock to you.'

'Do you suppose he killed himself?' she blurted out.

'There is no evidence to suggest so, but then there is no evidence to suggest anything else. There'll have to be an autopsy.'

'Poor, Jerome. Things were getting rough.' She glanced at Hugh, seeking affirmation.

'I don't believe he was very happy,' he said carefully.

They sat in silence for a moment, neither looking at the other.

'You've had quite a shock,' Hugh continued. 'But perhaps you should come and see him? I mean I've identified him, but . . .'

'I don't want to see it, I mean him. I'm sure I wouldn't cope. It's not as if you'd make up a story like this.'

'I could ring someone to come and look after the children.'

Madelaine remained silent.

'Will your family fly over?'

'No.' She looked sullen and began pulling at strands of hair around her face.

Pauline had always thought Madelaine's relationship with her family was quite offbeat.

'What about a friend? Nell or Danny?'

'I might get Danny over later,' she whispered.

'Fine.' He didn't like to offer his wife's name; not very professional. Chalk and cheese they were, anyway.

'Is there no one who could come and stay for a week or so? Look after you and the kids? Just put a meal on the table and help deal with visitors?'

'Off hand I can't think of anyone, but I'll try,' she promised.

She was stony faced and hadn't shed a tear, though that was not unusual; shock did funny things to people.

'Have a good cry, when you're ready. It's perfectly natural, necessary. And come and see me tomorrow, or ring me as often as you need to talk. Alright?' He patted her hand.

'Yes alright, Hugh. Thank you for your concern,' she answered woodenly, thrusting out her chin.

'Why don't you have a shower and wake yourself up while I make a couple of phone calls and fix you a coffee.'

She pushed her hair behind her ears and snorted. 'I expect I'm not looking gorgeous.' She went back up the stairs to the bathroom.

Half an hour later she emerged, hair wrapped turban-style in a towel, dressed in clean denims and a white tee shirt printed with a picture of a skeleton sitting on a bench with a handbag. 'Waiting For the Perfect Man', said the caption. *Strange girl.*

Hugh was so far behind now it didn't matter. He had rung the surgery and told them not to expect him until after lunch.

Danica's

The platypus gum had snapped; splintered from top to bottom. The jagged fracture in the green wood was oozing sap. The trampoline lay against the shed like a backstroker on a pool wall. The force of the gale had flipped it easily. *I should be a good mother and bring the children inside. They could get hurt.* Plastic sand toys rattled across the yard. Sirens blared, so she turned up the radio. There were fires blazing out of control in several parts of the state. The power was out and people were scurrying like rats to protect their property.

The phone had rung four times in the space of half an hour. Each time Danica had snatched up the receiver – 'Hello, Danica Divjak' – there had been silence, and then the click of someone hanging up. She was sick of it. Today was not a good day for phone harassment.

Jeleni was on her way to mind the children. Danica had called her, afraid of dealing with Madelaine, but Jeleni had insisted that Danica go to her friend. She would arrive with pursed lips, mind made up, and push her daughter out the door. Veiled in perspiration, legs stinging with flying grit, Danica would press an inadequate bunch of roses against her chest and get in the car.

Travel through the elements to what? Nausea rose and she

rushed to the toilet, her hands shaking. She panted until her lips tingled and she felt faint. She was hyperventilating. Hugh would be cross. *Calm down. Give yourself a job, make a cup of coffee, cut up fairy bread for the children, just a panic attack.* The coloured dots on the bread swirled in front of her eyes as she slammed them into her mouth.

What would Jerome look like? *He won't be there, at Madelaine's, will he? No, of course not.* It was such a wild day; you would expect people to die: on the roads, on a cliff-top. *Poor man.* The wind was like a whirling dervish trying to snatch his soul. *Is . . . was Jerome religious?*

She hurried the children inside. Any minute and her mother would be there. The fierce north wind had picked up its pace and was roaring past the front window, whipping and scouring trees along the roadside. *Are they creaking?* Everything was dry and brittle. *They could split and fall.*

'Oh my God, Jerome dead.'

Danica scuttled from the cupboard to the bin, the counter to the window, dabbing at the sink with a sponge. The back door slammed and the children appeared with hair in their face and running noses. *Colds, and it isn't winter yet.*

'Mummy, I wanna drink.'

'Go away. Can't you see Mummy's upset? You'll have to wait.'

'But I'm firsty.'

Give in. She reached into the cupboard for a plastic cup and filled it from the sink tap. 'Here quickly then, drink this up and then go play with Sonja. Take her to your bedroom. That's a good girl.'

Feeling agitated and terribly hungry, Danica paced. *Shopping day tomorrow. A chunk of bread won't do much harm.* She tore at the crusty part of the loaf and eased the lid off a half-finished tub of dip. Standing in the refrigerator doorway, she kept her eye out for her mother and thrust the bread, back and forth into the dip, splattering her hands. Wiping her fingers on her skirt, she made a horrible stain that wouldn't shift. *Now my dress needs changing.*

A stale packet of water crackers in the pantry would fill a gap while she got her agitation under control, her thoughts organised. *Dead, dead!* How could she go and see Madelaine? Hugh wanted her to, but she wasn't a professional person. How did you deal with someone whose husband was dead? She wasn't old enough to have a friend whose husband was dead. A family friend had been swept overboard during a storm, her second cousin taken by a shark. But she had been very young then. What if Madelaine was crying or shouting and throwing things? What if she didn't talk to her at all? *She might expect me to hold her, or touch her.*

'It's your duty, Danica,' her mother said. 'Not a very nice friend always, but still a friend, and you must go to comfort her ... Of course you can ... Try to think how she must be feeling ... Don't worry how you look. No confidence, Danica. You never did have.'

Hugh's Surgery

Any film-maker worth their salt knew what would happen next. Madelaine worked on the script in her head.

Hugh is driving his red Saab into the doctors' car park. He picks his bag off the passenger seat, scoops up his un-opened mail and tube of toothpaste, and pauses for a moment, his head resting lightly on the padded steering wheel. Soon after, arms loaded with bag and papers and retreating through a back door, he winces as the swing of the door clips his arm. Tears come automatically. He sniffs under one arm. His BO is toxic. An old man waves as he pedals past, kitbag on the handles of his bicycle.

Deep down, Madelaine knew that Hugh was sweet and probably really had loved Jerome. Boys are often close at school, but don't articulate their feelings. Text-book stuff. They needed a really good death scene to stir them up.

As usual, the waiting room is full.

'Good morning, good morning. Fine, yes,' Hugh says. 'Weather should break soon. Tired that's all.'

A plastic fountain plays out over a green-tinged mound of stones. Several sick children bark expectorant coughs over each other as they dip their fingers in the water.

Hugh moves towards his consulting room, but a red-haired receptionist interrupts him.

'Call for you doctor.' She passes him a folded note. 'She sounded upset. It was very difficult to understand her. Shall I put her through to your room, or will you call her back?'

'Put it through to my office, please. Just let everyone know, if you haven't already, that I'm at least two hours behind. They may wish to go for a walk or fill in time somewhere else, change their plans . . .' His voice peters out, and moves along the passageway to his office.

'Hello, Jo. You've heard then?'

'Nell called me. I know she shouldn't have, but I'm glad she did. Czaba heard it from someone at the health centre. Is it true, Hugh? Jerome? Is he dead?'

'I'm afraid so. It's ghastly, I know.'

'How did . . . what happened to him?'

'We don't know at this stage. I'm terribly sorry.'

'But you must have some idea. People don't just die . . . at his age.'

'That's why it's so difficult, to discern.'

'Did he . . . did he kill himself, do you think?'

'There were no obvious signs. No bottles, pills, wounds. But we can't rule it out. We're waiting for autopsy results.'

'Poor Jerome. I expected him at home last night, but he didn't come. He was going to tell me something. Now I'll never know.'

Madelaine's – Morning

Madelaine, smoking, glared down at Danica from the upstairs window. Danica arrived clutching her bunch of red roses. *What is she thinking? That the roses match my car?* The door was unlocked because Madelaine had always said that there were worse dangers inside a house than out. Danica plodded up the stairs: plunk, plunk, plunk on the rubber strips. At the top of the stairs she caught her breath and swallowed.

'Welcome to the wake.' Madelaine made a move to greet her, then slunk back as if she had changed her mind. She patted a space beside her on the couch. 'Cigarette?'

'Thanks. How are you? Silly question, I know.' Danica reached for the cigarette like a lifeline.

'I've had a shower. I've spoken to Hugh. I'm focusing on the sea.'

And drinking.

There was an empty glass beside the couch.

'I don't know what to say, Madelaine. It must have been a ghastly shock.'

'Life is full of shocks lately.' Madelaine raised her eyebrows, watched Danica and then turned away. Danica felt afraid; she leant across for the lighter and her hand shook as she held it under her cigarette.

Madelaine glared. 'What do you think then, princess? Jerome was a bastard. Led me to hell and back, then up and leaves.'

'Please, Madelaine. Don't talk like that. People won't understand.'

'What a darling, to want to protect me.'

'You don't know what happened. Jerome must have had a heart attack. Or a brain haemorrhage.'

'Why wasn't Hugh looking after him? All that twag they talked together. Why didn't they discuss his health, run a few tests?' She poked her cigarette at Danica. 'What if it was deliberate? Maybe things weren't going so well with Madam Josephine.'

'Do you mean suicide?'

'Maybe, or flirtation. A few grogs. Too many pills.'

'He'd have to have been very unhappy.'

Madelaine shrugged. 'Selfish – how did he think we would manage? He always kept the financial side of things completely up his shirt. I have no idea how to organise our affairs: the mortgage, the practice, the stocks and shares,' she warbled, reaching for her glass.

'Have you been drinking all morning, Madelaine?'

'Absolutely, and I intend to continue until I feel better. Join me.'

'Alcohol might make things worse.'

'I'm feeling better. And I'll work things out. No one's indispensable. Look at bloody Hugo. You thought you couldn't live without him and hey, look at you,' she waved a shaky hand, 'surviving away.'

'I miss him. And I'm very nervous at night. I'm thinking of buying another dog.'

'See, infinitely replaceable.'

At this Madelaine began to cry. Deep rasping sobs racked her body, followed by a round of coughing. Stubbing out one cigarette, she immediately lit another. Her face contorted with misery, she crawled behind the couch to a small cabinet. She hauled out a bottle of brandy and second tumbler. Danica moved towards her to take the glass, her hand moved to pat Madelaine, then retracted to her side.

'I've been waiting for you to come. You're the only person I know who doesn't judge me, or try to change me. You're my closest friend. We could fade away together. Make a great headline: *Desperate friends make tragic pact*. What do you think?' Madelaine lurched against her, slinging her drink around Danica's shoulders, slopping brandy down her back. Danica shuddered and shifted her feet.

'This is a wake, my dear. There are certain protocols. You must promise never to tell anyone this . . . or I'll have to kill you. Before he died, I was so angry with him, *I* was going to leave . . . Do you believe me?'

Danica drew in her breath sharply. 'Madelaine don't.'

Madelaine moved on. 'Let God be the judge. Buddha too. All the deities can have a go for all I care. Everything is karmic. I thought my husband was so uncomplicated. Now he's ruined my life, probably the children's, and Jo's as well, although she deserves it. You live by the sword you die by the sword. *That's* fair.'

'Madelaine, Jerome was only young.'

'Is he suffering now? Is *he* in pain?' Madelaine hunched over her cigarette, blowing angry spurts.

Danica clutched her brandy. 'Are you eating, Madelaine?'

'No, are you?' she laughed.

'Don't tease. I've put on weight.'

'After the official mourning period is over, we'll catch the afternoon plane to Adelaide and go nightclubbing. We've both been missing out on life. Vlado snatched *you* from the schoolroom. I know, he loves nouvelle cuisine: tiny baby carrots, weeny peas, prepubescent beans.'

Danica almost laughed. She picked up her glass and soldiered on. 'Vlado will eat anything, but you've forgotten, he prefers to be a carnivore.'

Madelaine was impressed. 'Veal, then.'

'Madelaine, I want to help you, but turning on everyone around you won't help.'

'I did love Jerome. Really, I'll be good. I promise. I do wish he were alive. Do you believe me now?'

Madelaine began to cry again. Danica moved across the room and put her arms around her, crying as well.

'I don't want to upset you, Danny,' said Madelaine, her voice catching in the back of her throat. 'Yesterday everything was so loud ... Now, I almost feel as if I'm disappearing. Jerome promised to help me. Don't you leave me ... promise, won't you.'

Madelaine had spilled her brandy down her front. She cried without a sound, as if she were leaking. Danica could see her struggling, as if she'd been wading confidently then dropped off a sandbar into deep water. When she crawled forward, her head flopping at her friend's feet, Danica reached out to her and stroked Madelaine's matted hair, patted her wet cheek.

Madelaine's – Evening

Hugh struggled out of bed and lurched for his clothes hung on the bedside chair. No point in putting them away at night. Murphy's Law decreed that the phone always rang the moment he took his clothes off and fell into bed. Sometimes he waited in the lounge room, expecting calls. He watched late-night television and had an occasional cigar on the patio, where Pauline wouldn't detect the lingering odour. He cut his nails or flossed his teeth. At these times the phone never rang. Always waited till he dropped his pants and slid exhausted into bed.

'What's up?' grunted Pauline, rolling over. 'You coming or going?'

'Going. Got a call,' he mumbled through his teeth, pulling shoes and socks on in the dark. He felt his way along the wall to the hallway, where he could see, to do his buttons up.

'Be long?' she slurred.

'No idea. It's Madelaine. She's vomiting.'

'What time is it?'

'Two,' he called over his shoulder as he grumbled down to the bathroom to brush his teeth. Most patients weren't worthy of fresh breath at this hour, but it was a habit. More likely to spit in his face or try to punch him, as he ducked and wove suturing thread past their drunken protests.

Come straight in, Madelaine had said. The door was wide open; that was her style. From the doorway he could see her perched on a footstool in front of the lounge-room window. As she turned her head to face him, bloodshot eyes bored through him. Her face was ashen, her hair bedraggled. *Poor girl. She's doing it hard.* But the nails on her hands and feet gleamed in unchipped plummy perfection.

'I'm sorry Hugh, to drag you out like this. I thought I might have credit because I've never done it before.' She shimmied off the stool and dragged her feet across the room to touch his arm before sinking onto a two-seater couch.

'No worries. I don't mind coming for genuine calls. Stick out your tongue. Are you taking any fluid? Do you feel light-headed?'

Funny odour. In pretence of leisure, he had taken the opposite couch and leant towards her. 'How's your day been otherwise? Got through it alright?'

'Well enough,' she said, defensive. 'Danny came over and we talked. It's not her forte, looking after people.'

'Probably good for her. Take her mind off her own worries. Did it help you then? That's the question.'

'I'm very fond of her – we've been friends since I first arrived here and Nell started up the playgroup – but she's no Einstein. I guess one friend can't cater to all your needs.'

He thought about the size of her ego. She wouldn't have struck him as particularly clever herself, but then he hardly knew her – just superficial stuff. She was sharp enough to cut you with her tongue.

'Einstein may not have been all that adept at grief coun-selling.'

'You doctors are so pit-a-pat. Run on automatic after midnight.'

'You need some sleep?'

'Plop – bloody despotic, the lot of you. I feel ill. My head's thumping.'

'Did you have a drink with Danny this afternoon?'

'We had a few, yes. Not enough to make me throw up. Might be a virus do you think?'

'Possibly.' As if thoroughly diverted, he fiddled with his pen. *She's drunk alright.* 'I think you'll be okay, Mad. I'll give you a needle to stop the vomiting. Make you feel better. Roll up your arm.' She watched him draw up the needle from the ampule. *She isn't squeamish.* 'Come and see me in the morning and we'll have a chat. I believe you should view Jerome's body, say goodbye. You'd be fine, I know, and it might help.'

Madelaine didn't blink as the needle went in. 'Hugh, I accept the finality. Okay?'

'You sound angry.'

'I am angry. I feel deserted, betrayed.'

'Anger, however irrational, is normal when someone dies. We haven't established the cause of death yet, although it looks at this stage like a severe cardiac arrest.'

'Jerome never could just work nine to five. And then there was Jo. That was self-indulgent.'

'He certainly worked hard. Are you sure about Jo?'

'I went to see her and confronted her. She as much as admitted it to me.'

'That was brave. Was it out of character?'

'I was showing off to tell Danny. When I saw Jo squirm I was glad I went. She was a perfect lady and gave me a lot of old cobblers about them comforting each other over their respective break-ups.'

'It's possibly true Madelaine. Perhaps they were just friends.'

'I don't think so. Jerome couldn't spend a day out of touch with the engine room.'

'Sex?'

'Hoary, hairy. That same old chestnut.'

'Sexual drive does vary enormously.'

Hugh begun rolling up his stethoscope and reached for his bag. 'You look as if you're feeling better.'

'He died in love with me, you know.' She toyed with a cushion, turning it from corner to corner on her lap, eyes steadily fixed on Hugh.

'I'm sure he loved you Madelaine. You'd been together a long time. In fact, both of you just needed more time to work through some of your problems.'

'I mean present tense. We reached an understanding before he died. He was finished with Jo.' She paused. 'We made love again and he was coming back to me.' She stared harder at Hugh, compelling him to listen. 'Now it's too late. He should never have left me.'

'With respect, too late for you too Madelaine, but I'm glad you reached some kind of understanding. Perhaps he died the happier for it.'

'After all he put me through, he didn't deserve to. Now I'm a widow, standing one-legged on a rock in the living room,' she gurgled.

She's raving.

'I think you need a good night's sleep. Why don't you take one of the pills I gave you?'

'Typical, blot me out for a few hours, so I won't call you again.'

'It's important that you rest, not just for your own sake but also for the children's. Grieving all day is gruelling enough.'

'Well I might. Thanks for that, Hugh,' she said, arching her foot and wriggling off the couch. 'Does it surprise you that Jerome and I were together again?'

'Frankly Madelaine, the world holds few surprises for me now. Try and get some sleep and I'll see you in the morning. Just ring the surgery and the front-desk staff will squeeze you in somewhere. When you get organised, no hurry.' He picked up her hand as if to take her pulse, held it firmly for a brief moment, then let it drop. 'Goodnight, Madelaine.'

Louth Bay

It was a grey day but its wetness was just a veneer. Water had not penetrated the hard ground, but ran across the surface in sheets, seeking entry to the cobbled sods and finding none. Eager ploughing and harsh winds had eroded the unforgiving ground. It lay ravaged, stark. Only a few lithe grey tussocks had survived the harvester, the raw sun, and the lack of rain, stunted as they were, along the fence line.

Jo slumped on top of the sandhills while the children dashed along the water's edge. They flipped like butterflies, excited by the wind, flying along the sand, sea lice kissing untidy red welts on their summer-brown calves. Jo buried her head in her hands and cried. How strange life had become. Six bridesmaids in ivory-shot silk seemed like an age ago. She'd made her own decorations for the pews and the cottage circlets for their hair.

'Good luck darling.' Her mother had pressed her tearful face against Jo's neck. Her father had walked her down the aisle: his little girl who never shared anything distressing with him. She was a real coper, and he was proud of her. Now, Jo felt the mockery of her vows. All the effort and investment in the day had rapidly dissolved, in a partnership where an absence of goodwill made all her requests demands, and every plea for peace unreasonable.

Now Jerome was dead. Already cut and dissected, scraped and analysed; his essence extracted through tiny pipettes and slides and tubes, to discover what, that he was unhappy? *Is there a test for that?* That he gave in to death, and now whatever remained of him would crumble cell-by-cell, become no more than a part of the landscape he was unhappy in.

In grieving him, Jo had no legitimate role to play. She, who had licked his salty back, felt his hot breath through her blouse, and arched against him at the kitchen sink, was no one, just an interloper; an adulterer, her mother would certainly say.

When the police came that morning, Jo had been shocked that she, a decent law-abiding girl, should be so frightened. Had she seen him, the evening before? She had waited achingly for nothing.

'No,' she said.

The policeman had been stern but kind, treating her as he would a nervous child. The beach, he prodded. Had she made love to Jerome and left him there? For there was semen. *Semen, so sordid.* Her mother would die if she knew that Jo was being associated with semen.

The gulls wheeled in graceful arcs across the sky. Storms were on the way to rinse water deep into the land's pores, to roll back the lips of the sea and lift them grimacing over the sand again. *Poor Jerome. What next?* He'd thought she was so uncomplicated. He had felt relaxed with her. Now events buffeted her like the wind. She swayed, wiped her eyes on her skirt and called the children in for tea.

Danica's

Heart pounding, Danica sat up in bed with a start. *What was that? Not the wacko caller again? Why would someone keep ringing me like that? Someone who knew Vlado was away? But it could be anyone.* Before he left, Vlado and his mates had been on a pub-crawl along the foreshore. Half the patrons on the front-bar drag knew he was away. A random dialler? A strange demented only son who lived at home with his mother, secretly ringing, relishing her terror, her anguished breathing, her quavering answer: Hello. Hello? Hello, who is it? Bored with her, he might move on.

'Don't be silly,' Vlado would say. 'It's just some nutter.' And she would slide into bed behind him, knees beneath his buttocks, arms around his waist, locking in to warmth and safety, careful not to touch his genitals and arouse him.

Pulling the quilt around her, she sat quite still in the dark, breath held tight and ears straining. The lemon-scented gum scrunched down like a brush broom on the roof. A shower of gumnuts catapulted across the iron. *What a pig of a night and Vlado isn't home.* The wind surged and was still, by turns. Wooden beams creaked and groaned. Tin shifted and scraped. Something was flapping. *If only I had a dog.*

Now there were creaks in the house and she must check

the children. She mapped a path around the darkened house, keeping clear of doorways and open windows, sliding her hands up under blinds to check catches, fingering keys and pressing the lock buttons on doorknobs. She refused to look out into the whirling black night, fearing an ethereal face, a pale disturbed creature, watching her. *No one can get in now without my knowing.* She swung Vlado's squash racket under the beds, in the wardrobe, behind the couches, then crept back to bed.

There she huddled down again, listening until her head subsided on her chest, refusing vigilance. Tap, tap, tap ... she started again in terror. *That had to be something more than a branch nodding against glass.* Leaves skittered along the cement walkway between the bedroom wall and the side fence. She jumped again as a swift arpeggio ran along the fence and then subsided. *Someone is out there.* She felt sick with fright, wanted to go to the toilet, but flushing could mask the sound of breaking in and she was immobilised by terror.

When the fence clanged again she began to whimper. *If only Vlado were here.* Nell would confront her fear by taking up her hockey stick and marching to the window. *I'll put the porch light on and ring the neighbours.* Danica was afraid to look, afraid of being afraid. What could she say, It's Danica Divjak here and I'm frightened. I can hear noises. *Laughable — a wife and mother!*

When the steady tramp of footsteps were near enough to crackle leaves beneath her window, she began to dry retch. Sliding out of bed to crawl across the floor, she willed control of her arms and legs, part of her wanting to retreat to the window where she could face impending danger. Cradling the phone in her lap, she dabbed at the numbers, losing

181

concentration halfway through the sequence and then re-dialling. *What if they jemmy open the window before I can dial the number? The dialling is so loud. Can it be heard outside the window?*

She was cowering by the phone when she heard the deep, reassuring voice of her neighbour at the back door. 'I'm sorry to ring you at such an ungodly hour,' she said.

'Sorry, Danica. Can't see a damn thing. This filthy wind has got everything moving around. Could have been a possum. Or someone dragging a tree branch along the fence on the way home from the pub. I might have scared him off.' Danica bleated thanks at him and hovered at the side window to watch him in his dressing gown and heavy boots, striding home across the road.

Powerhouse Beach

What should I do while everyone else is having fun? Madelaine scribbled 'Mourning' on the spine of a videotape. *There has been a great loss. Someone is lost. It must be Jerome. I'm not dead, am I?* She couldn't remember the morning, except for unplugging the telephone after Nell had rung to say she was lunching with a new Labor minister who'd flown over on the mourning plane. No, that wasn't right – the morning plane. In the afternoon, Madelaine lay on her bed and tried to read the newspaper someone had kindly tossed onto her lawn. None of it made sense – private health out of the consumer price index, rumours about new trading banks, economic progress with practical social reforms.

In the end she gave up and lay on top of her bed, fiddling with the pause button on her camera. It had been sticking lately, and she felt lost. She wondered if Hugh would let her video Jerome's body, lying on the table at the surgery. *Surely he'll understand that first and foremost I'm a film-maker.*

In the evening, she had put a favourite tape on. *Elgar.* Madelaine had always loved unbearably sad music. She turned up the volume to cover all the crying. She thought of going for a walk and fastened her sandals, then wondered if she had remembered to eat. Something wasn't right, because she was losing weight and she certainly hadn't stopped drinking. *I will make myself eat.* She sat cross-legged on the lounge-room floor, nibbling buttered toast. The band of her black skirt had slipped below the waist, and butter dribbled over her belly and into her lap.

Madelaine use a plate dear, her mother would say. Not her father, no.

She dabbed at her buttery skin with the hem of her skirt, and when she looked up, she could have sworn she saw Jerome's reflection in the lounge-room window, ironing. He loved ironing. Had always taken a great deal of care, ironing both sides of the collar and cuffs, gently probing darts with the nose of the steam iron. Spraying with ironing-aid and pressing, pressing, pressing, until the surface of the fabric was gleaming smooth. Problem creases persisted, but they never bothered Jerome. He was happy enough to strive.

Madelaine climbed onto the couch and lay back with her arms behind her head, not daring to turn around in case he really was there, set up with a glass of beer in easy reach, happily ironing by the window. When she did turn around, she imagined speech bubbles erupting round his head:

Engage with life, darling. There's nothing like ironing to lift your spirits. Do get off the couch, put down your drink, and *do* something.

'Shut up, Jerome.' *Even when he's dead he can't leave me alone.*

There was no moon when she slid off her sandals and decided to pad away without them, into the friendly dark. She wanted words of comfort to come from the sea – strings of them, towed by little planes across its shimmery surface, standing up like cue cards along the horizon. Some of the letters could be missing, and she wouldn't need that Adrianna what's-her-face who used to be on television, to help her. She knew exactly what the sea was saying: *be strong, stay afloat.*

She snatched up her cigarettes and a box of matches and limped out of the house. It was almost three o'clock in the morning, so the beach was deserted. Her match scratched and fizzed in the warm air, lighting the dark around her hands and face. Her cigarette glowed as she drew back. She felt raw with pain, but the sea would heal.

She padded along to the wharf, looping her skirt high to clamber through the slippery rocks and over the wooden balustrade. Back curved, hands deep in his pockets, the last lonely fisherman pushed against the wind along the wooden decking towards her. She ducked out of sight. Home he went with something in a bucket for his wife.

Lights blazed on the wharf, standing as it always did, toes dug in against the sea. Madelaine scurried towards the end of it, keeping in the shadows of the big boats until she slid behind a solid hawser. Merchant sailors laughed and talked all at once in a quiet garble, smoked on deck before their curfew. Japanese? South American? She couldn't tell. They couldn't see her.

She shrank back, sniffed and fidgeted like a wharf rat as she stared out across the smoky water. She shivered and groaned. Flags flapped against a mast. She stood there like a rag herself, hair whipping around her face. *I'll run away. I'll climb aboard one of these boats and go back to where I came from.* How silly would that be? She could end up in Peru, or worse still, in Adelaide with her father.

A light glowed at the end of the wharf and she could hear the boats knocking against the massive piers. She imagined corridors inside the boats, tumescent with men, or more likely, acned boys with ugly haircuts, tight white tees and boxer shorts.

When a man stuck his face out of a doorway, she retreated along the wharf and back to the beach, where she lit another cigarette and waded into the water. She rolled onto her back, her smoking hand aloft, the water licking round her face and hair.

After marriage, skinny-dipping at night had lost some of its flavour. Jerome hovered with towels and jackets, and hissed at her about being quiet, not splashing and staying low, while he fondled her uneasily.

'Why didn't you wear your bathers?'

He hadn't dared to say that she belonged to him as irrevocably as a Vesuvian pimple, or a reckless relative. He hadn't yet articulated that she was now part of his public and professional persona. Port Lincoln was a small regional city; Jerome's new prudence was quite likely connected with the weight of the street that rested behind them.

The cigarette sizzled in her fingers as she dived beneath the surface and tried to lie along the bottom. Sound swelled in her ears. Lights refracted in the water above her head. Something brushed against her body and slid away. A jellyfish? She tumbled over and broke the surface, swam towards the horizon and imagined the shadowy beach receding behind her.

A current sucked at her body. Her limbs ached, bucking against constant hunger; her stomach had shrunk to a small plug. She swallowed water and coughed, wondering how smoothly lungs could absorb water? *If I dive below and breathe deep, will the water take me?* The sea could never make up its mind, whether it wanted her or not, pulling at her one moment, ejecting her the next.

For all his tests and technology, Hugh had found out nothing about Jerome—no coronary or cardiac damage, blood alcohol measured .04, small traces of minor tranquillisers, superficial abrasions on the lower back. It was purported that there had been some transient heart arrhythmia. Whatever that meant. Hugh had explained. It had made complete sense at the time.

Dead was dead. Hugh preferred that Jerome had topped himself. That would make him happy. He, being so patently alive and coping, could make out a case for Jerome's self-conscious anxieties, and badly managed stress. Madelaine could then be safely blamed.

She trod water.

Of course Jerome would have been happier with one of those nice, stay-at-home, embroidery, hearth-fire wives. Do they call them firedogs? Perhaps a blow-up one sitting in the bay window with pursed lips, the house a shambles around her. They should be issued gratis with degrees, for busy men – and women – who required a supportive partner and ready sex.

What about the children? Madelaine stopped treading water and almost sank. The girls had been so unsettled lately, wandering around the house in the middle of the night. And it had been so hot. *I will not be happy if they go outside looking for me, and start wailing on the lawn.* Paige couldn't get out now, surely, not with her arm in a cast. But Georgia could. *What if they wake the damn neighbours, who are out of control as it is?*

Madelaine made for the beach, pulling hard across the current, working with it where she could, drifting along when she couldn't, moving steadily up the beach towards her clothes. *I should make a film about them. Call it 'Neighbours Agog'.* Even with the curtains drawn, no washing hung and the garden dry or dying, the curious came.

'You should pick your fruit up under the tree. It's rotting. Terrible waste,' *he* said, the conservationist next door. She blew cigarette smoke into his face.

'I'll make you a cuppa, love. And wash up,' *she* said, who had pushed open the rusty gate behind the shed, and tiptoed across the lawn in her Footrest shoes and stockingettes.

'No,' snapped Madelaine, gripping the sliding aluminium door.

'I'll take your rubbish down to the gate,' *he* said, the man from the other side, who ran the hardware business in the main street. 'It stinks.'

'Kind.' She waved her whisky tumbler, commanding him gone.

They weren't so perfect, or so in control of their lives, any of them. Slouching against their walls, prowling in their yards at night to insert the black nose of her camera below blinds, between curtains, over ledges and into their lives, she had filmed them all.

By the time she reached the sand she felt exhausted; her arms had turned to jelly, her legs dragged like weights behind her. She had only just managed to reach a depth where she could touch the bottom.

Falling forward on her knees in the shallows, she rested her head sideways in the water. Hair floated around her face as she clawed at handfuls of shells and weed, pebbles and sand. The sea heaved over her. Just for a moment, she knelt up like a girl in a Renaissance painting, hair wild, breasts sandy, water surging between her legs, but there was no large conch shell to clasp against her abdomen. Remembering the children again, and the neighbours, she struggled to her feet, and waded up the beach to haul on her clothes.

When she padded barefoot away from the beach, the road was empty. She lit a cigarette and glanced about at shadows, moving leaves and sly cats scuttling. It was a long way to Danica's house, and tonight she was too tired. Tomorrow she would take the car and pick her up. They were going out. It was all planned. She hoped to God Jerome wasn't still at home doing something horribly methodical, like polishing all their shoes. *Now I'm being silly.*

Don't make a song and dance about it, her mother would say. Put your nonsense to one side. Jerome's just gone to see a man about a dog.

As Madelaine slipped into her street, she could see the windows of her house. She felt okay about it. The house wasn't the problem: walls, roof, doors, windows ... nothing worrying there. The girls' room was still in darkness. And the family room. Jerome had given up his ironing. *Can I rest now?*

Whalers Way

'You won't believe this, me so organised.' Madelaine flipped back the side flaps on the wicker picnic basket and began lifting out plastic containers and parcels wrapped in grease-proof paper. Danica was not sure she wanted to be there, perched on top of a smooth rock at Whalers Way, chill winds waltzing straight off the Southern Ocean and into the gulf, penetrating her body. A gust inflated her dress and flapped it round her waist. She sat down suddenly, drew her knees up under her chin and tightened her skirt around her.

'We'll blow the cobwebs away,' Madelaine said. 'It's been a hell of a week.'

Whalers was a lonely, isolated place. They had left the city early, and the journey had taken only half an hour. Then they'd bumped for kilometres over the corrugations of an unsealed road, through the checkpoint and along a powdery track bordering the cliff-tops. Apart from occasional grey-haired tourists with stickers on their combies, it was a very private place. All the way until they neared the point, Danica had sucked one jelly baby after another. Kept her mouth busy and her mind off vomiting.

'What do you want to talk about, Mad?' she asked as they parked the car beside the track.

'Nothing special. For one thing, I want to sit with you in a peaceful place, without interruption. We can turn back the clock and be a pair of girls again. Tell secrets. Would you like that?'

Danica smiled, non-committal.

'Had any interesting phone calls lately?'

'Not interesting, no.'

Madelaine clicked her tongue.

They had carried the picnic basket and a tartan rug to the rocks at the top of the cliff. Madelaine chomped on an apple, and gushed about the sea as if her mind were on something else. 'It's like a woman's sex organ; so much more extensive than anyone ever realised, don't you think? Men have been wrong about so many things. How could they ever think the earth was flat and that women had a button.'

Danica ducked her head and concentrated on the sensible parts of the conversation.

'See that silver spilling. It's rain, way out at sea,' uttered Madelaine, clapping as if the display was for her personal entertainment.

'It is beautiful,' said Danica, turning her head away from Madelaine's sudden feverish animation.

'The whales are on the move. One more month, they'll be here.' Madelaine jumped up and fossicked in her basket.

'I know. Miranda loves them. Years ago, did they kill them here? Is that why it's called Whalers Way?'

'I imagine so. I love them too. Last winter, in the middle of the night, I followed our street right down to the back of the caravan park and there were two of them making a lot of noise right in front of me in the water. I know people have heard them snoring, but they weren't snoring. They were whistling and groaning and bumping. I laid on the beach and listened, wanting to get in with them, until finally they swam away. Did I tell you about it?'

'I think you did.'

'This year I'm going to swim with the whales.' Madelaine looked out across the water as if summoning them, then shook her head and turned back to her basket. 'Here, look, I made this especially for you.' She unscrewed the lid from a small silver flask and poured green fluid into the silver cup. 'Just for Danica. I've written on it.'

'What is it?'

'A perfect concoction to lift your spirits. I copied the recipe out of a book.'

'I'll try it in a minute, but I should line my stomach first.'

Madelaine passed a wad of sandwiches and demolished the last of her apple as she lay back on her elbows with her knees up, staring into the sky.

'Ever seen a white sea eagle on the prowl?'

'No.' Danica glanced up, failed to see the bird, then looked down again, to sniff at Madelaine's brew. The shadow of the eagle passed over. *Damn Madelaine.* It probably had oodles of alcohol in it, and cream. Danica slid her hand behind a tuft of grass and poured some of the drink into a small bowl-shaped rock formation. She flicked a glance at Madelaine, now spread-eagled across the rock, eyes closed, hair spread out behind her like an oriental fan. The eagle had disappeared.

'Packs a punch, Madelaine,' she said, sipping a token mouthful from the bottom of the beaker.

'Thought you'd like it. There's plenty more where that came from. By the end of the afternoon you'll be feeling wonderful.' Madelaine's laugh was just a rasp. She sat up, drawing back her arm to spin her apple core into the whirling air above the cliff.

'Why are we here, Madelaine?'

'I love the wild. Don't begrudge me. Just enjoy it.' With a sweep of her arm, she gestured along the rugged coastline. There were signs in front of them about freak waves and taking care. Great curtains of foam flew up around them at rhythmic intervals. 'I want to be a stone scoured smooth by events.'

'I'm glad you're feeling better but it's bloody cold,' said Danica shivering. 'If I'd known we were getting out of the car I would have worn pants. Just a drive, you said.'

'Walk near the edge. Dare, dare and double dare.' Madelaine flung back her hair and licked her lips.

Danica stood reluctantly, turning up the collar of her dress to follow Madelaine. 'I don't like heights, but I'll come a little way.'

'We won't go too close. Come on, chicken.' She gripped Danica's arm and tugged at her.

Danica felt uneasy. 'Don't pull, Maddy, I'm coming. Don't tease.' There was a hysterical edge to her voice as she dug her heels in. Schoolyard scenes flooded back into her consciousness, of grappling with her will, wanting to be a good sport, but feeling terribly frightened. Madelaine pulled harder, the grip on her wrists tightening to an iron clench. They slid, together. Danica felt dizzy. She was just a push from a nauseous tumble through metres of salty nothingness, to surf churning over rocks as sharp as razors.

Quite suddenly Madelaine released her, and Danica stumbled hard against her. Madelaine flung an arm around her shoulder. 'There you are,' she whispered hoarsely. 'You aren't dark. You want to live. Do you feel it?' She shifted her arm and bumped their hips together.

Danica staggered sideways. Shale cascaded. She put out her hand to break her fall and landed on her backside on a small platform at the very edge. Madelaine was reaching out to her. She could feel her arm in the small of her back.

'No, Madelaine.'

'Coming here is important. We're grains of sand, specks of salt, molecules of water – insignificant. We could so easily disappear forever. Just an accident.'

'Madelaine. Please don't. Let me go. I feel sick.'

'Probably drank too much of my special toddy.' Madelaine moved away along the eroding cliff-face and Danica scrambled up the slope to safety, staring back at her, wide-eyed.

'Madelaine, please come up here with me. The sign says it's dangerous. I hate it when you're reckless. A freak wave could sweep you off. Please, Madelaine.' She felt tearful. *Poor Jerome. No wonder he couldn't manage her.* Danica dug her fingernails into her palms.

Legs crossed like a deity, Madelaine subsided on the clean surface at the point of the cliff. The wind whipped her hair around her long body and her eyes were closed.

'You're afraid, but nothing will happen Danica. It hardly ever does. Life is beckoning, not death.'

Danica retreated to gather up their picnic, waited on a rock like a child not picked up from school, and was almost overcome by an urge to see the girls. They were safe with Vesna and wouldn't miss her. But she was shaken and wanted to touch home. The afternoon was sour.

When she stepped away with the basket, Danica noticed a little trickle of fluid oozing from a hollow in the rock.

She'd poured too fast. She dabbed with her tissue; then stashed it up her sleeve.

After half an hour she called out to Madelaine. 'I'm waiting in the car. I want to go home,' and Madelaine rose and followed her.

Danica's

'What's wrong?' Vlado rolled across her body, curving an arm round Danica's head on the pillow. Their faces locked, her eyes fled. He kissed her lightly and stroked her cheek.

'Come on Danny. Spill. What's wrong? The kids getting you down? You've put on weight? Madelaine was rude to you?'

She winced. Tears welled. *Jesus, he thinks I'm so pathetic.* 'I've got a problem. A big problem,' she croaked.

'Tell me and I'll fix it.'

'That's what I'm afraid of. I don't think you can.'

'Danica . . .'

'What I think . . . it couldn't be true. I might be imagining everything.'

'Try me.'

'You'll be heavy handed.'

'Two courses open to you then. Sit on it for a bit longer, although I don't think it's healthy. Or tell someone else, in a What-would-you-do-if . . . sort of way.'

'It might be dangerous. I'm frightened.'

'Danny! What have you been up to? Gambling? You need money?' He looked severe.

'No. No.'

'What then? Is Jerome's funeral worrying you? You don't have to go, although I think you should.'

'No. It's not that. You don't have to baby me ... This afternoon, will you mind the kids?'

'I'd like to help but I can't. I told Milan I'd meet him down at the boat at quarter-to-two. I need to go over the catch sheets with him and talk about a new deckie. Give Mum a ring.'

'I wouldn't like to Vlado. She was here this morning.'

'Can't they play in Nell's backyard, with her kids?'

She sighed. 'Yes, don't worry. I'll work something out. I might take them with me.'

'Sorry, love. Cheer up now and make me the happiest man alive.' His big blonde head bunted at her chin, his long legs coerced her own apart, and he tugged with his teeth at the tie on her blouse. He was safe, predictable. She snuggled in and closed her eyes.

Port Lincoln Airport

Curled like a foetus, Madelaine rocked back and forth in her bed. She had woken early. When she pressed her fist against her eyes, blackness came first, and then little jagged flashes, golden squizzles, and red stars shooting through her brain. Father was coming on the morning plane and there was no avoiding it. She erupted out of the bedclothes and landed on her knees in front of the window. The sea was so far away. Even with her cheek pressed against the glass she couldn't hear it.

Danica couldn't know how lucky she was. Vlado was so uncomplicated, such a nice solid man. It would be tempting to write him off as a great lump who left his fishing boots behind the door and thumped the table at dinner. But he wasn't like that. Despite his size and obvious strength, there was a fineness about him. He evoked a Mediterranean languor, and that he liked the company of women was quite transparent. When she visited Danny he offered her tea and coffee and smiled at her politely. If he were her husband he would stand between her and anyone, even her father.

But neither Vlado nor Jerome could help her now, and an airport greeting would demand public demeanour. Hello Mother, hello Father. Not, Daddy, don't hurt me, and Mummy, don't let him. Madelaine hid her face behind her fingers, then sighed and swept the tissue box from the bedside table. She lurched after it and stubbed her toe on the end of the bed. Her parents made her feel so dangerously unbalanced. The least setback and she could tumble, fall away, disappear inside herself. Jerome had always handled them, made them behave. And they had, for him.

'Don't come,' she'd begged on the telephone, the prospect of dealing with them as dreadful as what had happened with Jerome. 'I'm fine.' They said they had to come. What would their congregation think if they didn't, in such a circumstance? She knew that her father would hold her an indecent half second too long and a great shame would suffuse her body. Jerome's carefully plastered-over effigy of a wife and mother would be put aside. A clumsy wooden child would lumber forward.

Somehow she had cleaned the house. It would torment her more to watch her mother do it. The floors were still drying as she fastened the girls seat belts and drove away.

Madelaine flew around the bends and across Stinky Creek, that ridiculous unglamorous waterway. Beside her in the air outside the car, sea birds floated, back-pedalled and darted away, their shadows swift across the sand to the sea. Boats anchored along the coast dipped and rocked like empty amusement-park rides. She gunned the car down the straight and then slowed. In her rush for punctuality she'd forgotten her reluctance to arrive at all, and a wave of nausea rushed through her as she rumbled over the cattle grid at the airport gate. There was no turning back now.

The plane was almost in. She saw it circle in a wide arc from the north, and then despite the wind pulling at the windsocks, descend hard and firm on a keen trajectory. After a little bump and a wobble, it headed up the runway.

A crowd milled in the besser-block construction that sufficed for an airport. Car-hire workers completed their last-minute tallies and waited, smiling, keys in hand, behind small lecterns. As toilets flushed and cigarettes were lit, disembarking passengers would appear, before the part-time airport became deserted half an hour later. Baggage trolleys would lie abandoned behind the building until the next flight.

Madelaine watched her parents cross the tarmac. Her father wore a dark suit and carried a briefcase; her mother a polyester frock with permanent pleats in the skirt. They were tall and, to an outside observer, elegant. They were not speaking. Her father used the small of her mother's back to steer her. Madelaine bit her lip as they pushed through the small wire gate leading into the terminal. Paige curled like a comma below her chin, head nodding into her sling. Georgia dragged at her arm.

'Hello, Mother.' Peck, peck – on the cheek. Overpowered by wafting lavender, Madelaine drew back.

'No black, dear?' An invitation to the first skirmish.

Madelaine turned away.

'Hello, Father.' Her face brushed against the stiff white dog collar. Tears came to her eyes and she sniffed as he pulled her head hard against his shoulder. Scrabbling desperately in her pocket for a tissue came to nothing, and she wiped her nose on her sleeve. Stupid tears, after all these years when the tears wouldn't come. She wanted to scream at them, that she hated them; hated them because she still loved them, and they didn't deserve either. *Why did they have to come now when I'm in such a mess?*

'Mummy's shaken up by the flight, Madelaine. It was rather turbulent, especially descending.'

'I'm sorry. Do you want a glass of water, Mother? Or shall we collect the bags and go?' Madelaine gathered herself together and tugged at Georgia's hand.

'I'm alright, dear. Oh dear little woman,' crooned her mother, laying her cheek against Paige's brown one. Georgia stared up.

'They're so sweet and perfect, Madelaine. Rather like you, both of them.'

'Not so perfect, but we try, don't we girls?'

'Oh Madelaine, they're only babies. Come to Grandma, Georgie. You don't remember me, I suppose. It's been such a long time.' Georgia peered from behind her mother's legs and offered a tentative smile.

Hauling Georgia forward, Madelaine led them through the swing doors to collect the baggage piled on a trolley behind the building. Her father picked through the packages, cartons, bales of daily newspapers and golf bags until he found their two neat overnight bags. They started towards the car park.

Near the car, her mother's voice quavered, 'How are they coping with . . . you know . . .'

'They're very young.' Madelaine drove the key into the lock and leant in to snap up the buttons.

'They are old enough to miss their father,' chided her mother.

'Yes, of course they miss him.' She'd love to scream at them that things hadn't been right for a long time. Allowing them to mediate her grief was one thing. They couldn't have it all. *Sweet Jesus, why did I say they could come?*

She moved a sandy rug aside and stacked the overnight bags in the boot. *I must shake it out and wash it.*

'And you, little Madelaine,' her father smiled at her. 'We have been praying for you. Too late for Jerome, he is safe with his maker.'

Christ, they're always praying for me. She lifted the girls into their bolster seats and snapped the seatbelts into place.

'Shame you weren't praying for Jerome earlier,' she bit.

'We always have of course, ever since he met you. It is tragic that a man should be struck down in the full flush of his manhood. God must have a special plan in all of this.'

She hesitated for a long moment before she tossed her handbag onto the dashboard and leapt into the driver's seat. Her father hated to be driven, and she had almost offered the keys as a courtesy, a meek obeisance. *No.* She clenched the keys in her fist. Her life belonged to her now.

'As I understand theology,' she said, 'God is all-knowing. He would have been aware of Jerome's imminent demise and grieved with all of us and for the circumstances that led to it. I can't believe your God would plan a death.' *Now I'm using his language.*

Her father stared ahead, his feet braking beside her on the bends. 'Humans can affect their destiny and disturb God's pattern. Never underestimate the power of prayer.'

Madelaine tried to concentrate on driving. The road home from the airport never failed to fill her with a sense of wonder, remind her that some things remained the same. As she swept around the last curves, the water swathed the coastline like grey silk moving over an undulating body. Sun burst between the clouds, spilling silver on the inky shales and the soft grey pebbles in tiny coves. Dark cloud shadows chased across the shallows. Bobbing in a red dinghy, a rounded back shrugged and bent over a fishing chore.

If I can endure the next few days, I will survive.

St Thomas' Church

Rain drummed steadily on the iron roof and Danica could hear cars skirting the swollen gutters, the noise of spray on the footpath as fierce as steel cutters. Thunder rumbled and the dim lighting inside the church seemed to flicker in sympathy with the distant storm. The change had roared through the pale light of dawn from the west, dousing and spraying, whipping and churning. *Summer is almost over.* She pressed her knees together, wanted to wee. Rushing storm-water and overflowing gutters combined with cold and nerv-ousness had made her bladder jumpy, and she'd been twice before she left.

She hated the smell of wet wool, the dampness around her black-clad ankles and the decrepit strands of hair, once a hairstyle, now matte against her cheeks. The church felt unfamiliar, strange and potent. Vlado reached across and squeezed her hand. Curled in a tight knot of anxiety, she squeezed back politely and batted him off. When she birthed the children, it had been the same. So irritating to be dis-tracted by a clumsy well-meant hand massaging the back or stroking the brow. She had mustered her whole body to deal with pain, had not wanted the flow of energy interrupted. Vlado turned his head away. Now stoked, an automatic guilt caused her to lay her fingers briefly on his thigh, before she straightened up to peer over the rows of mourners.

White-faced and stricken, Madelaine had thrown a black jacket across her shoulders like a cape. Her dark hair was swept back and caught at the nape of her neck. There were small pearls in her ears. Pearls were for tears. During the hymns she stood between her parents with Paige on her hip and Georgia wriggling on the pew beside her. Danica had met the parents only once before, but the mother's beauty had softened and rounded with middle age. Madelaine's proud svelte look was missing from her. She wore fussy bows and a jet necklace, and she was large with strong hips and firm round breasts. Her shoulders were slightly hunched, like those of many women her age. A narrow belt encircled her thickened waistline.

Madelaine's father held his hymnbook aloft; his face was leonine, and out of place in the ordinary mass of the congregation. It was a strong sensual face, with a large forehead like Madelaine's, rough bushy eyebrows, two or three craggy undulations like warts and large full lips. Danica could imagine him gripping the lectern with both hands and leaning forward to emphasis a point as he shouted about hell and damnation, his face alight with his knowledge of a thousand sinners.

Madelaine was hemmed between her parents, her face devoid of any easily interpreted expression.

Jerome was not a churchgoer but the pastor's words were kind. He sketched a picture of a good man, well loved in the community. Danica tried to nudge the hard lump in her throat, which rose and bobbed like a ballcock between her swallows. Her eyes misted over and she sniffed and blew her nose.

At the end of the pastor's long soliloquy, Madelaine stepped up to the pulpit and tried to speak, but couldn't. She didn't cry. Danica knew that didn't matter; she had heard her mother talking after funerals. *She was very good,* she'd say. *She didn't cry. It was very well-conducted.* If they cried it didn't matter either. She'd say, *She had a little cry, but was very good.*

Jo was crying. *Not so good,* Jeleni might say. Jo and Doug were seated next to each other near the side door. *Has there been a truce?* Doug's hissing voice broke the silence in the church. Two rows of mourners in front of them swung their heads in a smooth parabola. Jo was pink with distress. She placed her hand against her forehead as if to hold it up, and moved away. Doug leant against the wall of the church, arms folded and face grim. *Not happy. Does Doug know about Jerome and Jo?*

Pauline, elegant in black crepe, frowned as Hugh dabbed his eyes. *Does she think he shouldn't cry? That he shouldn't intrude on his patients' grief.*

Danica found it difficult to imagine the body, lying still and perfect inside the wooden casket. Madelaine had ordered South American mahogany from the master furniture makers on Whalers Road because Jerome liked nice things, and hang the expense, he would have been pleased with the craftsmanship, Danica was sure. Madelaine's first major purchase outside Jerome's tacit embargo on her aesthetic taste. The patina of the wood glowed in the darkened church. Nell, leaning on a walking stick, winked and smiled at Danica from across the aisle. She must have had an accident. Czaba hovered near Nell, passing handkerchiefs and hymn sheets.

At the end of the service, everyone had rushed through

the rain to their cars. Most were caught short without umbrellas. Danica saw Jo stalk through the vestibule ahead of Doug, then she had lost sight of them. Pressing her nose against the passenger-side window, Danica wondered why there was a hold up.

The funeral procession had snaked its way at a frustrating pace along the main highway towards the cemetery. As if in respect, the rain had eased and passers-by stood to attention to mark the passage of the hearse.

'Okay, love?' inquired Vlado.

She sniffed. 'I felt strange when the priest talked about what a good man Jerome was. It doesn't seem real. I can't get a picture of Jerome, especially his face. As if he never existed. As if he really is dead because he's disappeared for me.'

'He'll come back to you later. I can picture him quite easily. He would be pleased if he were here today. It's a good turnout.'

'Vlado don't be silly. You can't measure your popularity in terms of how many people turn up for your funeral. And Jerome *is* here,' she answered, shredding her tissue and picking loose threads from her hem.

'It's as good a place to start as any. Don't be so serious. Death is part of life and Jerome was well respected.'

'I don't want to talk about it. I think death is the end of life, not part of it.'

As he steered the car through the ornate wrought-iron gates and across the gravel to the car park, Vlado took one hand from the wheel to curl his fingers under the hem of her skirt and stroked her knee.

A door slammed behind them and a car spun its wheels taking off on the gravel. Vlado withdrew his hand to watch through the rear-view mirror as the speeding car veered away from the gates. 'Doug's not happy.'

Danica turned her head. Jo was hesitating before the gate as if deciding whether to walk away or gather her dignity and walk in solo.

'Wait, Vlado.' Danica leant into the back and opened the rear door of the car, beckoning Jo with her free hand. It was going to be awkward with Madelaine, but she couldn't leave Jo standing on the road. *Where are the children?*

Madelaine's

Her mother had organised a light lunch after the funeral, but Madelaine threw up in the upstairs loo, and was presently leaning against the balustrade, making running commentary as she panned the room with her camera. She raised her voice over the murmuring people and clinking cups, and zoomed in to mock the sandwiches. 'I can hardly leave them out; they're set pieces: ribbons of cheese and gherkin, beef and pickles, ham and mustard, tomato and pickled onion. All the colours in order on every plate.' Her father was looking at her with daggers.

Curious guests swung their heads when Jerome's brother Luke laughed up at her as he came up the stairs. Madelaine abandoned the sandwiches to grin at him. She tilted the camera down his body before zooming in for a close-up.

Her mother looked severe. 'Come down, darling. And put that silly thing away.'

Madelaine drifted over to the balcony stairs to hug Luke.

Work the room, Madelaine, he would have once said. Don't run aground with the wrong people.

After Madelaine and Jerome got engaged, Luke had returned from New Orleans where he was writing computer programs for a pharmaceutical company. The two brothers were like best friends, so they started going out, the three instead of two. Luke was nocturnal in a pathological way; the moment darkness fell he lit up like a Christmas tree, leading them on crazy romps from one nightclub to another, the kinds of nightclubs where no one had a partner and everyone vibrated in a seething mass like larvae under lights.

One night after a late dinner at Madelaine's flat, Jerome had fallen asleep on the floor and she and Luke had talked deep into the night, lighting cigarettes off each other and getting rather drunk. He had told her that he was the bad egg in the family, had been gambling his life away; in fact their ailing father, who was sick of paying off his debts, had kicked him out that morning.

'Jerome is the golden boy,' he'd said, leaning across the couch to kiss her, one hand reaching for her breast.

'You're very drunk.' She'd waggled her cigarette at him, attempting a perfect smoke ring.

'Jerome won't mind, all in the family,' he'd lied.

'You can stay here, if you want,' she had said, in the spirit of the moment, and had kissed him back. But then Jerome had snorted and woken, blinking, and Luke had struggled out into the harsh bright light of early morning. Within a fortnight he had moved to Perth.

Now Luke had changed. Zooming closer still, Madelaine could see his face was plumper, his hair thinner, his jacket cheap.

'Not travelling well?' she asked. He raised his hand to block the lens. Rain splashed against the plate-glass windows, the sea was grey and moody like the party. She swayed against him, twisted her head to graze his lips and smelling Eau Sauvage, snaked a weary arm around his neck. Her mother went into spasms and materialised immediately at her side.

209

'Get your father a cup of tea please, Madelaine.'

'Christ, why can't *you*?'

Her mother's face fell, but Madelaine moved away.

She's always been a bit casual, her mother would say to Luke.

Madelaine moved across the room, filming silently, focussing on one couple and then another. If they spoke, she lifted her eyes from the viewfinder, lowered her face in greeting for a half second, and resumed filming. Some reached out to draw her into their arms, but she was gone, gliding sideways, disconnected.

'Put that down, Madelaine.' Her father was picking through the bookshelf, thumbing Jerome's copies of Faulkner, Lawrence and Kafka. He turned towards her, his face pink with irritation.

It was only righteous anger. 'My mother said you wanted tea.'

'No, Madelaine. Madelaine . . .'

'Don't speak to me – about anything. I am on my way to get my friend a drink.'

She laid the camera on the bookshelf, then, observing her father's stitched-up face, changed her mind and picked it up again, replaced the lens cap and wound the strap around her hand. She scooped up two wine glasses with her free hand and jiggled them at Danica and Vlado, who stood in silence by the window. Vlado raised his thumb.

Madelaine slid past her father and lifted the glasses over guests, turning her body away from him to wink at Danica. Vlado reached forward to receive the wine before it spilled. *At least they've given Jo the flick. Appearing graveside was outrageous enough.*

'Are you alright, Mad? What a terrible day.'

'I'm pissed actually, but don't tell Mummy and Daddy.' She swilled her glass of wine, spilling some on her hand and then, off balance, clutched at Danica, who tried hard to look supportive. 'Did I ever tell you that I euthanased your dog?' She patted the camera under her arm. 'We should have a video night.'

'What?' Danica whispered and looked to Vlado.

Madelaine was annoyed when Vlado raised his eyebrows and turned his face away in disgust. 'I'll get some coffee,' he said.

Damned rude.

'Don't suppose video evidence would suit you two.'

'Don't be an idiot, Madelaine. Come on. You can do this. One more hour at most and everyone will leave.'

'It's true darling. I really did it. Guess how? Nellie's insulin. Nicked it from her refrigerator the week before because I thought it might be handy.' She giggled.

'Stop it, Maddie. You're being hysterical. I'll get Hugh if you don't.'

Madelaine pouted but continued undeterred. 'One or two mils, just like Nellie said, and down he went, nigh nighs. I popped him under the fuschia. The colour suited him. I did it because I love you. You should know that.'

'Madelaine stop it. Don't think I don't know about the phone calls, but don't give me this dog crap. You need to go and see Hugh and get some pills.'

'Where's Jo? I saw you canoodling with her at the f . . . funer . . .' Madelaine hiccupped.

'Vlado and I took her home. She wasn't feeling well.'

'It's not like her to miss a party.' Madelaine's glass slipped out of her hand and smashed.

Vlado slid black coffee into her hand and closed her inert fingers round it with his own. 'Drink.'

'Oh, I've been told,' she said. 'I've been told.'

Strawberry Farm

Nell and Danica had arranged to meet at three for a quick coffee at the Strawberry Farm. Nell needed to be back before the shops closed. The rain had cleared but it was a peculiar day; beaten-egg-white clouds clung effortlessly to the bowl of the sky, rich indigoes swirled through the mixture. Who knew what the weather would do?

Following the snaking road to the farm, Danica swept past Little Swamp. At this time of the year the swamp was dry and the strawberries were finished. Bowls of freshly picked strawberries and mounds of local honey ice cream were available for most of spring and summer. The farm was also a small zoo. Visitors entered through the bowels of the shop, stepping down into a shady circular walkway. On either side of the path were aviaries of birds including peacocks, yarded deer and donkeys, small cages of kangaroos and rabbits.

Never tiring of the exhibits, Danica's children trailed across the wooden bridge to prod at the goldfish in the pool below, and strained at their mother's hands to race ahead. Nell's boys peed in the pot plants.

'I'm so glad to sit down,' sighed Nell, adjusting the contours of her lap and swinging her arms up in great arcs to shade her face. 'If only it doesn't rain for an hour.' She clutched the table for support to cross her legs, rolling from one buttock to the other. 'Now, what's up? What's so important we have to discuss it before playgroup tomorrow? Are you unhappy with the new roster?'

'No, of course not. You know I don't care about that.'

The children jigged up and down at a safe distance from the sulphur-crested cockatoo. He mimicked them, bobbing and bowing and occasionally snapping as they teased him with their milky fingers. Nell waited patiently, toying with her straw.

'I'm worried about Madelaine, about some things she's told me,' Danica whispered.

'Oh, come on. You don't want to take any notice of Madelaine.'

Danica paused, automatically checking the children and resumed. 'Do you remember when Hugo died?'

'Yes, of course.'

'It was mysterious, even to the vet.' Voice wavering, she looked over her shoulder through the shop doorway, as if expecting company. 'At Jerome's funeral, Madelaine told me she put Hugo down for me.'

'She was just pulling your leg,' said Nell.

'At first that's what I thought, but she said she stole your insulin.'

'My God. Do you believe her?'

'She could have. She was babysitting for me the afternoon before I found him.'

'Yes, but surely she wouldn't. How would she get my insulin?'

'Easily. You keep it in the fridge. I bet you don't check it, do you? She's been erratic lately. Sometimes I feel as if she hates me, that she would do anything she could to hurt me.'

'It sounds as if you two need a rest from each other.' Nell looked at her thoughtfully.

'I've had some disturbed nights. When Vlado was away there was an intruder in the yard. And mysterious phone calls, lots of them. But when I answered, no one spoke. I'm sure it was Madelaine. She's not a bit frightened herself you know. She often wanders around at night.'

Nell was observing her with some concern. Danica's eyes darted about like an anxious bird's, as if she expected Madelaine to appear at any moment.

She stumbled over her words. 'I'm alright, Nell. I talk to Hugh sometimes. I get low when Vlado is away and Madelaine is unkind, but I'm okay.'

'Why do you think Madelaine would ring like that? You could have the call traced.'

'It's the only thing that makes any sense. At first I thought it was just a nutter. But she takes an unnatural interest. Rings me every day to ask how my night went, and then laughs, as if it's a great joke. A few days ago on the cliff-top at Whalers, she deliberately frightened me. I thought she was going to push me over.'

'Now you are being silly.'

Danica clutched at the table and whispered hoarsely, eyes entreating. 'No, I don't suppose she would, but ... That's not the worst of it, Nell.' She gathered herself together. 'Can't you see, there's Jerome. What about Jerome?' she cried. 'I keep thinking of how he died, and how Hugo died; both so neat and clean and young.'

Nell drew in her breath, shocked. A small spider dropped on a dragline between their faces. It shimmered and spun as it caught the few small rays of sunlight glimmering through the shade-house panels. Danica shivered and leant away from it. Nell batted at it with a folded paper serviette and it scurried up the swaying line.

'Of course I see what you're driving at. Insulin is a naturally occurring substance. It wouldn't show up in an autopsy. It would be quick, no noise or fuss. Oh lordy Danny, she wouldn't. People just don't go round knocking off pets and husbands.'

'She says Jerome had it coming. He was acting crazy . . . Jo and all. She's very angry with him, still.'

'Raised in the church and all.'

'I know, I've thought so much about it I feel ill. She's angry with her father too. I think he abused her,' said Danica and hung her head.

'And Jerome. He was a good, kind husband.'

'He hit her once, but . . .'

Nell scooped her skirt up around her thighs, and ran her fingers lightly over her own white flesh, pocked with cellulite and old abrasions. 'Just assuming we give this any credence at all, how would she get away with it? There'd be needle marks, surely.'

'It might not show, just one. There was an autopsy. They would have looked, but there might be places to do it where it doesn't show, ears or navels or somewhere.'

'God Danica. I can't believe you dreamt this up.' Nell shook her head.

'I'm frightened, Nell. I do love her and I feel sorry for her . . . But she's always watching me, she seems more intent, as if now that Jerome is gone I'm flapping around in the net by myself.'

'You should be careful, I think. Saying, Oh that's just Madelaine, won't do any more. I can see that.'

215

Danica could feel tears pricking. 'I have to go, Nell. Will you ring me later?'

They rose and hugged.

Homemade crafts and jars of clover honey lined the shelves of the Strawberry Farm gift shop. As Danica slapped down coins at the old wooden counter she felt frail, but relieved to have unloaded her burden on Nell. The dried-fruit balls were her reward for speaking up. She just hoped Nell wouldn't betray her.

A few minutes later, nosing the car back onto the road to the city, she chafed at second gear and, unable to wait any longer, slid her fingers to the bottom of her handbag, eagerly breaking the cellophane to ferry secret mouthfuls.

'Don't be silly,' she told the children. 'Of course you're not hungry. We just had afternoon tea. We'll go home and make something nice for dinner.'

It was best they didn't see her sneaking. They were far too young to make sound decisions about nutrition.

Louth Bay

Playgroup had been rostered for Jo's, but Madelaine wasn't sure if she was up to that. In the end she wore red because it matched her eyes and wearing bright colours might shock the socks off all of them. Luckily her parents had flown away within days of the funeral. Since then, as far as she remembered, she hadn't been to bed at all. *Damned if I remember what I've been doing. Will they expect me to come?*

Danica was perched on Jo's piano stool, shivering. Madelaine pinched her cheek. 'Cold? Haven't seen you for a few days. Been a good girl?' Danica touched her cheek and ducked away.

'Come and sit over here, Madelaine,' ordered Nell. 'How are Mum and Dad?'

'Gone, vamoosed. Praise the Lord and thank Him for His endless mercy. They were entrenched. Sat on the couch every morning, like worn barnacles, their faces turned up to the sun at the window. I started calling the family room the pensioners' lounge. They tried to corrupt the children until I put a stop to it.'

'Weren't you glad to have your family with you? You don't see them often,' said Nell, polishing her glasses.

Madelaine pointed a finger at Nell. 'That's a trick question, right?'

'Not at all.'

'Okay then. It's quite apparent they think I'm a bad parent. Mother crept around the house, secretly dusting and polishing and scooping up the children like war orphans. Every meal my father stared me down, questioned my humility and harped on about my disjointed grieving process.'

'Have you been managing, Mad? You haven't rung any of us,' said Pauline, oaring in.

'Sure. Fine, you know.' She hoped they wouldn't ask a hundred questions. *I might have to tell Pauline to back right off.*

Madelaine glanced around the room. Beams of light conveyed dust motes to the floor in a dappled cinematic way. Madelaine felt nauseaous. There seemed to be a change in the lighting. *Am I just imagining it? Are they all watching me?* She rubbed her eyes and technicolour squizzles leapt about. All at once she had double vision. There were two Nells, and two Danicas and ... The picture kept breaking up. *It wasn't such a good idea to come.*

The two Nells spoke quietly to her. She suffered their gaze. The two Paulines rolled and thumped dough into snakes, sausages and baskets for the children. *God, do we need that many? Are we going on a picnic?* Madelaine wanted Danica to hold her, but realised there wasn't really any point. *Coming was a very bad idea.* She leapt to her feet, listing to one side as she yanked at Georgia's arm and scooped Paige up around the waist, her sling arm dangling. *I'm, not going to fall now. Not in front of everyone.* Georgia whined and pinched the flesh under Madelaine's arm. Lately, Paige had been jumpy, frightened even. Madelaine was sad about that. *Jerome has a lot to answer for.*

'I can't stay. I think ... I feel rather ill. Virus, is all.' Madelaine left.

Madelaine's

When Danica pulled up at the curb, Madelaine's BMW was slewed across the lawn, its nose against the verandah. *Hell, she almost drove it through the front door.* Danica wound down the windows of the car, gave the girls strict instructions not to speak to any strangers, and walked up the path to push the front door open. Television blared from Paige and Georgia's bedroom. The room was stale and stank of gammy nappies. They were clutching bags of Twisties before a small portable.

'Where's Mummy, darlings?' inquired Danica. Her expression bleak, Georgia gestured with her hand, then sank back into her chair.

'Madelaine. I need to talk to you,' Danica called, mounting the stairs. 'Are you up there?'

On her knees on the floor of the bedroom, Madelaine grunted as she stuffed clothes and papers into an old leather suitcase. 'Can't. Too busy.'

'Please, Madelaine. I'm terribly worried about you.'

'Worried about me. All along I thought you were only worried about you. That's so sweet, but you're awfully late. Pop out of the way now. I'm cleansing my sins and I haven't got time for yours. You and Nell should be proud of me. Women are strong, like tea bags; don't know their strength until you put them in hot water and all that ... Aren't they Danica? Remember that joke about the tea bags. Nell embroidered the words for me on a pincushion. No idea what I should have done with it. I stuck a few pins in it, thought a few bad thoughts.' Camera thumping heavily at her neck, she slammed shut the bulging suitcase, dragged it to the landing and bumped it down the stairs.

Danica followed her helplessly. 'We're all worried about you, Madelaine. What are you doing?'

'I'm burning things out of my life. Don't touch the girls; they're coming too.' She manoeuvred sideways through the back door, grimacing as she struck her elbow on the handle and then strode across the unkempt lawn where a burning bin was smoking gently. Madelaine dropped to her knees, lifted the grid and shoved in clothes and books and papers. 'It's not healthy to smoulder,' she laughed, returning from the garage with lawn mower fuel in a jerry can. It splashed as she tossed it in and a little purple flame trickled along her arm. Madelaine panted and swatted at her arm with her other sleeve. Danica recoiled from the singed-hair smell.

'Madelaine, stop. This is crazy, what you are doing? I want to help, but you have to be reasonable.'

'I'm over him, you know.'

'Jerome? Is that why you're burning his things?'

'Yes. No – him, him. For years, he made me bleed. I thought Jerome's love would be enough, that it wouldn't matter much about my father. He was here you know, at the funeral. Did you see him?'

'You know I did,' Danica said.

Watching the flames leaping towards the garage roof, Madelaine began to wind her hair around her face and rock back and forth on her knees. The video camera swung wildly, crashing against her chest, and Danica tried to remove it.

'I needed you at the funeral, you know. I needed women to wail with. It's traditional,' she sobbed.

'I was there, Maddy. You remember. Vlado too.'

'Vlado?' Flames shot high in the air. Parcels of newspaper caught and flared, little pieces leapt into the wind and danced over the fence. The garage roof caught on fire. Danica darted back towards the garden tap.

Madelaine yanked at her arm, snatched at her hair, moved hard up against her. 'I loved you Danny, but you never had time. All you thought about was you, you, you: how *you* would cope, and what *you* would do. I was in pain ... and you rabbited on and on about eating things.'

'I'm sorry, Madelaine.'

'I am the resurrection and the life. Whosoever believeth in me shall not perish, but have everlasting life. Ha!' Madelaine closed her eyes.

Danica stared, mesmerised, wanting to pull away, but her body was frozen in dismay. 'Madelaine, I do care about you,' she whispered. 'Why make it so complicated? I thought you wanted to kill me ... when we went out to Whalers ... you frightened me.'

When Madelaine released her, Danica stumbled and then righted herself before seizing the opportunity to run to the tap and unroll the hose. She played the water along the gutters where dry leaves flared and downpipes had begun to melt. Madelaine dropped to her knees and rocked beside the empty suitcase. 'I am the resurrection and the life. Whomsoever believeth in me shall not perish, but have everlasting life.' She cleared her throat, sniffed and began again. Her nose ran and she smeared it with her hair. 'He told me when I was little that God would punish me. Now I know why. I was unworthy; and my father was God's instrument.'

'Let me help you, Madelaine.' Danica had managed to quell the highest flames and hauled the mesh lid down over the burner. 'Come inside and I'll run a bath, make a cup of tea. I'll take the children home with me.'

Madelaine ceased rocking. 'No, not the children.'

'You can lie down. I'll get Hugh to come and see you.'

Danica felt as if danger had finally passed her by.

'I don't want you,' Madelaine groaned. 'I need a man to find me worthy. I didn't want to hurt *you*, just to wake you up. Didn't you know?'

Danica hovered uncertainly, arms folded. Madelaine pushed herself into a squatting position and bounced on her knuckles like an angry primate.

'Bring Paige and Georgia here and I'll take them down to the sea,' she quavered. 'I'm almost ready to go.'

She began to scuttle away from Danica, settling behind the diosma. 'The sea is my womb. It will hold me safe. I will curl up on the shore, and effervesce.'

The furnace threw a shower of sparks and Madelaine shook before the flames died down again. The old lady neighbour had smelt the smoke and stuck her nose over the gate. Danica waved her away while Madelaine remained half obscured from view by the bush she had backed into.

Finally, Danica left the garden and went inside. If she gathered up the children and telephoned Hugh, they would all be safe. *Madelaine isn't herself. But will she stay put?* Hugh would know what to do.

Powerhouse Beach

Madelaine strode through the back door to write 'Ululations' on the spine of her last tape. *Tapes can be like journals, though less subjective.* Later, when there was more time, she would edit them.

The biggest problem now, was that Madelaine couldn't find her children. She had searched the house high and low, upstairs and down, the yard and the driveway. The television had been burbling away at two empty chip packets and a half bottle of milk. Paige's doll had fallen behind the couch. It was all too much. *How can I be a good mother with so much interference?*

Her father had kept a diary in his desk drawer. At the age of ten she had tried to read it, and he had slapped her down. Fathers of the cloth spent their time reading the word of God, philosophy, theology and literature. They trawled the newspapers for contemporary hooks to hang a sermon on. Every morning the double wooden doors of the study at the manse were closed and he was not to be disturbed, not for tea or phone calls. Only Maddy.

Curled up in a corner of his office, she read while he pored over scripture. Now and then she would look up to watch his perfectly manicured fingers flicking pages. Even in the

Bible, family provided no protection: Cain killed his brother, Amnon raped his sister, and Abraham would sacrifice his son on a burning pyre – for God. When David slew Goliath, God was good. And when John the Baptist's head was served on a platter for Salome's happy delectation, she didn't shed a tear. The Old Testament was brim full of darkness, degeneracy and sin.

On Sundays, rejoicing in God's love, Madelaine's father rose from the pulpit like a great dark bird. Every week he beat back the sins of his people. Madelaine wanted to kick in the pew with her patent-leather shoes, and run into the sunshine where she could breathe. After the service he would glide along the aisle, perspiring faintly in his stiff white collar, greeting and touching fresh new souls at the door.

Madelaine snatched up her camera, crying, and backed down the street to the sea, filming the house as it shrank away from her. With the beach deserted, and 'Ululations' loaded into the camera propped against a rock, Madelaine pressed RECORD and flew into the water, tossing angry arcs of spray. Trailing her red dress behind her, she pushed against the rising tide. In deep water she had walked right out of her shoes.

Madelaine struggled out of her dress and knotted it around her waist. She swam up and down, back and forth, parallel to the road, like a kite on a string. Periodically she stopped to howl at the camera and cough. *Swimming is the only thing that works.* Head dipping in and out of the sea, small feet flapping below the surface, she left no impression. Clouds gathered and the sea moved beneath her like an amorphous being. Her fingers wrinkled and her eyes squinted against the sun. Heavy machinery droned in the sheds by the silos, gulls screeched over the wharf. There was a rotten fish smell.

When she grew too tired to swim, she settled back, the

water lapping round her neck, and she stared at the shape of a figure beckoning on the beach. Her eyes stung so badly she could barely make it out. *It's Hugh. God love him, but what on earth does he want?* She shook her head, felt savage about Danica. *What did she say to Hugh, before she whisked away my children?* She'll go down to the beach, that's what she'll do, Danny would have said.

Madelaine waved at Hugh and croaked, 'Go away. Leave me alone. Where are my children?' Breathless from shouting, she turned her back. *I will not give in.* When darkness fell, Hugh and Danica had waded out to get her. She had given in. They had each held an arm and brought her to the shallows, where her tired legs crumpled under her like the spokes of a battered umbrella.

Soon after her reluctant rescue, Madelaine sat stiffly at the window, her face locked against the stillness of the sea, her eyes fixed like a newborn drinking in a mother's love. Wet hair weighed heavily against her neck. Her hands were cold. Food arrived on trays and left that way as well. Ash piles grew and fell away from neglected cigarettes. Smoke shrouded her face. Paige and Georgia tugged at her clothing, placed pudgy fingers on her face, and wet kisses against her lips.

Days and nights merged. Answers were subsumed by questions. Flashes of lightning over the sea lit up the blasted placards: Unresolved Grief, Post-natal Depression, Children at Risk. Everyone had been at her: Jerome's partner Gregory, who counselled her about money, and winding up the practice; Hugh, the cold fish who had countersigned the forms transporting her from the sea to a red-brick mausoleum in the city; and the detective who stank of takeaway food and interviewed her breasts – he must have had a name – was it Zan, Stan? For over a week, Madelaine had slid into a fog where memories and nightmares became indistinguishable.

Nell came. How perverse, not to speak to Nell. Danica had cried. What could be wrong with her now? Jo had the nerve to visit, twisting her handkerchief, plucking at her pearls. Pauline brought florist flowers. Madelaine willed them dead. When the worst darkness descended, Jerome had pressed his distorted face against the glass.

She tried to shout, I can't see the sea! But no sound came.

Glenside Hospital

Who has taken my children? Rare lucid moments flashed past as if she were skimming across the tops of waves, and the children were lights on shore. In moments of terror she thought she might have hurt her babies. Their inexplicable absence was her only fear as she lay strapped to a barouche in the belly of the tiny plane, which leapt like a fish through the thunderstorm, on its way to Adelaide. The ambulance crew patted her hand and turned their faces to the flash and crash of the bucking sky. Madelaine shut their earnest faces out. Storms were nothing, measured against the certain knowledge that she was hurtling away from her girls.

Alone again, she had come full circle.

As they wheeled her across the tarmac a blast of cold wind bit into her face and she began to shake. If the barouche was stabilised, it didn't diminish the sensation of a speeding vehicle chopping lanes along the highway to the hospital. At times they stopped, and Madelaine heard traffic curdling, music belting from open windows, and boys shouting. Once a siren wailed.

The days that followed felt like a blow in slow motion. She was heavy and sullen, light and brittle, and so dark she could wither the faces of the staff with her intensity. Something they were used to.

'Where are the girls?'

'Safe with your mum.'

'Why have they got them?'

'You need to get well.'

Madelaine threw her head back in despair. *I can't smell the sea? What have I done?*

One afternoon Madelaine watched her mother shepherding the girls along the cement pathway bordering Paterson House. The visit was a reward for Madelaine's compliance. Georgia and Paige, it seemed, were only pawns in her recovery. They wore sashed dresses and patent-leather shoes. Their hair was licked up like the plastic painted coifs of cupey dolls, and, they were clutching white paper bags of mixed sweets.

'Jesus Christ, what have you done to them? They look like me thirty years ago,' Madelaine cried. Her mother stiffened, cast her eyes about for a nurse. Georgia tossed her constricted head and Paige pushed her bag of sweets against her quivering mouth.

'Madelaine. Think of these little people. You should always put them first.'

'You, outside.'

'I'm not supposed to leave them alone with you. If this visit doesn't work out, we will have to wait until you are feeling better.'

Madelaine turned her back on her mother, seizing Georgia's fingers to draw her closer.

'George, have you been down to the sea? Is it still there at the end of the street?' Georgia grinned and snuggled into her mother's shoulder. Paige burrowed beneath both their arms, holding up her bag of sweets in triumph.

'Mmm. Any love-hearts for Mummy?' begged Madelaine. Paige's sticky fingers worried through the bag.

Madelaine's mother held herself upright on a vinyl chair beside the door. She placed her handbag at her feet, folding the girls' cardigans over her lap. Cardigans, for God's sake.

'Daddy is teaching Georgie to read. She's very bright for four.'

'I wish he wouldn't,' answered Madelaine swiftly.

'Beatrix Potter.'

'Beatrix Potter,' repeated Madelaine, stroking Paige's anxious face before turning back to her oldest child. 'Georgia, remember the Flopsy Bunnies? In the garden where the lettuces are soporific.'

Georgia nodded sagely. 'It means sleepy.'

'Did Papa tell you there is danger everywhere, for little bunnies?' Madelaine reached for the child's hand and drew her closer, whispering, 'Promise me, that you will stay with Paige and keep her safe. Always.'

'Don't say silly things to the children, please. We have all been through so much.'

Madelaine swallowed hard and continued whispering into Georgia's face, a hand curled around the child's neck. She heard the chair scrape across the wooden floor, the snap of her mother's purse, the scrabble for a clean handkerchief. Her mother was crying.

'What's wrong now?'

'Madelaine, I didn't want to do this here, but . . . your father has a cancer.'

Madelaine started. 'A cancer.' She felt strange. *Could it be my fault? Is that what she's saying?*

'Did you hear what I said, Madelaine?'

'Yes, of course I did. I'm sorry. What is he going to do?'

'The specialist is doing tests. It could be inoperable. You must get well, Madelaine, as soon as possible.'

She thinks I have a choice.

'I'm not sure how long I can keep the children', her mother added, her mouth in a grim line.

'I didn't ask you to, remember? That wasn't my fault.'

All Madelaine wanted to do was rest, take time out from the voices in her head, decide on the next step. She couldn't understand why the court had supported her parents' application, especially if her father wasn't well. Nell had offered. Danica too, the brave little sherpa. In the end, Madelaine had lost her sole portfolio and her right to reply. *All those years of voting Labor. And there was a women's adviser for God's sake.* The girls had been whisked away on an afternoon plane, like refugees, no doubt clutching sugar rations in white paper bags.

At the end of the visit, Georgia and Paige had cried.

'Can you come home with us now, Mummy?' said Georgia, her heart-shaped face flushed.

'Soon. I promise.' Madelaine had helped carry them to the door and Paige had clung hard, clamping her heels around her mother's waist. The nurse had torn her from Madelaine's arms and carried the kicking child to the car park. Georgia had dragged at her grandmother's hand, throwing angry glances behind her. Madelaine wanted to hold them in her arms and never let them go. *And what about my father? Do I want him dead?*

She made her way to the showers, the only place she could cry for a long time without scrutiny. Then she had gone to the occupational-therapy room and found Annie gluing tiles into a mosaic.

After that, Madelaine spent unknown lengths of time facing the white-calcimime wall. She eventually stopped dipping her fingers in the upended plates of food and tracing the meandering contours of the world's oceans in smears on the wall. There were no memories of visitors; only white night-stingers with armloads of leads and syringes, who circled her bed in their rubber-soled shoes, and manhandled her. They observed her from the glass windows of the nurse's station. She bartered with them for cigarettes, and a trip to the sea.

In the early hours one morning, she was wrapped in a blanket and transported in the back of beat-up station wagon, driven by someone whose hands smelt like rubber. They were alarmed when she ran straight into the sea, and struck out like the clappers for Port Lincoln. They hadn't taken her again, and her neck was wry from the rescue.

But she had survived, moved on, and the future grew brighter when she met Annie – small, thin Annie, with spoggy hair. *Everything might be alright, after all.* Madelaine's films were waiting in a vinyl bag in her bedside console. She and Annie began to workshop storylines, to think about awards and competitions.

Madelaine wanted to ring her mother and shout about her plan. But she didn't. Madelaine was excited but tried to remain calm, attending group therapy in the hope of cementing diplomatic ties with the ward sister who ratified access visits. Not that she offered more than a word or two during sessions. There was no need when the others were always spilling confidences, offering their convoluted tales of loss and rejection, fear and hope.

On the first morning it had been Annie, who had been a marine biologist, and was now making films. Madelaine thought this was pure serendipity: they had so much in common. *God has not forsaken me after all.* During coffee break on the second day of therapy, she took the plunge, swam through the group to talk to her, and was relieved when Annie confided in her. She had been to the Galpagos Islands, and her next film was about pearls. Her pamphlet on the leafy sea dragon was available to the public, on the counter at Seaworld. The girl looked awfully young to have done such wonderful things. There was something odd about her, but Madelaine liked her.

Annie had been a serial visitor at Glenside, admitting herself around school and university examinations. Madelaine never tired of being with her, and questioned her voraciously. Annie's voice was soft, her manner diffident, her eyes darting. When Madelaine was discharged they would collect her children and drive through the Tanami Desert, working in Aboriginal settlements along the way, making their way to Broome to work on their first collaboration. Madelaine focused all her energy on their grand escape.

Back in her room, she visualised a starfish in the flat of her hand, and fingered the points like a mantra: warmth, safety, ninety miles of beach, a mudflat staircase to the stars, new films.

Things will work out. She wouldn't tell Mother about Annie. She would just call past one day, in a taxi, and grab the kids.

Paterson House

When Danica came to visit, Madelaine was alone, seated on a wooden chair, her hands curled under her thighs, staring at the window. Her hair hung thick and corrugated past her shoulders. Self-conscious, Danica edged across the polished hospital floors. *This place feels more like a prison than a hospital.* She imagined teams of green uniforms hovering up and down the corridor everyday.

'Madelaine . . .' Danica's voice fractured, caught somewhere in the back of her throat.

Madelaine started when she saw her. She lifted a light hand to her hair and, head half-cocked, smiled. *I've surprised her.* But almost immediately, Madelaine withdrew the smile and a shadow crossed her face. Just as quickly she blinked back tears and reached out to touch Danica's arm. *No, she's just confused.*

'Dear girl, is it you?' Madelaine sighed. 'You're looking well. Are we still best friends?'

'Of course. I've missed you, but I am well. Very well, and happy.'

They brushed cheeks.

Turning from the window and moving over, Madelaine patted the edge of her chair and drew Danica down beside her. Danica sat straight on her bottom, rolling on the chair edge as she took up the strain with an arched foot. Madelaine moved closer, dropping her head on her friend's shoulder. She picked up her hand and stroked it.

'You're looking fat,' she probed.

'I'm pregnant.'

'Ah, another shot in the dark for the heir.'

'Of course Vlado hopes it's a boy and I want to retire.'

'I hope you aren't madly jiggling this one around, and starving it to death.'

'Don't ... Hugh is very happy with my weight and diet. What about you? Are you okay?'

'Absolutely.'

'Things are settling down?'

'Do you mean am I rattling with pills and acting compliant?'

'I've been worried about you. I visited the girls at your parents' and I heard you weren't happy to begin with, but that you're getting on better with the new doctor.'

'I was admitted by a fossil from the Cambrian Period who thought I had FITH Disease. Telling nasty tales about Daddy, with a capital *D*, prevented me seeing my kids.'

'You'd think it might help. What's FITH Disease?'

'Fucked in the head.'

Danica swallowed. 'It must be hard to know the girls are with your parents.' She glanced up, a sympathetic question burning in her eyes.

Madelaine wafted a hand in front of her face 'It won't be for long.' She crooned. 'Listen up. Once upon a time, not so many years ago, there was a Ha–Ha wall, around this institution. From outside on the road it was low enough to climb, but on this side there were deep moats.'

'Why did they call it the Ha-Ha wall?'

'On a first glance at the wall, people saw freedom; they ran towards it. But on this side of the wall the ground dropped away; there was a deep moat, and their hearts tumbled in. Kerplunk. Ha, bloody, ha . . . Now they don't have walls. They have Ha-Ha drugs.'

Danica bumped against Madelaine. She bumped back. They bumped each other a few times and laughed. Like old times. Danica stopped when she saw Madelaine wiping her eyes with the back of her hand.

'I thought I would die here.' Madelaine's voice sounded croaky. 'There were pink pills and green pills. They didn't all go down the way they planned. But now I know, to get the girls back I have to be perfect.'

'What did they make you take?'

'Things to make me sleep, things to make me calm, things to make me shit.' She dropped her head on Danica's shoulder again. 'Nothing gives me pleasure. Print dances. Food is grey. I can't remember anything important. I feel cauterised.' Madelaine sat up abruptly. 'Come outside.'

She drew a crumpled packet of tobacco from her pocket, took out two ready-rolled cigarettes, and offered one.

Danica gripped the sides of the chair to accommodate Madelaine's jerky movements, stood and followed. 'I hardly smoke when I'm pregnant.'

'Four or less a day makes no difference. I remember someone told *me* that. Here.' Madelaine led the way through the door, across the backyard, and onto a path leading to a wooden seat beneath the trees.

'No I won't, thanks.' Danica lifted Madelaine's hand and took the papers past her nose.

'Do they mind you smoking? Isn't it like a hospital?'

'Almost everyone smokes here. Staff, specialists in the corridors between ward rounds. It's not like you think. Stuff isn't smuggled over the wall. I have some money.'

'I don't really like rollies.' Danica squeezed the ends of the cigarette between thumb and forefinger, took it to her mouth for two quick breaths, then curled her lip.

'You must hate it here.'

'What do you think? I have recurring nightmares. Someone is chasing me. I stumble through my own front door. Think I'm safe. Dash into the bedroom and slam the door. I hear the slightest sound at the window, a throat clearing.'

She's so dramatic.

'The dream always ends the same way. I know I'm in the presence of a killer. I'm mesmerised by the curtain rippling across his face. Some nights I can even feel the breeze from the open widow. I am my heartbeat. I'm going to die. When a hand reaches out and grabs me, I wake, screaming. It's my father, behind the curtain.'

Danica felt a desperate sadness, concentrated on a poor attempt to cross her legs, wobbled. 'Does he visit?'

Madelaine ignored her.

'Do you know why they built the wall in 1876? To keep people out. Trespassers, thieves in the orchard, were disturbing the patients.'

'Oh, that's so funny.' Danica smiled. 'Do you think about Paige and Georgia a lot?'

'Every minute of the day. But what happened wasn't my fault.'

How can she bear it?

Madelaine reached across and placed the cigarette between Danica's lips.

Danica drew back on it with pursed lips. Almost immediately, she felt her womb harden and contract.

Madelaine lit another for herself and stretched her hands above her head.

Goodness, no bra.

'Are you feeling better, Maddie?'

'Exciting things are on the horizon. Soon, I'm going to get my girls. I have a trip planned for all of us, and when I get back I'm going to apply to go to university: film-making. I've latched on to a nice new friend. She keeps me sane.'

'That's good.'

'Come and meet her. We're going to Broome to make a film together. She's awfully sweet.' Madelaine sprang from the chair, tugging at Danica's sleeve.

'Wait.' She waved the cigarette at her, and drew back on it.

'How are all my old friends then? Nell rang, once. I told her about a princess who had seven years bad luck – not me; I was the toad. You can ask my mother.'

Danica sighed. 'Pauline is in a quest and spends a lot of time raising money. Poor Hugh is lonely and working harder than ever. Jo is in love.'

'Mad woman alert. You must spare me the Jo details.'

'Madelaine, tell me about what happened? Please.'

'You know the most important parts. I was ill. They took my children. *You* took my children. When I first came here I had such convictions about everything – not shared by anyone, it seems.'

'I'm sorry. I was worried about you. And them. I'm sure you'll be back together soon.'

'Oh, yes.'

Is she angry? Danica stubbed out her cigarette. 'Jerome?'

Will she turn on me? She glanced over her shoulder for a nurse. Through the window she could see someone bending over a trolley.

Madelaine eased back onto her seat, crowding Danica and nodding. 'I'm careful. So much depends on it. I have a responsibility to my children,' she said, looking stubborn as she crushed her cigarette against the edge of the seat, and let it drop. Danica could feel Madelaine's breath hot in her ears, on the side of her face. *She is so intense. She could say anything.*

'I am very excited about taking this trip and making a film with Annie. I can hardly concentrate on anything else.'

'Are you sad about Jerome? Is that why you want to run away?'

'Jerome infected our nice life with his doubts. Nothing would have happened, if he'd been steady like Vlado.'

'Madelaine, did you kill him? Like they charged you. Remember?' She tried to place her hands lightly together, move her face around in front of Madelaine's without losing her balance. She spaced her feet below the rungs of the seat: she was poised for flight.

'I've told you, all of you, a hundred times. *I* believe Jerome killed himself,' Madelaine answered. 'He must have.'

'Yes, but Madelaine; can't you tell *me?* At the end, when everything was crazy, did you help him? Did you make it possible?'

'I don't see why you think I know *how* it happened. As you said, I wasn't well.'

Danica's heart lurched with familiar helplessness. She rested protective hands over her belly. She decided to change the subject, leave on a happier note.

Madelaine shrugged and jumped up, tugging at Danica's

arm. 'Come on. Come and meet Annie. I asked her to wait for me.'

Madelaine bounced away and Danica followed. *She looks energised. As if she can hardly wait to get back to this Annie. Good for her.* Madelaine turned down the side of another brick building.

Through the glass, an abysmally thin girl, holding a book against her chest, sat so still she seemed part of the garden. *Noticing thinness is pleasing.*

Madelaine tiptoed over, gathered up the girl's lank blonde hair and trussed it into a knot on top of her head. The girl started and turned to face them.

'Annie, meet Danica. She was, is, my dearest friend. Fatty isn't she?'

The girl smiled and ducked her head.

'Annie's a smart little sausage – marine biologist. She and I have some secrets, haven't we, Annie? We're going to make a feature film together, about the sea.'

Madelaine prodded her arm. The girl winced and reached for a spray of frangipani tucked in her belt. She crushed a flower between her fingers and lifted the bruised petals to her nose.

They made small talk about the weather, Annie contributing little.

'Maddy, I have to go. I'm booked on the five o'clock plane,' said Danica. 'Take care.' She leant towards Madelaine and grazed her cheek. Comforting her after Jerome's death seemed a hundred years ago. Grey clouds skittered across the sky. Danica took a few steps away and turned back to watch Madelaine and her friend.

Madelaine had taken her jumper off and was arranging

her hair at the nape of her neck. Her lips were pressed over three or four hairpins as she watched the other girl with studied indifference. Annie was crying, wiping the back of her nose with a skeletal hand. Madelaine released her hair and reached forward to run a hand down the girl's cheek, then laughed.

Danica stepped along the corridor and zipped her jacket to her chin. It looked cool outside. On her way to the car park, she remembered a parcel of crystallised fruit, which she had brought for Madelaine but left in the glove box. By the time she had travelled back with it, Annie and Madelaine had disappeared. She tugged at the door to Paterson House.

'Thank you,' she said to the nurse who caught the door above her head. She had imagined psych nurses to be rough and beefy, a little mad themselves perhaps, but he was small and delicately built, with layered blond hair and startling long eyelashes. His eyes were kind, his smile good-humoured.

'Madelaine looks more cheerful now that she's teamed up with Annie,' he said.

'Yes, she's very excited about the film they're making when they both get out of here. Madelaine worked in a film studio before she was married. She goes crazy with the camera.'

'She hasn't told me about that, although I saw her bag of videos.'

'Yes, and she loves the sea. Who would have thought she would meet a marine biologist who wants to make a film, in here!' Danica exclaimed.

'Why not?' The nurse glanced through the window, hesitated, and then placed his hand on her arm. 'But Annie's not ... either of those things.'

Glenside Hospital

When Danica caught up with Madelaine, she found her talking to Annie about a film they had both seen.

'What's wrong?' Madelaine asked.

Annie melted away.

'I had to come back.'

'You missed me already?'

'I brought you some fruit. I left it in the car.' Danica handed her parcel over.

'Okay, thanks. But remember, you can't stay here. There's an entrance exam.'

Danica scanned the room. 'I want to talk to you about Annie.'

'Are you jealous of Annie?' Madelaine looked flustered and glanced around.

'She's not what she said.'

'Danica,' Madelaine whispered. 'I can't hear the sea here, at all. I can't smell it either. I can't swim. Things aren't good. Annie has been my salvation.'

'I'm so sorry, but she's not a marine biologist, or a film-maker. She must have made it up. She ran away from home when she was fourteen and lived on the streets. I know that doesn't mean she couldn't be either of those things … but she isn't, Mad. The only job she had was in a roadhouse on the Nullarbor. She has nice parents who are pulling their hair out.'

Madelaine looked impassive, her eyes had fled. Then she shivered. The sun had moved behind a cloud. 'This place is the pits. Who told you that? People make things up to get at me. They jerk me around.' She snapped forward and placed her hands on the shoulders of Danica's leather jacket, ran them down the length of the arms and pressed her thumbs firmly against her friend's wrists. 'Let me borrow your jacket, please. It's so cold here after five. When I get out, soon, maybe next week ... I'll bring it back to you.'

Danica felt the weight of Madelaine's fingers, her sour breath in her face, the penetrating sadness in her eyes. 'Yes, of course you can. I have another coat in my luggage.' She struggled out of it and Madelaine hugged it to her chest. The nurse watched them from the verandah, squinting into the dying sun.

'And Danny, can you lend me some money? Two hundred dollars. I'll pay you back as soon as I can.'

Vlado had given Danica some cash to shop for the baby in Rundle Mall while she was in Adelaide. After she'd counted out money into Madelaine's hand, she felt a little sick.

Madelaine looked eager, restless. *Perhaps she's taking it better than I feared.* Danica had felt mean doing it, as if she'd told a child the truth about fairies. She wondered if it mattered that Madelaine had been misled. It was harmless enough. But she hadn't wanted Madelaine to get hurt. What if Annie thought she was Jesus Christ as well as a film-making marine-biologist, and that Madelaine was the devil?

Danica thought about her jacket, wondering if it would

be traded for some illicit pleasure, and the money used for a ticket to Broome. And she was worried about Georgia and Paige. Would things be better or worse for them now?

She took off suddenly, waving to Madelaine as she walked towards the hire car. As she left, Madelaine had been putting on her jacket and brushing back her hair. At the airport, Danica bought chocolate and a miniature bottle of schnapps – secret treats for the flight home.

The Harbour

From the moment Danica pulled away from the hospital car park, Madelaine began to shake. Seized by anger so luminous, she had closed her eyes and let the white heat of it sear across her brain. Annie had lied. Madelaine had been so eager to find a solution to her life that she had failed to register it – her unprofessional language, the lack of relevant detail in her CV. Meanwhile, Madelaine's girls remained at risk, locked down with her father. Ill though he may be, they must be extracted, soon. The Broome plan had been so appealing. Now she would have to take them on her own.

Madelaine placed her hand against the wall and steadied herself before rushing to her room. She flung Danny's leather jacket across the bed and dropped onto her knees in front of the bedside console. All her films were gone. 'Goddamn, Annie.' If she wanted to make films, passing Madelaine's off as her own would make perfect sense. But why had she left the camera behind? Now, after all Madelaine had been through, no one would ever understand. Only the films could tell the story. Annie had sabotaged everything.

It only took minutes to track her down. Annie hovered at the laundry door, looking as guilty as hell.

'What have you done?' Madelaine shouted at her. 'Where are my films?'

'I don't have them. I was waiting for you and a nurse came. I shoved them under your bed.'

Madelaine turned her head towards Paterson House. *What if Annie is lying, again?* By the time she returned the girl would have fled.

'What have you got there?' asked Madelaine.

Annie blanched, attempting to hide something behind her back. 'Pantyhose.'

'You don't wear pantyhose. Do you? You're stealing them.'

'I need a pair to clean the crud off my mosaic.'

Madelaine grimaced and changed tack. 'You have so many talents. I told Danica how excited I am about the film we're going to make. And about the trip to Broome.'

'Danny was nice. You're lucky to have her for a friend.' Annie's hands flipped the pantihose like landed fish as she fixed her gaze on Madelaine's face. Pale, thin, and stricken, she was further diminished by her oversized Indian jacket, its tiny stitched-in mirrors flashing like scales as she moved. During the few weeks Madelaine had known her, Annie had skulked in the shadows. If someone blew on her she would collapse like a pack of cards.

Madelaine seized her arm and pulled her towards the trees. 'Why did you lie to me?' she hissed in her ear.

Towed in Madelaine's wake, Annie quivered. 'I don't know what you mean.'

'You do. About being a film-maker and a bloody marine biologist. Why did you pick on *me*? You must have realised how much it meant to me. You could have told anyone else and it wouldn't have mattered.'

'I did. I told everyone in the group. Remember?' Annie dug her heels in, tried to resist.

Madelaine pulled up hard and reached out with her other hand, to get a better grip. Almost in the same motion, Annie bent and bit her hand. Madelaine released her, staggering back, as the girl shoved past her, running towards the rear fence. Rubbing her hand, Madelaine retreated to her room. *Surprise.* Beneath the bed the boards were bare – no films.

'The lying little puss.'

Madelaine felt self-loathing overtake her. It had been desperate-Madelaine, gullible-Madelaine, who had followed Annie after the therapy session, and dropped her dreams into their conversation. It had been Madelaine who had raved on about working at the film studio, about the films she'd made, and wanted to make. Annie had furnished the details about Broome, but it was Madelaine who had suggested they could run away and make a film together.

Madelaine took cigarettes, matches, a notebook and pen to a space beneath the hedge. She would write another script – the darkest ever – to clear her head. She had to make a plan, but didn't know what to do about Annie. Leave her behind? Let her flap her mouth to staff and make it worse for Madelaine, ruining any chance of access to her children? Her pen flew across the pages.

Once, when the storm of words abated, she laid back her head and closed her eyes. She imagined tilting her camera to frame the red-brick building looming over Annie, who would be crumpled like a wet rag on the lawn below the clock tower. Dusk restricted Madelaine's depth of field, but shadows and sepia tones enhanced a certain kind of film.

Madelaine had never made a genre film before. The set was perfect, gothic: imposing trees, gloomy buildings blocking out the moon, untidy pathways. She wondered if there were instruments of torture in the back wards of the hospital.

Madelaine flicked back to the beginning of her notebook, to the laundry scene.

Her Madelaine character would lunge forward, snatch the panty-hose from Annie's twitchy fingers and tie them round her neck. She would try to knock her over but Annie would put up a fight. They would both be panting.

They would be interrupted by a balding woman with a missing tooth, who would grin at them and murmur, 'Cat fight,' as she lugged her plastic washing basket into the laundry. Annie and Madelaine would fall back, looking awkward, traffic sounds from the main road swelling to fill the space. A gust of wind would whip hair around their faces. Annie would hiccup. In the distance a large nurse with a clip-board would be bustling towards the administration building.

There Madelaine had stopped to sketch a cameo of Paige. She fingered the smears of dirt and tears that blurred the little face, and continued with the script.

The Madelaine character would use her grip on a hank of Annie's hair, to drag her behind the building and deep into the trees. Annie would gag and choke as Madelaine forced her up against the fence and tightened the pantyhose ligature. Annie's pale fish eyes imploring, Madelaine's would remain stern.

Madelaine had felt sorry for her, then, and began to write a different film, in which the silly cow, dark and hurt by Madelaine's outburst at the laundry, would take herself into the trees to twist the pantyhose around her own neck.

A reluctant witness, Madelaine would screech, 'I will not be part of this. You'll get me into trouble, and I'll never be able to leave and get my children.'

But they were shitty films, both of them, and there were

some casting issues: the loony extras, finding actors to play her and Annie. She wondered if she should junk the film notes, and began to cry. Spots of rain mingled with her tears. She used her arm to shield the page and laboured on, reading, correcting, thinking. Two patients kicked a ball back and forth across the oval. Madelaine could hear the shouting, the thunk of their boots against the leather, then, the sudden quiet. She jumped when she heard male voices close by, and the crunch of their boots on the gravel behind the hedge. She pulled her head in, eased her body deeper into her burrow. Apart from an eerie column of light descending over the eastern hills, the sky had become quite dark, rendering her script a blur of angry flourishes. Soon patients and staff would be getting ready for dinner. Someone will notice that she was missing. *Damn Annie.*

While the dissatisfied, addled part of her brain remained consumed with Annie and the films, in another chamber a plan was crystallising. First she would go to the sea. She slammed her notebook shut and stood up.

All she needed was her camera. She hurried back to the room to get it, placing it on the bed while she zipped Danica's leather jacket high under her chin, and felt for the money in the pocket. Running away had always been in the plan. She scraped her hair back from her face, so tight her eyes were oriental, and then twisted the bulk of it in a tight wad at the nape of her neck, like the sisters did. No one would look twice at a tall nurse in a black jacket, rushing from the wards between showers.

At the back of the administration building, the staff were distracted catching rain entering a room through damaged tiles, so she passed with her head high in an attempt at anonymity.

When they finally got wind of it, that she and Annie had gone AWOL, the alarm would go up. Breakouts were common. They would beat the suburb, expecting her to subside on the front lawn of a nearby bungalow, or press her nose against the bevelled glass of someone's front door, ready to unload her particular tale of imprisonment and drugs.

After she passed the work sheds, avoided the path through the trees behind the laundry, and with some difficulty, scaled the high back fence, Madelaine almost dropped her camera as she landed in the laneway. Mud spattered her shoes. Anxious about being observed, she looked around too fast and pulled a muscle in her neck. The sudden pain increased her disorientation. She recovered her balance and veered left to hurry north along Conyngham Street.

She was confused by the looming presence of the silos, thought she was back in Port Lincoln. *But there is only one silo, how odd.* With one hand easing the spasm in her neck, she angled her head, accepting the spatter of rain against her face, and noticed the four levels of slits before the concrete lid. They looked like foreskin. *No, Madelaine. It's a water tower.* And the sky was wrong; it was a city sky, low and tight like a lid. The rain fell harder and she ran on as if swept by tides.

People sprinted through the rain, seeking shelter in doorways and their cars, barely glancing at her through their windscreen wipers. She followed the belt of parkland trees, first west and then south, heading for the sea.

In her scramble for freedom, she hadn't forgotten the children. She hoped they were safe for the moment, with her mother, until she could pick them up. Soon they would be in her arms. She imagined phoning her mother from a phone box along the way.

Hello, Mother. Can I speak to the girls?

They're in bed, dear. Fast asleep.

Please, I haven't got much time.

Madelaine, where are you?

Her mother would be sharp and Madelaine would hang up. They would go to Broome just the same. She fingered Danny's money in her pocket. *How much will a ticket cost?* Annie wasn't the only film-maker with initiative.

It hadn't seemed so smart to walk along the main highway to the sea. She slipped along backstreets, keeping an eye on the streaming lanes of cars and trucks, and the changing furniture of the median strips.

Sirens penetrated the night air, water swirled and splashed against the gutters. Public buses made rumbling gear changes. Planes shrieked through clouds, splitting them like atoms. *Are they flying to Broome? Port Lincoln?* Were the pilots aware of her scuttling along in the phosphorescent darkness?

At the last intersection before the port she drew in a deep breath of satisfaction. Not far now. She followed her nose – salt, weed and diesel oil – and her ears – shrieking gulls, sonorous booms, curdling machinery.

Madelaine's feet hurt. Rain had trickled under her collar and down her back. She almost fell when a blue-singleted worker spilled from the waterside pub on the corner. The man had reached out a hand to steady himself, dipped his face into hers, and moved his thumb across her breast. She shrugged him off and righted herself, then took off, glancing sideways into the fug of cigarette smoke. The usual roar emanated from the pub – expletives, laughter, clinking glasses.

Passing Victorian buildings that loomed and leered like gargoyles, Madelaine rushed along the wharf, with one hand thrust deep in her leather pocket. The moon had moved behind a knot of clouds as she slid into the darkness by the water. She walked along a while, then sat on the edge, her feet dangling, and envisaged herself home with the children, at the Powerhouse Beach. More than anything she wanted to be on a boat pulling through the quickening silver water, away from the shore. If there had been a time when she wanted to lie back in the arms of the sea, close her eyes forever, and drift away from everyone including Paige and Georgia, it had passed with the revelation of Annie's careless duplicity. Instead, Madelaine focussed on her enduring love for her children, which had always anchored her disjointed thoughts. What a life they would have in Broome, meeting vibrant people, attending outdoor screenings of her own short films, learning indigenous languages.

A sudden gust of wind hurled her forwards, depositing her on her knees by the water, and she peered into the oily depths, imagining herself flung on a dolphin's back, screeching into open sea. Water slapped against the hawsers, sprayed her face. Gulls swooped and bickered over putrid waste on the decks of fishing boats, and a tanker rested heavy in the water. Rubbish drifted past, shining briefly as the moon broke through the shifting darkness.

Annie's plan had sucked her energy and left the children vulnerable. *What is it about me that people prey on?* Was there something inside her, diamond-hard and intractable, dislikeable? Or something fragile, begging to be fractured? She would go back to ask her father. She would confront him on his deathbed and make it clear that it was not about her, but about Paige and Georgia. Annie or no Annie, she would make it up to her children. She would then take them as far away as possible, to Broome, where they would live once again by the sea.

Madelaine hummed as she limped back along the highway, turning south, away from the port in the direction of her children.

Acknowledgments

I thank the people who read early drafts of this book: Madelaine Brunato, Elvin Crouch, Leigh Jennings, Jill Kelton, Andrea Lloyd, Wendy Lloyd, Brian Lynch, Marion Mackenzie, Chris Matthews, Fran Knight, Doug and Tina Stevenson, Trish Stringer, Janice Virgin and Helen and Rod White.

Eva Sallis offered invaluable feedback, and Franny Kelly gave long and loyal support.

Thanks to Sue Crouch, who answered questions about Glenside; John Stewart, who knew about fishing; and Gary Lloyd and Brian Lynch, who answered questions about killing pets and people. Thanks to Alma Muftic.

Special thanks to the people at Wakefield Press: Michael Bollen, who showed early enthusiasm for my bitchy characters, and gave me the opportunity to develop the manuscript; Julia Beaven for reading critically and enthusiastically; and most of all Ryan Paine, who not only contorted himself into various physical situations to check the plausibility of my scenes, but carried such a strong sense of my big picture that his structural suggestions were invaluable.

The House at Number 10

Dorothy Johnston

Sophie Harper is abandoned by her husband, not for another woman, but 'a raft of girls – a floating, open-ended freedom'. Left with a four-year-old daughter to support, Sophie finds work in an old house in Canberra that is being used as a brothel. *The House at Number 10* is a novel about the complex relationships people develop with the buildings they live and work in, about betrayal and the will to vengeance, but most of all it is about the resilience of friendship, and the transformative power of the imagination.

'Johnston weaves wonderful metaphors of building and construction, of revelation and concealment.'

– Toni Johnson-Woods, *Sydney Morning Herald*

For more information visit www.wakefieldpress.com.au

Ash Rain

Corrie Hosking

A bushfire in Dell's childhood still haunts her. She dreams up new starts, but her spilling stories cannot over-write the past.

Evvie dances into Nell's life. She has run as far as she can from her family, but her country keeps calling her back.

Evvie's daughter, Luce, is most at home in the company of creatures. All she wants is her collection of bugs and a guinea pig for Christmas.

Dell meets Patrick in the pub, but he's going back to Scotland. Her life finally rupturing, Dell follows. She leaves a hole that Evvie and Luce struggle to fill. They must find each other again, without Dell. And Dell must discover how love works half a world away.

Ash Rain explores the corners and crevices where love can grow in unexpected ways.

'Corrie Hosking's prose sizzles and burns. It is unforgettable.'
— Eva Sallis

For more information visit www.wakefieldpress.com.au

Also from Wakefield Press

Poinciana

Jane Turner Goldsmith

'Café au lait' *she calls him, the young nurse who finds him in the wet mud on the riverbank, hours after his birth. He is too shocked to wail, would have died in the tunnel of bamboo leaves feathering gently above him.*

Catherine Piron is in Nouméa, searching for traces of the father she barely remembers. She meets journalist Henri Boulez, her only lead in a foreign country. Their journey into the remote regions of New Caledonia uncovers an extraordinary story that, like the island itself, *brille à la fois claire et noire au soleil*—shimmers light and dark in the sun.

'*Poinciana* is a special novel . . . a story of passionate attachments and burning divisions told with subtle understanding that brings to life the troubled world of the French Pacific with all the sharpness and intensity of a personal quest.'   – Nicholas Jose

For more information visit www.wakefieldpress.com.au